The Wings of the Eagle

A World War 2 Spy Thriller

by

JJ Toner

D1065897

First published as an eBook 8 January 2014

This paperback edition published 15 September, 2014 by
JJ Toner Publishers PO Box 25, Greystones, Co Wicklow, Ireland

ISBN 978-1-908519-18-4

Other books by JJ Toner

The Black Orchestra, ISBN 978-1-908519-17-7

Ovolution and Other Stories, a collection of fun SF short stories

St Patrick's Day Special, a thriller featuring DI Ben Jordan

Find Emily, The second DI Jordan thriller

JJ Toner lives in Co Wicklow, Ireland.

http://www.JJToner.net

DEDICATION

For Judy

ACKNOWLEDGEMENTS

Sincere thanks to Lucille Redmond for her editing skills,
to Anya Kelleye for a marvellous cover, to Karen Perkins of
LionheART Publishing House for formatting the book for print,
and to Pam, Judy, and all my other intrepid beta readers.

The Wings of

the Eagle

Part 1 - The British

Chapter 1

Friday April 9, 1943

It was time to jump, but Kurt's legs refused to move. The officer grabbed him by the arm and dragged him to the open door.

Outside, powerful searchlights lit up the sky and the plane rocked and juddered as anti-aircraft shells exploded all around them.

Waves of panic swept over Kurt. His stomach heaved. He tried to remember what the instructor had said. Spread your arms and legs like a starfish. Tuck and roll, tuck and roll on landing. And there was something else... Count to ten slowly before you pull the cord.

At that moment there was a blinding flash in the air outside. The plane bucked under the accompanying explosion.

"Don't think about it," shouted the officer in his ear. "Just count to twenty and pull the cord. You'll be fine."

It was that 'count to twenty' that did it. It distracted Kurt just enough to allow him to let go. He fell through the open door, spread his arms and legs, and counted to twenty.

As soon as he pulled the cord he knew he was in trouble. Only half of his parachute filled with air. One of the cords that should have been attached to the canopy was flapping uselessly around his head, and he was dropping like a stone.

Chapter 2

Three weeks earlier

Kurt Müller stood in darkness staring through the window at the Dublin street below. Diffused by a heavy drizzle, the light from the street lamps perfectly mirrored the conflicted state of his thoughts. To his right, Anna lay sleeping in her bed, clutching her rag doll. Like any ten-year-old, Anna's view of the world was uncomplicated and innocent. Since the day of their escape from Nazi Germany, she had accepted Kurt as her papa, and she was as dear to him now as if she were his own. How could he explain to her that he had to leave, that he might never return?

Gudrun appeared by his side, wrapped in a dressing gown. "Come back to bed, Kurt," she whispered. "We can talk about it in the morning."

He shook his head. "No, Gudrun. I've made up my mind."

She gripped his arm. "You agreed to wait a year. You wouldn't last a day in Berlin. You know that."

The Third Reich had suffered a number of serious reversals in the 10 months since their escape, but the latest news was of a successful counter-offensive on the Eastern front. It seemed the war would never end.

Kurt said, "I can't wait any longer–"

"Keep your voice down, Kurt." Gudrun peered at her daughter in the half-light. "At least wait until after Anna's birthday."

He lowered his voice again. "Every day that passes is killing me, Gudrun. Can't you see that? I have to go back."

The light from the street lamps caught tears in her eyes. "What can you do? You are only one man."

"You may be right, Gudrun. But I have to do what I can."

She moved away from him, then. "And what about me? What about Anna and me? What if the Gestapo catches you and you die over there?"

He reached out to her. She put her arms on his chest to push him away, but he drew her close. "They won't catch me, and I will come back, I promise."

#

Professor Stephan Hirsch welcomed Kurt with a firm handshake and a broad grin. "By all that's holy! It's Kurt Müller, the Nazi killer! What are you doing back in Ireland?"

The professor's American accent hadn't changed, but he had aged 10 years in the 12 months since Kurt had last seen him.

"Things got a bit difficult for me in Berlin after the death of Reinhard Heydrich," said Kurt. "I barely got out in one piece. I expect the Nazis are hunting me."

"You're right," said the professor solemnly. "There's a price on your head since the assassination."

"You're still in touch with the Black Orchestra in Berlin?"

"I am, although my role has diminished somewhat since Heydrich died. I communicate with your friends in the Abwehr from time to time. I take it you plan to sit out the rest of the war here?"

The university was in recess. Professor Hirsch's rooms, on the third floor overlooked a Front Square almost denuded of students.

Kurt shook his head. "I intend to go back to Germany."

The professor coughed. "Not a good idea, Kurt. If those bastards catch sight of you, you'll be dog meat. If you're looking for work, I could find you something in the maths department."

"Thanks, Professor, but my mind's made up. I thought I might work for the British."

The professor snorted. "You're crazy! The British will never trust you, given your background in the Abwehr."

Kurt tapped the side of his head. "I have some solid intelligence to trade."

"That could make a difference," said the professor. "But if they do decide to use you, they're certain to want to send you back to Germany."

"I'm banking on it, Professor. What I need from you is a name, someone in British Intelligence to contact."

"I can do better than that, Kurt. What are you calling yourself?"

"Kevin O'Reilly."

The professor picked up the telephone and spoke to the operator. "Get me Huntington two-six in Cambridgeshire. Tell them Professor Stephan Hirsch would like to speak with General Sir Hugh Anderton."

"They've agreed to meet you," said the professor as he replaced the telephone receiver. "They'll make contact when you arrive at Euston Station."

As Kurt was leaving, the professor gave him one last word of advice. "Trust no one, Kurt. Treat everyone you meet as a potential double agent."

#

Captain Johnson of the Office of Strategic Services, US military intelligence, sat at his desk in a dingy office in London WC1.

The door opened. A US marine entered and saluted. "We've had a call from Piper, sir. That's the math professor in Ireland."

The captain took a sip from the grey liquid congealing in his cup, and grimaced. "I know who Piper is. Professor Hart. What does he want?"

"That's Professor Hirsch, sir. He's sent us details about a member of the Abwehr who's in Dublin and planning to join the British operation. He'll be travelling to London in the next day or two."

"Could be a Nazi plant. What do we know about him?"

"Name of Kevin O'Reilly. Something of a math genius, according to the professor. And Hirsch reckons he's legit."

Captain Johnson snorted. "Who do we have free?"

"I've asked Willoughby to sit on his tail."

"Okay. Keep me informed. And get me a fresh cup of... whatever the British call this revolting dreck."

#

As the mailboat *Cambria* slipped away from the dock at Dun Laoghaire and headed for the mouth of the harbour, Kurt stood at the railing and waved to the three people who meant the most to him in the world.

He was facing an uncertain future. If the British rejected him he would have to spend the remainder of the war behind bars in a British POW or internment camp. If his plan succeeded and the British took him on as an agent, he could expect to find himself back in Germany risking capture, torture and death. Either way, he might never see Gudrun, Anna or his mother again.

In the pocket of his jacket he carried a parcel containing a set of forged German papers in the name Frederick von Schönholtz. This was the bogus identity he had used to escape from Nazi Germany nearly 10 months earlier. It was the one thing that could get him out of a jam – his trump card – and the one thing that he intended to keep secret from the British.

The sun sank below the land to the west as the ship turned into the choppy waters of the Irish Sea. A cold wind laced with spray drove the passengers inside. Kurt found a stool at the bar and ordered a pint of Guinness. The man at the next stool tried to strike up a conversation, but Kurt picked up his beer and moved away.

At disembarkation in Holyhead he was met by a military checkpoint. A British soldier in uniform checked his passport.

"Kevin O'Reilly from Dublin. And where are you headed, son?"

"London," Kurt replied. "I'm enlisting."

"Good man," said the soldier, handing the passport back.

Chapter 3

SS-Hauptsturmführer Bismarck Lange lowered his portly posterior into a chair, and dropped his leather briefcase on the floor beside him. He was sweating, although the temperature in Necker's office was not uncomfortable.

"Glad you could come," said his host. SS-Sturmbannführer Necker was wearing his dress uniform and a supercilious smile. "We have a lot to talk about. When was the last time we met?"

Lange ground his teeth. Necker knew the answer to that question. Surely the aristocratic prick was not about to bring up their last encounter and rub his nose in it?

Before Lange could frame a suitable reply, Necker jumped from his desk. "Give me a moment," he said and he left the room, closing the door behind him.

That was typical behaviour for Necker. The man was all smoke and mirrors. This latest illusion was of a man with important business that required his immediate attention in another room – a subordinate who needed to be reprimanded, perhaps, or an important report that had to be checked before it was handed to someone upstairs.

Lange ran his eyes over the top of Necker's desk. He was itching to see what his nemesis was working on, but the folders on there were tantalisingly just out of reach, and it was an obvious trap. Instead, he lifted his briefcase onto his lap, flipped it open, extracted a silver hipflask and took a quick swig. Seconds later the flask was back in the briefcase and the briefcase was on the floor.

Necker swept back into his office and returned to his seat. "Now where were we?"

SS-Sturmbannführer Necker of the SD was from an aristocratic family. Thin as a coyote, he was 1.85 metres tall, with blond hair cut short in the military style. Lange, on the other hand, was the son of a barber. He had a glandular condition that made it difficult to control his weight, and he barely met the minimum height for the SS. The fact that, despite these disadvantages, he had risen to his current rank was a continual source of personal satisfaction to him.

Lange seized the initiative. "You agreed to let me read your notes on deserters from the Eastern campaign."

"Yes, indeed I did, and you were to share your latest information on subversives in the universities. I take it you have the information with you?" Necker nodded toward Lange's briefcase.

Lange opened his briefcase and extracted a thin file. Then, like duellists at dawn, Necker handed an equally thin file across the desk with one hand while accepting Lange's offering with the other. Both men opened what they'd been given and began to read.

"There's nothing but numbers in here. Don't you have the names of the deserters?" said Lange.

Necker really was an unbelievable bastard. Six months earlier they had been of equal rank, two ambitious young Gestapo men competing for a single promotion and transfer to the Security Service, the SD. It had gone to Necker. Right up until the moment when the announcement was made, Lange had been convinced that it would be his. He had earned it. He had sweated blood for it. But Necker had the breeding and the height, and they had given it to him. Since then, Necker and Lange had shared three major investigations and in each case Lange had done all the work, it was Lange's men who had found and arrested the guilty party, it was Lange who had extracted the confessions, and yet Necker had somehow managed to claim all the glory.

"This file contains nothing but a few names," Necker countered, touching the jagged duelling scar on his right cheek – a souvenir of his time at Heidelberg University. "What I wanted was an indication of the numbers involved, the number of universities suspected of harbouring subversives, the numbers of students and staff arrested and so forth."

Lange pried his portly frame from the chair. Necker stood up to face him. That was when Lange first noticed that Necker's desk was mounted on a pedestal of three or four centimetres, making him appear even taller than he was.

The two files were returned, each to its owner. Lange dropped his file into the briefcase and stepped toward the door.

"I shall have my staff send those figures to you," said Lange.

"And you shall have those names," replied Necker.

When hell freezes, Lange thought. Before leaving, he turned, clicked his heels and saluted "Heil Hitler!"

Necker gave a limp wave in reply and returned to the papers on his desk.

#

On the train to London, Kurt found himself sharing a carriage with a young Irishman in an ill-fitting suit. No words were exchanged, but Kurt noticed his travelling companion casting a curious eye in his direction from time to time.

London was more grimy than he remembered it, more grim. Euston Station was largely unscathed, but there was a smell of charred wood and rubble in the air.

The young man presented his ticket at the barrier and made a bee-line for a pub across the road.

Before leaving the station, Kurt placed a small parcel with the left luggage office. A passing pedestrian gave him directions to the nearest public lending library, 15 minutes' walk away.

The streets had been torn apart. There were piles of rubble where houses had been, their neighbours on either side propped up by wooden struts. The people looked weary, their clothes worn and faded, but all were quick to smile.

In the library, he found an obscure corner of the non-fiction section and slipped his left luggage ticket inside a copy of *Einstein's Theories: Space, Time and Relativity* which had clearly never been borrowed.

Back at the street outside the railway station he joined five others who were obviously waiting to be picked up.

Thirty minutes later Kurt was alone and still waiting; his five fellow passengers had all gone. He wondered if General Anderton had forgotten to arrange for someone to meet him or if he had missed his contact during his short trip to the library. He could imagine having to take the train and ferry home, his tail between his legs.

He decided to get something to eat. He hadn't eaten for several hours, and his insides were churning. Maybe he'd be able to work out what to do next on a full stomach.

As soon as he stepped inside the pub, he spotted the young man from the train sitting at the bar. Nearby, four Tommies in uniform sat at a table, drinking pints. Kurt took the stool beside the young man, and ordered a cheese sandwich and a pint of bitter. The stool to his right was occupied by a heavy-set man reading a newspaper.

One of the Tommies stepped up to the bar between Kurt and the young man, and ordered a round of drinks. Speaking out of the side of his mouth, he said, "You were on the train from Ireland, weren't you?"

The young man smiled at him, but said nothing.

"Where are you headed?" asked the soldier.

"I'm here to meet someone," said the young man.

"Oh, you're Irish," said the Tommie. "I knew you weren't a squaddie. I wondered..."

The soldier took his drinks back to his companions at the table.

Almost immediately the barracking started, as the Tommies took it in turns to call out to the young man, accompanied by raucous laughter.

"Who needs the Irish drinking our beer?"

"Taking our jobs."

"Humping our women."

"Why don't you go home where you belong, Paddy?"

"They're neutral, these Irish bogmen, y'know."

"Should be neutered, the lot of them, if you ask me."

The young man put his glass down and slipped off the stool.

Kurt put a hand on his arm, caught his eye and said, "Leave it."

The Irishman shook his head. He went over to the table and said, "What is your problem?" to the Tommies.

"I should have thought that was obvious," said one of the soldiers. "You do know there's a war on, Paddy?"

The Irishman leaned across the table and knocked the man's drink over. There wasn't a lot left in the glass, but what there was ran toward the squaddie's lap. He shot to his feet, knocking over the table and the drinks of his three mates.

The landlord let out a yell from behind the bar. "Oy! Take it outside."

"Suits me," said the Tommie.

"And me," said the Irishman, and they both headed for the door.

The other Tommies crowded outside, and Kurt followed them. The young man removed his jacket and handed it to Kurt. The Tommie handed his to one of his mates, and the two men faced off, fists raised.

They circled each other like prize fighters, feinting, ducking, fists rolling. The other three Tommies stood around, jeering and encouraging their man.

"Show 'im what a Brit can do."

"Give 'im one for me, Nobby."

"Queensbury rules?" said the young man.

"Whatever you like, Ducky," said the soldier, and he threw a wild punch.

The young man avoided that easily and countered with one of his own that struck his opponent on the ear.

"Come on, Nobby. Give it to 'im!"

A crowd was gathering, and Kurt noticed the heavy-set man from the bar watching with a broad grin on his face.

Nobby swung a second punch that caught the young man on the side of the face. He threw an uppercut, in reply, but failed to make contact.

The Tommies cheered. "Finish 'im orf, Nobby."

Then the Tommie switched to wrestling, wrapping his arms around the young Irishman's midriff and knocking him to the ground.

The Irishman broke free, but the Tommie landed a roundhouse punch that knocked him to the ground. The Tommie aimed a boot at the Irishman who turned away in time, grabbed the Tommie's foot and twisted.

The Tommie gave a howl of pain and fell, face down. Leaping to his feet, the Irishman placed a boot in the small of his opponent's back, effectively immobilising him.

The other three Tommies crowded forward to help their man. Outnumbered four to one, the Irishman would soon be fighting for his life.

"That's enough," shouted Kurt, stepping forward. "Let him go, soldier. He's had enough."

The spectators roared with laughter at this.

"They're only getting started," complained one of the Tommies.

"Kings regulations forbid public brawling," said the heavy-set man. "Break it up."

The Irishman released the Tommie who regained his feet, scowling and brushing dirt from his uniform. Kurt handed the Irishman his jacket.

The heavy-set man said, "Which one of you clowns is Kevin O'Reilly?"

"That's me," said Kurt.

"Major Weir." They shook hands. "General Anderton sent me to meet you."

The Irishman fished a pound note from a pocket and waved it in the air. "The next round is on me."

The Tommies cheered and went back inside the pub with their new-found friend from Ireland.

Kurt and Major Weir set off together at a brisk walk. After sitting on the mailboat and train for the best part of a day and a half, Kurt was glad of the exercise. London and the Londoners looked surprisingly cheerful considering the hammering they had been receiving from the Luftwaffe. Kurt saw little signs of the bombings, just two thin plumes of smoke rising in the still air to the north.

They walked for 15 minutes before turning into Kensington Palace Gardens, a wide, tree-lined street containing a row of stately houses. Weir pressed a buzzer on the gatepost of one of the houses, gave his name, and the gates swung open. The front door opened as they approached it. Kurt and the major stepped inside, and the door was closed behind them by a soldier in uniform.

Taking Kurt's bag and handing it to the soldier, Major Weir said, "Welcome to The Cage."

Chapter 4

Two Tommies escorted Kurt down a flight of stairs to a basement corridor and into an interrogation room. There they strip-searched him. Kurt found the procedure humiliating, dehumanising, although a small part of his mind found it comical. When the search was complete, his clothes were returned.

The room was drab, grey, lacking windows, poorly lit and equipped with two canteen chairs on either side of a plain wooden table. Within 30 minutes the door opened and Kurt was joined by a rotund man in his early sixties wearing a shabby military uniform.

The officer sat down facing Kurt. "Welcome to England," he said, in perfect German.

"Thank you," Kurt replied.

"You may call me Colonel Scott," said the officer, continuing in German. "What is your full name and rank."

"Kevin O'Reilly, Oberleutnant."

The colonel pursed his lips. "Your real name if you don't mind."

"Please understand, Colonel, I need to protect my real identity. I am a wanted man in Germany with a price on my head."

"You're going to have to trust me," said the colonel. "I promise your name will not pass beyond these four walls."

Kurt took a deep breath and said, "Kurt Müller, Oberleutnant."

"A deserter from the Abwehr, I'm given to understand."

The word shocked Kurt momentarily. He had not considered it before, but that's exactly what he was. A deserter. The word carried unpleasant connotations. Deserters were the lowest form of life in the eyes of the Wehrmacht. They could be shot on sight.

"I'd like you to tell me your story," said Colonel Scott, switching to English, "from the beginning, if you would. Leave nothing out."

Kurt noticed a trace of a Scottish accent. He took a deep breath and began, "I was born in Ulm. My father worked in local government, my mother–"

The colonel held up a hand and smiled like a dried prune. "I don't think I need your full life story, Müller. Please start from when you joined the Abwehr."

Kurt told how, operating from Abwehr headquarters in Berlin, he had been in charge of running German agents in Ireland, and how he uncovered and joined the German resistance. He made no mention of his nefarious uncle, the late Reinhard Heydrich.

"You are now a committed anti-Nazi? Is that your position?" Colonel Scott was wearing round spectacles that gave him the innocent look of a child, but behind the lenses lurked a pair of eyes that betrayed a mind as sharp as a diamond.

"It is. I wish to return to Germany to do whatever I can to hasten the end of the Third Reich."

Colonel Scott cross-examined him about the Nazis, their leadership, their creed and policies and the progress of the war, clearly fishing for the truth: did Kurt harbour any affection for the Party or any lingering hopes of a German victory. Finally, he said, "And you have come to us for what purpose?"

"I thought I could become an agent for British Intelligence."

"And do what, exactly?"

Kurt stood for a moment to stretch his legs. He lifted a shoulder. "Whatever you wish."

"Right. And how can we be sure that you are who you say you are? You could be sent here by Admiral Canaris to infiltrate and undermine our intelligence operations."

"I assure you that is not the case," said Kurt.

"Why should I believe you?"

"I have brought something that may help, a token of my good faith," said Kurt. "I can give you a list of call signs used by German agents."

"These are agents operating in England?"

"Many of them would be. The call signs I have are allocated to agents as they are deployed, all over the world. The list includes call signs in operation now and some that will be used in the future."

"And how will these be of value to us?"

"I was a signalman with the Abwehr. Believe me, Colonel they will be of value to your code breaking teams."

Colonel Scott adjusted his glasses. "Where are these call signs? We found nothing like that among your belongings."

Kurt tapped the side of his head. "I'm a mathematician, Colonel. I have them committed to memory."

The colonel left the room and returned with a single sheet of paper and a pencil, and Kurt wrote out the call signs that he had liberated from the Abwehr, adding two columns of variations.

When he had completed the list he handed it to the colonel. "These are the call signs of 30 agents, 10 - 12 in use, the rest waiting to be allocated to future German agents overseas. As you can see, each has two variations that will be rotated in random order."

The colonel folded the paper carefully and left the room with it.

A Tommie entered, set up his camera, and took two head and shoulder photographs of Kurt – full face and profile – with Kurt holding a piece of cardboard with a number stencilled on it.

When the photographer had finished, a different soldier entered and took down Kurt's details: height, eye colour, distinguishing features, scars, tattoos, etc. He also took a full set of Kurt's fingerprints.

Kurt felt like a criminal. All that was missing was a charge sheet and a pair of handcuffs.

#

The colonel returned carrying a folder. "It will take a while to verify those call signs," he said. "Is there anything else you can tell me in support of your story?"

Kurt said, "You know that Reinhard Heydrich was ambushed and attacked in Prague on 27th May last year? He died on June the fourth."

Scott nodded.

"I played a small hand in that." Kurt explained how he had advance knowledge of the assassination attempt, but had done nothing to prevent it.

"That was helpful," said the colonel, pursing his lips. "But the reprisals were horrific."

Kurt had read about the Nazi reprisals. The Czech village of Lidice had been obliterated, and every male over 16 years of age massacred. The women and children were taken to labour camps. The village was levelled, leaving nothing but rubble.

Kurt said, "I read about that in the newspapers. Do you know how many were killed? The reports I read gave no numbers."

"No one knows for certain, but we estimate over 500 people must have died as a direct result of Heydrich's death. The news was broadcast from Berlin. They made no secret of it."

Once again guilt and shame weighed heavily on Kurt as they had when he first read the story. He shared the guilt of all Germans for the horrific actions of their government, but he also had to bear his own special guilt, for, if he had intervened and saved his uncle from the assassins, the Czech village would still be there, its inhabitants still alive.

"Is there anything else you can offer as proof of your bone fides?" said the colonel.

Kurt could think of nothing.

The colonel said, "Can you give me the names of any agents operating in England?"

"I'm sorry, Colonel, I don't have any."

"Not even one?"

"No. All I have is the call signs."

"You ran the agents in Ireland. Give me their names."

"There was only one at the end," Kurt said. "His cover name was John Dolan, his call sign was Stallion and he lived in Cork. His reports were mostly low-level stuff about steel production in the Cork steel works."

"Only one agent? You expect me to believe that?"

"I went over to investigate the disappearance of another agent and to meet with Professor Hirsch."

Colonel Scott said, "What can you tell me about the Black Orchestra?"

Kurt's blood turned to ice. "What is that," he said, "some sort of American jazz band?"

The colonel blinked. "It's a secret underground movement that opposes Hitler and his Reich, with members in high positions within the Abwehr. You must know about it."

The colonel was well-informed, but whatever Kurt said next he needed to be as vague as possible so as not to put anyone in danger. He said, "Never heard of it. But I have seen a signal altered in the Abwehr before it was passed on to the Wehrmacht High Command."

"Just one? What was it about?"

"It contained the monthly production figures for RAF aircraft. The figure was exaggerated."

"What else did you notice?" said the colonel.

Kurt answered hesitantly, "Well, it seemed to me that the training of agents for overseas operations was inept, and I saw a couple of German agents operating in England withdrawn or silenced for no obvious reasons."

"You can name these agents?"

"No. I don't have their names/"

"Was there anything else?"

Kurt shook his head.

"Tell me what happened in Ireland. Leave nothing out."

Kurt took a deep breath and gave the colonel an abridged version of his trip to Ireland, his meeting with Professor Hirsch and how he killed two Gestapo officers before returning to Berlin. He mentioned no names apart from the professor's.

When Kurt had finished his story, the colonel made no comment. He pulled two photographs from his folder and placed them on the table. These were pictures Kurt had carried with him from home. "Tell me who these people are."

"That's my mother, Mary O'Reilly. She reverted to her maiden name after my father died, and these are my family, Gudrun and

Anna. They are with my mother in Dublin."

"Your father, who was he? What became of him?"

A knot was forming in Kurt stomach. He could see no logic to the colonel's interest in his family.

"Walter Müller. He was shot in 1934 on the Night of the Long Knives."

"Tell me about the Abwehr deciphering operation," said the colonel.

Kurt told the colonel how the Abwehr routinely deciphered British Naval Cypher3 messages, and that British TypeX signals could be decoded by the Abwehr, but only after receipt of the daily keys from the Spanish Legation in London. This information was greeted with a sceptical flicker of the colonel's eyebrows, before Kurt added, "The flow of daily keys from Madrid stopped about a year ago. I expect you know what happened there."

The colonel made no response to this. "Is there anything else you can tell me to prove your story?"

Kurt said, "Contact Professor Hirsch in Dublin. He will vouch for me."

Colonel Scott replaced the photographs in his folder and stood up. "We will be in touch with the authorities in Eire about these people. If they are German citizens they will probably be interned. Or they may be deported."

Chapter 5

It was 7 pm by the time the interrogation resumed. Colonel Scott went over Kurt's story again. Kurt protested that he was exhausted, but the colonel insisted on revisiting every detail.

By 8 pm, the colonel had run out of questions. He accompanied Kurt to a room at the rear of the house that served as a mess. The colonel left, and Kurt found himself in a queue behind a young man with fair hair, dressed in civilian clothes. Kurt ordered a plate of minced meat and potatoes and a mug of tea. He took a seat at an empty table and the young man sat down beside him.

"Welcome to The Cage, Kevin." He spoke in German.

Kurt was surprised. "You know my name?"

"Everyone here knows who you are. My name's Pilgrim."

Kurt detected a trace of the north in Pilgrim's accent. "You are from Saxony?"

"No, I'm from Mecklenburg."

"But you are German?"

"I'm half German half English," said Pilgrim.

"Is Pilgrim your family name? What's your first name?"

"It's Pilgrim. Just Pilgrim."

Kurt wolfed his food while Pilgrim picked at his. When the meal was over, Pilgrim showed Kurt to a room at the top of the house equipped with two military cots.

"This one's mine," said Pilgrim. "That one's yours."

Kurt was not unhappy about the arrangement, as Pilgrim seemed pleasant company, but he wondered if Pilgrim was there to spy on him. He resolved to say nothing to his roommate that might lead to new lines of interrogation.

Pilgrim revealed that he was 26, and had lived all his life in England, although his German was flawless.

"You have family in Germany?" asked Kurt.

A shadow passed over Pilgrim's face. "Yes. And you?"

Kurt shook his head. "Not in Germany, but I have a girlfriend – Gudrun – in Ireland and she has a ten-year-old daughter called Anna. Do you have someone special?"

Pilgrim paused before answering, "There is this girl. We've had a start-stop affair for a few months. I'm not sure how she feels about me."

"You're very fond of her, obviously."

Pilgrim flushed before changing the subject. "What's it like in Ireland, Kevin? Do they have rationing over there?"

"It's fine. And they do have rationing. How long have you been in The Cage?"

Pilgrim shrugged. "Long enough."

Kurt sorted out his cot and climbed in. Within minutes he was asleep.

He awoke in darkness. Pilgrim was tossing in his cot, shouting in his sleep. Kurt shook him by the shoulder to wake him.

"You were shouting."

"Sorry about that. What time is it?"

"Three thirty." Kurt filled a cup of water for Pilgrim. "We can leave the light on if you like. I can sleep with it anyway."

Pilgrim sipped the water.

Kurt returned to his cot intending to go back to sleep, but Pilgrim wanted to talk. He told Kurt of his childhood. His mother was German, his father British. Pilgrim lived all his life in England. His mother's nationality made him a target in school and even later when he joined the merchant navy and became an electrician and radio operator.

"How long since you were last in Germany, Pilgrim?"

"A long time. Do you know what happened in Mecklenburg... to the Jews?"

"The Jews? I don't know – I have heard that Jewish activists have been sent to labour camps..."

Pilgrim's knuckles strayed to his mouth.

"Pilgrim, when you were shouting in your sleep, I thought I heard some Yiddish words. Are your family Jews?"

Pilgrim looked sharply at Kurt, watching his reaction. "My mother is Jewish."

Kurt could offer no words of comfort or hope. If Pilgrim's relatives – his mother, his grandmother, his aunts and uncles and cousins, his brothers and sisters – were Jews, they were lost to the concentration camps by now, God knew what their fate. "My name's not Kevin," he said. "My real name is Kurt." He didn't divulge his family name, and Pilgrim didn't ask.

He tried to think of something else to take Pilgrim's mind off his family, and started to tell him a series of old jokes. "An Irishman went into a bar in Belfast with a crocodile on a lead. 'Do ye serve Catholics?' he says..." When he looked over, Pilgrim was sleeping peacefully.

Chapter 6

Friday April 2

Kurt was woken at 6 am by a soldier in uniform and taken down to the basement interrogation room again. The soldier closed the door and stood by it with his arms folded. Kurt asked him a couple of questions, but got no response. He took his usual seat and waited for the colonel to arrive. He was hungry again, the minced meat and potatoes of the evening before having stimulated his gastric juices.

The door opened and Major Weir strode in, carrying the colonel's folder.

"Colonel Scott is not convinced by your story. Kindly tell me again how you first made contact with Sir Hugh Anderton."

"Professor Hirsch called him from Ireland. Sir Hugh arranged for you to meet me at Euston Station."

"This Professor Hirsch, how does he know Sir Hugh?"

"I'm not sure. I assumed the professor was working with British Intelligence."

"We don't know this professor of yours." The major pulled Kurt's passport from the folder, and slapped it on the table. "Who the fuck is Kevin O'Reilly?"

Kurt was taken aback, not just by the question, but by the aggressive way it was asked. "That's the name I used to travel from Ireland," he replied. "I explained that to Colonel Scott."

"You travelled here under a false name, using a forged passport. You do realise this is a serious offence?"

Kurt said, "How else could I get into the country without being immediately detained? Are you suggesting I should have travelled under my own name?"

Weir came around to Kurt's side of the table "Stand!" It was an order. Kurt got to his feet, and Weir immediately drove a fist deep into Kurt's solar plexus. Kurt doubled up and dry-retched.

Weir shouted, "I'm suggesting that you are a lying Kraut. Stand up!" and when Kurt remained bent over, the young soldier grabbed him from behind by the elbows. Placing a knee in Kurt's back, he forced Kurt into a rear-vertical stance, and Weir hit him again.

The soldier released him. Kurt hit the floor and lay there.

Weir stood over him. "I might as well tell you, here and now, O'Reilly, I hate Germany and the Germans, and I hate the cowardly Irish even more. I come from Coventry, and when the city was bombed my family home was demolished. I lost my mother and my sister."

Weir nodded to the Tommie who pulled Kurt up from the floor and dropped him on his seat. The Tommie left the room. Weir headed after him. At the door he paused and ran a hand through the meagre strands of hair on his head. "For the passport offence alone I could have you shot as a spy right now, and no one would bat an eyelid. I've met quite a few Germans, and I've yet to find one that I'd piss on if he was on fire."

Kurt was struggling to catch his breath. He croaked, "I hate the Nazis as much as you do, Major. Why d'you think I'm here?"

Weir left the room, slamming the door. Kurt rubbed his bruised stomach muscles. He was fit enough to withstand most onslaughts, but the major's fist was like a hammer and he had been unprepared for the first blow.

Weir returned 30 minutes later. "You may as well know, Müller, that Colonel Scott is ready to sign your papers. All he has to do is sign an order to have you sent for trial as a spy, or summarily shot."

Kurt said nothing. He struggled to calm his racing heartbeat. The pain in his gut was competing with the ominous crawling sensation in his scalp. He had no reason to doubt what the major had said. The next 30 minutes would determine his fate.

Weir opened the folder again. "You have said that you travelled to Ireland to communicate with your spies. How did you get there?"

"By U-boat. I was dropped off the Cork coast."

"But you have given us the name of only one agent in Ireland. Do you expect us to believe that you travelled by U-boat to speak with one agent, an agent who was providing..." he consulted the folder, "...low level intelligence about steel production?"

"As I said, I wanted to meet with Professor Hirsch and to trace another, missing agent."

"This agent's name?"

"His cover name was Rupert Kinski. His call sign was Ornithologist. I forget his real name." Kurt's blood pressure rose. The major was exploring ground already covered in detail by the colonel.

"Did you locate him?"

"I found him living rough in Dublin. I tried to persuade him to come to the German embassy to arrange his passage home, but he refused."

"You expect me to believe that?" said the major. "How did he get into that state in the first place?"

"He received a warning that his cover had been blown and the British were about to capture him. He ran. His story failed to convince the staff at the German embassy – he had no papers – and they turned him away."

"I'm not surprised," said Major Weir with feeling. "I don't believe a word of it. Tell me about this professor. He contacted General Anderton on your behalf, I think you said."

"Yes. The professor is an active member of the German resistance. Living in Ireland he has more freedom than most, and he has contacts far and wide."

"With a name like Hirsch, I assume he's German?"

"He's an American of German extraction, but he cares deeply about the future of Germany."

"Tell me what happened when you visited the professor."

"I've already been through all that with the colonel," said Kurt wearily.

Kurt told the tale again. He omitted details concerning the professor's contact with Reinhard Heydrich and he made no mention of anyone else, but otherwise he told the story as it happened.

"That's your story?"

"That's what happened," said Kurt. "You can confirm the details with the professor."

"I'll be back," said Major Weir. He opened the door. Kurt heard an agonized scream echoing down the corridor, cut off by the sound of a door slamming. The British were torturing a prisoner!

Kurt shivered. He had tried to make sure that the answers he'd given to the major were consistent with what he'd told the colonel, but was it going to be enough to save his life? He had no doubt that the British wouldn't hesitate to have him tortured or shot if they thought he was telling them lies.

An hour passed before Major Weir came into the room again. This time, he had a nasty, triumphant glint in his eyes. The man exuded hostility. He remained standing behind his chair.

"Tell us about Reinhard Heydrich."

Kurt opened his mouth with no idea how he was going to respond, but before he could say anything the major added, "We know that Heydrich was your uncle. Don't try to deny it."

Kurt's heart did a backward somersault and headed for his boots. "Heydrich was my uncle by marriage," he said. "He was no blood relative of mine."

"And yet you say you could have saved his life and didn't. Your own uncle. What sort of fools do you take us for?"

"I've told you, he was no kin of mine. The man was a monster, responsible for the deaths of thousands of innocent people. I was happy to sit on my hands and allow the Czech resistance to kill him."

"The fact remains that you lied," the major bellowed. "You omitted to mention your family connection to this high German government official. How can you expect us to believe anything else you told us after that?"

Kurt leapt to his feet. The chair clattered to the ground behind him. "Why do you think I came here, Major? Isn't that proof enough that I am telling the truth? I have given you the call signs of German agents, present and future, information that will be useful in deciphering operations. How can you doubt that I sincerely wish to help to bring down the Third Reich?"

"Nothing you've said or done proves a thing. We know you are a German national. And you concealed the fact that you are a close relative of a senior member of the Nazi government. We can't afford to make a mistake, here. What if you are an enemy agent sent to infiltrate our intelligence service? What if those call signs you gave us are false, or call signs that will be used in the future for misinformation?"

The major stepped to the door. "I'm sorry, O'Reilly or Müller or whatever your name is, but there's nothing more I can do."

Chapter 7

Kurt spent that day and three more locked in a cell, staring at the walls, grasping at slim straws of hope. It was obvious that Professor Hirsch's initial contact with Sir Hugh Anderton was all that was keeping him alive.

He received three basic meals a day, delivered by a young woman wearing black-framed glasses. She told him nothing apart from her name: Melissa.

By the fourth day all hope had gone, and he was having serious doubts about the wisdom of his actions. The brutality of the Nazis had convinced him to stand against them, but he now knew that the British could be just as brutal and just as narrow-minded.

He began to dread the sound of the key in the cell door. They had decided to have him shot. His body would be buried in an unmarked grave somewhere on foreign soil, all record of his existence erased. Gudrun, Anna and his mother would never know what became of him. If only he could communicate with them just once more... He longed to let Gudrun know what had happened to him, not to leave her waiting, hoping for word for the rest of her life.

Early on the afternoon of the fourth day the cell door opened and Melissa came in.

"Come with me," she said.

Kurt's mood lifted. Surely Melissa would not be the one to take him before a firing squad. Perhaps he would be put on trial first.

She led him upstairs to the second floor, and stopped at a door marked MI14.

"What's MI14?" Kurt asked Melissa.

"The Germany desk." She knocked and ushered Kurt inside.

Major Weir sat behind a desk, writing. A nameplate on the desk read 'Bertram Weir'.

"Take a seat," said Weir without looking up.

Kurt and Melissa took the two chairs facing the desk.

Weir put down his pen and looked up. "We have a job for you, O'Reilly." Kurt's heart immediately began to pound. "I understand you are familiar with the area around Ulm."

Kurt noticed in passing that Weir used his Irish alias while Melissa was present. He was pleased that he was true to his word. Only Weir and Colonel Scott knew his real name, and they were happy to keep it that way.

"I was born there," said Kurt, his spirits rising. He had been concerned that the British might send him to Berlin, where his face was well known. The prospect of revisiting his home patch was an entirely different matter. He would have every advantage there.

"One of our agents operates in that general area. We have not heard from her for a week and we'd like you to find out what's become of her. Have you had any parachute training?"

Kurt's mood immediately swung from elation to dread. The thought of jumping out of a plane turned his blood to ice. "None."

"Right. That's the first thing we need to sort out. I'll make the arrangements. You will travel as a construction worker, a surveyor. Melissa will sort out your papers. Do you have any questions?"

"The agent's cover name and details? Do you have a photograph of her?"

"Melissa will fill in all those details." Weir walked to the door and opened it. "Anything else?"

"When will I be going?"

"Today's Tuesday. I'd like to get you on station by the weekend."

Melissa led Kurt to another office on the third floor. This one had "Director of Operations" on the door. A Union Jack flag hung limp behind an impressive antique desk.

Melissa circumnavigated the desk and sat in the leather chair.

"You are Director of Operations?" Kurt asked.

"No, silly," said Melissa. "I am General Anderton's personal assistant. This is his office."

Kurt took a deep breath. He found a chair. "What happened? I thought I was to be shot as a spy."

She opened a desk drawer, pulled out a folder, and passed it across the desk to Kurt.

"You were," she replied, "but Cleasby's disappearance has forced the colonel's hand. The major needs eyes and ears on the ground in southern Germany."

Kurt opened the folder to a photograph and a set of documents. Erika Cleasby, cover name Porsche Hoffbauer, aged 32, a broad-faced woman with thick lips and brown shoulder-length hair. She had been sent to the Haigerloch area, near Stuttgart, from Leipzig two weeks earlier. Kurt was familiar with the town of Haigerloch and its mediaeval castle.

He noted with astonishment that the agent had a physics degree from the University of Montreal. He could count on the fingers of one hand the number of German women he knew with any kind of science degree.

"A woman with a science degree. Is she Canadian?"

"She's half Swedish, half Canadian, but she has lived in Germany for many years and her German is perfect."

"Did Major Weir say that Cleasby has a radio transmitter?"

"She has a contact in the area with a transmitter. His name is Fritz Baum. But we have heard nothing from her or Baum for a week. It's as if the earth opened and swallowed them both."

"So what do I do for a radio if Baum has been captured?"

"You shouldn't need one. All you have to do is find Erika and get her out."

Melissa opened a second folder and pulled out a battered German identity card. It carried Kurt's photograph under the name Klaus Randau. Kurt examined it. It was an excellent forgery. The embossed Reichstag eagle was indistinguishable from the genuine article.

She handed him three more forged papers – all dog-eared. Kurt examined them. There was a ration book in the name Klaus Randau, resident of Mannheim, a travel permit, Mannheim to Stuttgart, and an NSDAP member's card issued in Mannheim.

He handed the NSDAP card back. "I won't be needing a Nazi Party membership card, thank you."

"Take it with you, Kevin," she said. "You might be glad of it."

"I don't think so," he said.

"Your cover story is that you have been sent from Mannheim to Haigerloch to join a construction site as a surveyor. Cleasby's contact, Baum, is a builder in the area. Once you identify yourself to him he will happily take you on. You won't have to do any actual surveying, maybe fiddle about with a surveying thingamabob."

"A theodolite."

"Exactly. And pretend you're doing something clever."

"You think this builder might still be at large?" Kurt said.

Melissa nodded. "It's quite possible that nothing sinister has happened to him. He's not a trained agent. He may simply be having trouble with his transmitter."

"So how will he know I'm coming? And how will I find him?"

"He won't. It should be simple enough to find him. Haigerloch is a small town."

"Yes, yes, I know the town and the castle. My parents took me there several times."

"There can't be too many building sites there. When you do find him, you have to say 'Winter will be late arriving this year.' and he will respond 'The geese will still fly south in November.'"

"Why Haigerloch? I know the town. There's nothing much there, apart from the castle."

"That was Cleasby's destination. It seems to be the centre of all the military activity in the area."

Kurt said, "I take it I'll be travelling alone."

Melissa shook her head. "You'll have a companion with you."

"Shouldn't I have met him or her by now?"

"You've already met his name's Pilgrim."

They left Sir Hugh's office and made their way to the mess hall. The place was deserted, but there was always tea brewing in an urn. Armed with a cup of scalding, sugarless tea each, they sat at a corner table. Melissa sipped her tea in silence and, for the first time since they'd met, Kurt relaxed. She removed her glasses and rubbed the bridge of her nose. Without them Kurt could see a serious, intelligent woman, somewhat careworn, but attractive. In his imagination he could see her untying her hair and shaking it down around her shoulders...

She blushed. "You're staring, Kevin."

Kurt apologised and averted his gaze. He sipped his tea.

"So the colonel believes my story?" he said at last. "He trusts me?"

"I wouldn't say that, exactly. Weir was going to send Pilgrim on his own. Pilgrim suggested taking you along. Colonel Scott risks nothing by sending you to Germany. You know nothing of British Intelligence operations. And if you fail in your mission what has he lost?"

"And if I succeed?"

"He may use you again." Melissa's smile reminded him of Lewis Carroll's Cheshire cat. It looked genuine, but she seemed able to turn it on and off at will.

Chapter 8

The third time was the worst. Kurt had no head for heights, and climbing the scaffold was terrifying. Jumping off with nothing but a flimsy harness to break his fall was a nightmare. The first time, everything was so unfamiliar his rational mind simply closed down and he did everything he was told like an automaton. The second time he had begun to appreciate the risks he was taking. His mathematical brain began adding up the number of ways that he could be injured. The third time, he was fully aware of the madness of what he was doing. All he could do was concentrate on keeping his knees from shaking so that he wouldn't fall off before he got to the top of the tower. As for jumping off, it took a supreme effort of determination to switch off every natural survival instinct, lean forward and let his body fall.

Kurt did his best to hide the terror roiling in his guts. Pilgrim, on the other hand, didn't seem to have any. Clambering to the top of the tower like a demented monkey, he seemed perfectly content to throw himself off time after time, trusting his life to the canvas straps and supporting apparatus.

By the twelfth jump Kurt's mind was numb and he chucked himself off the tower with abandon, laughing like a madman. After 25 jumps he was starting to understand what he could learn from the training exercise and attempted to carry out the instructor's commands. Tuck and roll on impact. Tuck and roll.

By the end of the day the instructor declared himself satisfied with both trainees. He sat them both down at a rough wooden bench and gave them the last piece of advice.

"When you jump from the aircraft..." Kurt shivered. "... spread yourself out like a starfish, face down and use the wind resistance to stabilise your descent. And remember to count to ten slowly before pulling the cord."

Kurt wondered whether it might be better to count to twenty at normal speed, but he was too exhausted to ask.

#

Placed in the hands of a combat training instructor, Kurt picked up a few new moves and some new bruises around his rib cage. At the end of a gruelling session the instructor had to admit that the unarmed combat training Kurt had received from the Wehrmacht was every bit as effective as what the British army had to offer.

Next, he spent a couple of hours at a firing range and proved that he was just as accurate with the British Sten gun as he was with the Schmeisser MP40.

The instructor had a field radio, but as both Kurt and Pilgrim were professional radio operators, he set that aside and turned to explosives training.

He handed Kurt a box no bigger than a matchbox.

"This is the latest thing from our boffins," he said. "It's a delayed-action grenade. Set the dial for five minutes, then pull the tab and see what happens."

Kurt pulled the tab, and the instructor placed the grenade at a safe distance. It exploded with a loud *crack* and a plume of smoke. Kurt checked his watch: five minutes on the nose.

The instructor produced another grenade twice the size of the first one, but still no bigger than a large matchbox. "We call this a RAG, a radio-activated grenade, it's triggered by a radio signal."

Pilgrim turned the grenade over in his hands. "How does it work?"

"There's a tiny radio receiver connected to a detonator inside. Send it the correct Morse signal and it will explode. Let me demonstrate." He placed the grenade at a safe distance and switched on his field radio. "Key in the word 'PILGRIM'."

Pilgrim tapped in the Morse sequence and the grenade exploded with a loud bang.

"What's the range?" Kurt asked.

"Five hundred metres in the open. Maybe one hundred if the signal has to penetrate walls."

"Each of these radio-activated grenades must have a unique code," said Pilgrim.

"Correct."

"How will we know which is which?"

"You will be given only one of the RAGs and five of the time-delay grenades," said the instructor.

"Why only one of the radio-activated ones?" said Kurt.

The instructor shrugged. "The boffins are churlish about handing them out. I expect they worry that they might fall into enemy hands."

#

On Thursday, April 8, Major Weir completed their mission briefing. "Your mission has one objective only: locate Erika Cleasby and get her out. If you can't locate her, then get out of there as fast as you can. Haigerloch will be your base of operations, but you'll need to find separate lodgings. It will be important not to be seen together."

Kurt asked what Pilgrim's cover story was.

"I'll be a Wehrmacht soldier on leave," said Pilgrim, scratching the back of his neck. For the first time since they'd met, Kurt thought Pilgrim looked nervous.

"In uniform?" said Kurt.

Melissa answered, "No, not in uniform. He'll be wearing civilian clothes."

Kurt asked if Pilgrim's clothes were all made in Germany. His own were.

"Every stitch. Would you like to check?" said Pilgrim with a grin.

Major Weir gave each of them 1,000 Reichsmarks and some small change.

"You'll need a rendezvous point," he said.

Kurt suggested the village square in Haigerloch. "I remember a café there – a little place that used to serve delicious dumplings in a Polish broth before the war."

Kurt enquired about their escape route and Weir said, "Melissa will give you the name and telephone number of a contact in Switzerland. All you have to do is get across the border."

"And if we can't?"

Weir ran a hand through his few remaining strands of hair. "In that case, you'll have to use your initiative."

"Why all this Wehrmacht activity in Haigerloch?" Pilgrim asked.

"That we don't know. People and supplies have been seen disappearing into a cavern under the castle. Some analysts believe that the Nazis are building an underground bunker for Hitler and his supreme commanders. Others have suggested that they may be using the cavern to store ordnance. Or it may be nothing more than a well-stocked beer cellar."

Kurt was unaware of any such cavern. "Do you want us to investigate that?" he said.

Weir replied emphatically, "No. I told you, your mission is to locate Cleasby and get out fast." He removed two small capsules from a box and handed them over. "Potassium cyanide. Just in case. They work within ten to fifteen seconds."

Kurt slipped his into a secure pocket. Pilgrim did the same before resuming his neck-scratching.

"When do we go?" Pilgrim asked.

"Tomorrow night," said Major Weir.

#

That afternoon Kurt got permission to go for a walk in the company of Pilgrim, his chaperone. They strolled toward Euston railway station and Kurt suggested a quick drink in the pub.

While Pilgrim bought two pints of bitter Kurt went in search of the toilet. Once out of sight of Pilgrim, he left the pub and sprinted to the lending library. Going straight to the non-fiction section, he ran his eyes over the spines of the mathematics books in search of the book where he'd hidden his left luggage ticket. It was missing. When a careful re-examination of all the books in the section proved fruitless, Kurt began to sweat.

Casting his eyes around in desperation, he spotted a man sitting nearby with three books in a stack on the table in front of him. *Albert*

Einstein's Theories: Space, Time and Relativity was the top book in the stack.

The man was reading a copy of The Times newspaper. Kurt spoke to him. "Excuse me, sir, but could I borrow that book for a moment?"

The man looked up from his newspaper. "Einstein's Theories? Sure. Help yourself. It's an excellent book, full of interest."

The man's accent was unmistakeably North American.

Kurt picked up the book. Turning his back to the man, he flicked through the pages. To his relief the left luggage ticket was still there. He slipped it into his pocket.

"Thank you," said Kurt, handing the book back.

"My pleasure," said the man, returning to his newspaper.

Kurt hurried to the railway station, presented his ticket at the left luggage counter and retrieved his parcel.

He sneaked back into the rear of the pub. When he returned to the bar, Pilgrim was finished his pint. "What kept you?" he said. "Another minute and I would have sent a search party to find you."

Kurt grinned and downed his pint in one. "Gippy tummy," he said. "My round."

On the way back to The Cage, they discussed their mission in hushed tones.

"Erika Cleasby is a wonderful agent," said Pilgrim.

Kurt was immediately struck by the way Pilgrim said this. There would have been no change in emphasis or tone if Pilgrim had said, "Erika is a wonderful *woman*."

Kurt said, "You've met her?"

"She's been in London a couple of times, and we worked together on a mission in Leipzig a few months ago."

"What d'you think of Melissa?" said Kurt.

Pilgrim looked at him sharply. "Forget about her, Kurt. She's spoken for." Kurt raised a questioning eyebrow, and Pilgrim added, "Why d'you think she spends so much time with the general in Huntington?"

#

In the London headquarters of the OSS, the marine saluted and said, "We've received a report from Willoughby about that Abwehr man, Captain."

Captain Johnson turned a weary eye toward his marine. "The Irishman. What was his name again?"

"Kevin O'Reilly. Willoughby says he's been to RAF Faversham for parachute training."

"Shit!" said the captain. "Do we know where they're going to drop him?"

"No, sir, but Willoughby's eyeballed a set of false identity papers in the name of Frederick von Schönholtz."

"Let's hope he uses them," said the captain. "Otherwise it'll be like looking for a needle in the proverbial hayloft."

"That's a haystack, sir," said the marine.

Chapter 9

On Friday afternoon, April 9, Kurt and Pilgrim were transported to an RAF airfield at Biggin Hill, where Major Weir of the Germany desk was waiting for them. He provided Kurt with a portable theodolite in a canvas bag. This Kurt secured to his chest with a leather strap. Pilgrim carried the six grenades in a bag strapped to his chest.

Then they were helped into their parachutes.

"The best of luck to you both," said Weir.

As dusk fell, Kurt and Pilgrim climbed aboard the plane. It had two pilots and a third passenger, an army officer.

"Your first jump?" said the officer.

Both Kurt and Pilgrim nodded.

"You'll be fine," said the officer. "Just remember your training."

The plane taxied to the end of the runway and took off.

#

The noise from the aircraft engines was head-splitting, the vibrations bone-rattling. Kurt found it hard to think, and all of his natural physical senses were disrupted. He had a sense of being locked in a tin can rushing down a fast-flowing river toward a waterfall, and had to keep reminding himself that this tin can was flying among the clouds, hundreds of metres from the safety of the ground. He lost all notion of how far they had flown, and his natural sense of timing was gone. Only continual glances at his watch told him how close they were to their destination.

Kurt took a look at Pilgrim, sitting to his right. He looked green. Kurt held out an arm and patted him on the shoulder.

"We'll be fine," he shouted.

Pilgrim pointed to his ear and shrugged. He couldn't hear a word.

And then they were over Germany, and the anti-aircraft batteries opened fire on them. The shells burst on every side, sending violent shocks through the plane. It shuddered and jolted and flew on doggedly.

The officer shouted something and waved his arms. Kurt gathered they were passing over some industrial area. The barrage should cease soon. But it didn't. If anything, it grew more intense as they neared the drop-off point.

The officer looked at his watch and stood up. Shakily, he made his way forward and spoke with the pilot. When he returned he held up one hand with five fingers splayed.

Five minutes to the jump.

The officer opened the door, and Kurt nearly lost his last two meals. There was a sensation of cold air rushing in, warm air being sucked out into a bottomless abyss. Anti-aircraft shells exploded all around the plane and the sky was lit up by powerful searchlights.

The officer gestured to them to stand, which they did with difficulty. He indicated that they should take the 'ready' position at the door. Pilgrim stepped forward first, and the officer attached Pilgrim's harness to a wire above his head.

It was only then that Kurt noticed the two lights above their heads, one red, one green. The red light was on.

The officer shouted "Brace!" to Pilgrim and Pilgrim grabbed the sides of the door, one in each hand. Then the red light went out, the green light came on

"Go!" shouted the officer, and Pilgrim disappeared.

The whole thing was like a dream; nothing seemed real.

The officer beckoned to Kurt to step forward. But Kurt's legs froze. Grabbing Kurt by the arm, the officer dragged him to the open door.

A blinding flash lit up the sky. The explosion that followed rocked the plane like a raft on a white water river. The percussion blasted his eardrums, muffling all the sounds, and the feeling of unreality was complete.

"Don't worry," shouted the officer. "Don't think about it. Just count to twenty..."

And then Kurt was hurtling toward the ground under a half-open parachute.

Part 2 - Haigerloch

Chapter 10

Friday, April 9, 1943

Kurt panicked. His worst fears had come true. He tried to collect his thoughts, but even catching a breath in the uprushing wind was difficult. He forced himself to calm down. Reaching up, he tried to shake the straps, to free the collapsed part of the parachute, but to no avail. He kicked his legs, but that had no effect either. He peered up at the canopy. Perhaps he was imagining a problem where there was none. It was more than half inflated. Surely that would be enough to get him down safely. No, he was falling too quickly. The British had interfered with his parachute and he was going to die! Angrily, he shouted Gudrun's name into the rushing air flow. He would never see her again. She would miss him. She would grieve and move on. His eyes blurred and he realised that he was weeping, his tears flying upward and away with his screams.

The ground was approaching fast. At least he would die knowing that he had done the right thing for his country. Germany would rise some day from under the Nazi jackboot and become a proud, compassionate nation again. But he would never see it.

His last thought as he crashed into the dark trees and hurtled through the branches was of Gudrun.

He awoke in the branches of an oak tree. A quick check of his limbs told him that only his left arm and shoulder had suffered serious damage. He checked his clothes. His jacket was fine – it had been protected by the parachute harness – but one leg of his trousers had split along the seam from ankle to knee, and several cuts on his leg were bleeding into his boot.

He unbuckled the parachute harness and checked the cords. There was no mistake: one of the cords had been cut clean through with a knife. Someone in London had meant to kill him before he could start his mission. He was lucky to be alive. He wondered if Pilgrim had made it safely to the ground, or if he was lying dead somewhere under a half-open parachute.

Unstrapping the theodolite in its canvas bag from across his chest, he let it fall. The sounds of the instrument rebounding off the branches told him that he was roughly eight metres from the ground. Next, he gathered the parachute canopy together one-handed, and stuffed it in among the branches where it couldn't be seen from the air.

Climbing down was difficult. His left arm was useless, every move he made sending daggers of pain through his shoulder. The lowest branch was three metres from the ground. Kurt had to jump, and the landing raised the pain in his arm and shoulder to new heights of agony.

Kurt checked his pockets. His false papers and money were safe, and he still had his secret alias in the inside pocket of his jacket.

Gingerly, he swung the theodolite onto his back, and tucked his injured arm into the strap. He looked up. The parachute was barely visible through the branches.

It was 3:30 am local time. He knew roughly where he was – somewhere in the Black Forest, several kilometres to the west of Haigerloch. He checked his compass and set off through the trees. A sliver of a moon threw a little light between the trees, but whenever the clouds moved across its face, the darkness was almost total.

After 30 minutes, he stopped. His arm needed medical attention, but he had found no path heading east. He would have to wait for daylight. He sat under a tree and tried to sleep.

He dozed on and off through the night. On one occasion he opened his eyes to see a bushy-tailed fox watching him silently. He spoke to the animal and it slunk off into the night.

In the morning Kurt set off through the trees toward the rising sun. The pain in his shoulder was as bad as ever, but dim childhood memories of a monastery on the eastern edge of the forest kept him pressing forward.

Within 500 metres he came upon a stream and followed it down toward the valley. The forest became fields, the stream ran under an arched bridge – part of a country road, and soon after that he came upon a substantial structure surrounded in tillage fields with sheep grazing. Kurt blessed his memory. This was the ancient monastery he had hoped to find. He hammered on the main door and waited. There was no response. Kurt thought maybe there were no monks left. Perhaps they had all been conscripted and the monastery closed by the Nazis. Then the door opened and an ancient, diminutive monk in a brown habit peered out. He looked Kurt up and down, his eyebrows registering the state of Kurt's torn trouser leg. The monk checked to ensure that Kurt was alone before opening the door fully and ushering him inside.

The murmur of voices and the clatter of cutlery on plates greeted Kurt's ears, reminding him that he hadn't eaten for 12 hours.

"I'm Brother Markus," said the old monk. "Walk this way."

Waddling with a swaying gait like a barrel on legs, he led Kurt to a large refectory where two other brothers – also extremely old – were at breakfast.

"Are you hungry?" asked the monk.

Kurt nodded.

"Take a seat, son, and I'll fetch some food."

Kurt joined the brothers at the end of a rough bench. Two pairs of eyes watched him, smiling and nodding. A plate of eggs and a thick slice of bread appeared on the table in front of him and he devoured the food without ceremony.

Brother Markus resumed his seat and finished his breakfast. Then the three monks recited a short prayer before rising. One of them stopped across the table from Kurt and said, "We'll have to see what we can do about that arm."

Kurt thanked him and asked, "What should I call you, Brother?"

"My name is Brother Ambrose," replied the monk.

While Brother Ambrose examined Kurt's arm, Brother Markus took his trousers away to be repaired.

"Can you move your arm?" said Brother Ambrose.

Kurt tried, but the pain in his shoulder quickly told him not to try a second time.

Brother Ambrose said, "I think you may have dislocated your shoulder, and your arm may be broken, I can't be sure. When your clothes have been repaired we should take you to the hospital."

"No, no, Brother," said Kurt. "I don't need a hospital."

"We know of a small clinic at Stahlbad where they have Röntgen-ray equipment."

Kurt shook his head. "I can't be seen in a hospital."

"I understand, but don't be concerned. The doctors and nurses there are most discreet. No one will ask how you came by your injuries."

Kurt thanked him and the brother left the room. Kurt marvelled at the way the holy men had come to his aid without once asking him who he was and where he'd come from. They must have been curious, and he could only guess at what they would make of the theodolite, but no one had asked any questions. Theirs was a true manifestation of Christian charity.

Once again his thoughts turned to Pilgrim, whether he had made it to the ground uninjured, where he was now, and if the two of them would ever manage to find one another.

Kurt was reunited with his trousers. Then Brother Ambrose handed him a monk's habit and a pair of battered sandals. "Better put these on," he said. He helped Kurt to put the habit on over his clothes, covering the theodolite strapped to his back. "You look like a hunchback." The brother chuckled.

Kurt thanked him again, and Brother Ambrose said sheepishly, "A small deceit that will make your journey easier. I think God will forgive us."

Kurt offered money, but Brother Ambrose refused to accept it. "We have no need of money here," he said. "Remember us in your prayers."

Brother Markus was waiting outside on a four-wheeled wagon, drawn by a carthorse.

"This is Matilde," said Brother Ambrose. "She's may be a bit slow, but she's strong and she will get you to the clinic."

Brother Ambrose helped Kurt up onto the wagon beside the driver, and handed up Kurt's boots. "Put your hood up, and keep your boots hidden under the habit."

With the merest touch of the reins on Matilde's back, she set off.

The roads were undulating. In the dips nothing could be seen but young green wheat rustling in the spring sunshine on all sides. On the highs, Kurt could see a good section of the landscape ahead.

Kurt asked how many monks lived in the monastery.

"There are only three of us left," said Brother Markus, sadly. "All the younger brothers were conscripted into the army."

After a couple of kilometres the silhouette of a castle perched atop a rock could be seen rising from the heat haze in the distance,

"That's Haigerloch castle," said Brother Markus. "It's a place of evil. Stay as far away from there as you can."

"What evil?"

"People who go there get sick."

"Since the Wehrmacht took it over? What sort of sickness?"

Brother Markus refused to say any more. Apart from the rattle of the wagon and the snorting and blowing of the horse, they travelled in silence for several kilometres more. Then Kurt caught sight of military vehicles moving in convoy in the distance. When he asked about them, Brother Markus said, "That's the main road from Stuttgart to Ulm. We won't be going anywhere near there."

They came to a sharp bend in the road and ran straight into a roadblock. There was nowhere to run. Turning the wagon in the narrow road could not have been accomplished without unhitching the horse, and they were in full view of the two soldiers manning the roadblock.

"I can't reach my papers. They're in my jacket," Kurt whispered.

"That won't be a problem," said Brother Markus. "Leave the talking to me."

Chapter 11

"Papers," said the Wehrmacht soldier.

Brother Markus produced two identity cards from the folds of his habit and handed them down.

"You are Brother Markus? You are from the monastery over the hill?"

"Yes, Herr Leutnant. I'm taking Brother Francis here to the hospital at Stahlbad."

"What's the matter with him?" said the soldier, handing the papers back.

"He's not been well. You can see..."

The soldier stared at Kurt, his face partially obscured in the hood, a grotesque hump on his back. Kurt kept his gaze on Matilde's rump.

"Very well," said the soldier. "But if you come across any Wehrmacht vehicles, be sure to give way to them."

"Yes, Herr Hauptmann. And thank you."

As soon as they were out of sight of the soldiers, Kurt asked what Brother Markus had shown the soldier.

The monk grinned toothily. "I borrowed Brother Francis's identity card for the journey. You look a little like him."

When they arrived at the Stahlbad hospital, Brother Markus helped Kurt out of his habit and sandals. Kurt managed to put his boots on one-handed, but he had to ask Brother Markus to tie the laces. Kurt thanked him, Brother Markus stroked Matilde's rump with the reins and with a final wave he was gone.

The hospital was indeed small, but it was bustling with activity. Kurt handed over his identity card at the check-in desk. The clerk asked various questions: "You are from Mannheim, I see, Herr Randau. Is this your current address?"

"Yes."

"Date and place of birth?"

Cold sweat ran down his arm. He had not checked the date. "Ulm, July 1, 1913," he said: his own birth date. He would have to take the risk that the British had used the one from his passport. She checked the date on the papers, grunted, and kept writing.

"Next of kin?"

"All dead. They were visiting Dresden when the bombs fell."

She looked up and her face relaxed into a wan smile.

Kurt took his place in a queue of waiting patients. When his turn came, he was admitted to the Röntgen-ray section and had Röntgenograms made of his arm and shoulder. Afterwards, he was seen by a doctor.

The doctor held Kurt's Röntgenograms up to the light. "What happened to you?"

"I'm a surveyor." Kurt tapped his theodolite. "I was conducting a survey in the Black Forest, stepped backward and fell over a low wall. I should have been watching where I was going."

"Your arm is not broken, but your shoulder has slipped from its socket. I can repair it quite easily." The doctor took Kurt's wrist and placed his lower arm across his chest. "Make a fist, but try to relax your arm."

"Will it hurt–?"

Before Kurt had completed his question, the doctor rotated Kurt's lower arm outward. The pain was excruciating. Kurt gave a yell. The doctor continued the rotation, until Kurt's shoulder slipped back into its socket. The level of pain dropped immediately.

"All done," said the doctor. "It will be painful for a week or two. We've no painkillers, I'm afraid. Your shoulder will require a course of manipulations to get it back to full health. Make an appointment with the physiotherapist on your way out."

Kurt went in search of the physiotherapist. He found her in an office, writing patient records, her head down. When she lifted her head her eyes opened wide in amazement.

"Kurt! You're back!" she cried.

Chapter 12

Kurt felt the blood drain from his face. Her name was Helga and she had been his clinging, passionate lover for two feverish years when they were teenagers. Meeting people from his past was inevitable this close to Ulm, but was it good or bad luck to run into an old flame?

He took the seat opposite the desk and handed her his identity card. "You must be mistaking me for someone else," he said. "My name is Klaus Randau. I'm from Mannheim."

She stared at him blankly. "I see. Well, apart from the scruffy beard and the missing tooth, you look just like my old friend Kurt Müller from Ulm." She examined the identity card. "I see you share his birthday, too."

There was nobody within earshot. Kurt whispered, "Keep your voice down, Helga, please. Just give me an appointment. I'll explain everything later."

She hesitated a moment before writing the name K. Randau into her book.

"What treatment do you require, Herr Randau?"

"My shoulder slipped its socket. The doctor said I would need a course of manipulations."

"Let me take a look." She came around to his side of the desk, and he stood up to meet her.

She helped him out of his jacket and shirt. And then they were standing close together. As Helga ran her fingers over his arm and prodded his shoulder, her hair touched his skin, and memories of their time together as teenagers came flooding back.

"You don't live in Ulm any more?" He risked a glance at her face. She had a few new lines around her eyes and mouth, but she still wore her blond hair pinned around her head in neat plaits in the traditional style.

"Too many memories," she said. "Those three years we spent together..."

"Two years," he insisted. "I'm sorry–"

She moved his elbow sharply backwards. "Did that hurt?"

"Yes."

"And what if I do this?" She lifted his arm to shoulder height.

"Ow! That was painful."

"Good, that's as it should be," she said, smiling.

She helped him put his shirt and jacket on, and returned to her own side of the desk.

"I can give you an appointment for next Monday. How long will you be in this area, or are you back for good?"

"I have some surveying work to do in Haigerloch," said Kurt. "It may take a week... I'm not sure."

"Where are you staying?"

"I'm not. I mean I haven't had a chance to find lodgings, yet. I thought I'd find somewhere in Haigerloch."

She beamed at him. "Nonsense, Kurt. I have a spare bed. You must stay with me."

#

Helga turned the key and opened the door into a minuscule apartment. "After you," she murmured.

Kurt squeezed past, sidled around a two-seater settee and scraped his leg on a coffee table. He looked around. "Where do you cook?"

Helga edged around the other way and pulled back a curtain to reveal a scrubbed sink with pots and pans hanging above, a dismal gas ring, and a larder with a meagre store of food in glass jars. No mouse was going to set up home here.

The bathroom had a bath and a toilet. No hand basin – and no door. There wasn't room for the former and the latter had fallen off its hinges sometime during the Kaiser's reign.

Every time she spoke Kurt was inundated with memories. Her laugh, the way she said his name, the tilt of her head, her hair, and especially the way she used her hands to emphasise her words. It was as if they had never been apart. There was something else, too, an ominous sense of unfinished business, of a reckoning to come.

He stuck his nose into the bedroom and emerged with a frown on his face.

"Sorry about the mess," she said. "I didn't have time to make up the bed this morning."

Kurt shook his head and smiled at her. The state of the bed wasn't what was worrying him; it was the piercing eyes of Adolf Hitler staring down at him from the picture on the wall above the bed head. She was from a solid working class family, Catholic and stubbornly patriotic.

"You don't have room for a guest," he said. "I should find somewhere else."

"Don't be silly," she replied with a wave of her hand. "There's plenty of room, and we have a lot of catching up to do."

He used her toilet and she sang loudly to disguise the sounds.

When he emerged, she said, "I put a curtain up there when the door fell off, but then I made a dress out of it. We all have to make sacrifices for the Führer."

She had put some vegetables on to boil, and soon the acrid smells filled every corner of the small apartment, making his eyes water.

Kurt's shoulder was aching. "You don't have any painkillers, I suppose?" he said.

She turned off the gas ring, helped him to remove his jacket and shirt and spent 20 minutes manipulating his shoulder, throwing questions at him as she did so.

"So, when you left me in 1935," - she gave a ruthless twist to his elbow that almost made him faint - "where did you go?"

"I told you at the time, Helga, I joined the Wehrmacht."

"So you did." Another sharp twist, and the muscles in his neck clenched in sympathy. "And did you decide not to write, or did you just forget to keep in contact with your fiancée?"

"We were never engaged!"

When she'd finished she turned her attention back to the vegetable soup, but the questions kept coming: where had he been, what had he done. She would have made an excellent interrogator if the Gestapo ever needed one.

In an attempt to stem the flow, he turned on the radio. The newscaster announced a major military operation in the Ukraine, the burial of the late French President Millerand in Paris, and the entry to the war on the Anglo-American side of the South American republic of Bolivia.

"Oh no! Not the Bolivians!" she said, hooting with laughter. "We should lay down our weapons and surrender now!"

She said she had a headache and switched the radio off. When Kurt threw her a questioning look she said, "It's nothing, Kurt. I get them all the time."

Helga seemed unwilling to let the conversation flag, filling their silences with trivial anecdotes. He was only half listening. While she prattled on – something about how she'd taken up gymnastics with a group that turned out to be Communists – the bitter memory of their last encounter came back to him and settled in his gut. They had tried to rekindle their love on his return to Germany from Ireland in 1935, but the magic was gone.

She laid the small table with a linen table cloth and took a dusty bottle from the back of a cupboard. "I've been saving this for a special occasion," she said, her voice husky.

The label on the bottle read 1936. He uncorked it and she poured out two glasses. Gazing at him, she touched her glass to his and toasted "youth and friendship".

She drank some wine. "Delicious!" she said. She took a second gulp and then kissed him full on the lips, spilling wine into his mouth. It was pure vinegar.

As they ate Helga resumed her questioning. Was he married? Had he had many girlfriends since they last met? Was he living in Mannheim now? Did he have a steady girlfriend?

He told her a little about Gudrun and Anna. Helga had a few amorous episodes to relate as well, and they extracted as much fun as they could from those. As he responded to her questions he threw in a few of his own, and gradually managed to get her talking about herself.

Her father had joined the Waffen-SS before the outbreak of war and was with the first wave that entered Poland in September, 1939. As reward for his gallantry in battle he had been promoted to corporal first class. Then he was wounded during the invasion of France and had to have a leg amputated. He was shipped home, developed gangrene and eventually died from his wound.

"He loved the Fatherland and the Führer with a passion right to the end," she said proudly. "His dying words were 'Sieg Heil'."

Helga gave him her vision of the future. Following Germany's final victory over her enemies, the Thousand Year Reich would be established. Czechoslovakia, Poland, and parts of the western Soviet Union would form the new Greater Germany, the backbone of a new Europe. France, Belgium, Holland and the other countries would be given limited powers of self-government under Berlin.

"What about Norway and Denmark, Spain and Portugal?" Kurt asked.

"Spain and Portugal will be happy to join the new Europe. Denmark will be integrated. Maybe Norway and Sweden, too. The Nordic peoples are racially pure, after all."

"And the English?"

Her nose wrinkled in disgust. "They have had every opportunity to join us. I fear for the English. Their betrayal will be punished severely."

Staggered by what Helga was saying, by the level of self-deception engendered by the ministry of propaganda, Kurt bit his tongue. He had no doubt that he was hearing what rank and file Nazi sympathisers believed.

"What about the Americans? Don't you think their entry into the war has made a difference?"

"Short term, yes, but in the long run the American Jews will follow the easy path to peace. They have no real interest in fighting a war in Europe. Once they have defeated the Japanese they will withdraw."

She showed Kurt photographs of her father in uniform, her mother, her brother – now serving at the Eastern front. She gathered the pictures together to put them away, but he put a hand on her arm to stop her. "Let me see the rest."

Shyly, she showed him pictures of herself in school uniform, and at 17, her blond hair in pigtails, dressed in her Bund Deutscher Mädel (BDM) outfit. Beside her in one picture stood an awkward-looking teenage beanpole called Kurt with dark unruly hair. He remembered that uniform and those pigtails. She was a big girl, even then, the buttons of her BDM blouse threatening to pop.

Kurt wondered what their sleeping arrangements would be. The spare bed on offer was no more than a pile of blankets on the floor. He was entirely in Helga's hands.

"How's your headache?" he asked.

"All better." She poured the last drops from the bottle into his glass and smiled at him.

Chapter 13

By morning Helga was draped across his chest, snoring like a steam locomotive. Lying in the semi-darkness, Kurt thought about Pilgrim. Had he made the jump safely, or had his parachute been interfered with? Was he lying dead in a field somewhere, or had he and his precious grenades fallen into the hands of the Gestapo?

Helga stirred, pushed herself up onto her hands and blew into his face. "Ready to go again, soldier?"

"Please, not again, Helga," he replied. "How about some breakfast?"

"Spoilsport!" She leapt out of bed and he watched as she dressed.

The night had been spent playing an old game that Helga called 'hide the bratwurst'.

Kurt had refused at first. "I don't have a condom."

"We don't want to worry about that," she said. "Just give me whatever you've got."

When Kurt stood his ground she rummaged in the bedside locker and handed him a heavy-duty condom with a sigh.

She was insatiable. His injury, coupled with the pricking of his conscience ensured that his involvement had been no more than passive. Helga didn't mind. In fact she seemed to prefer it that way.

Breakfast consisted of diced cabbage on dry black bread.

"Is this all you've got?"

"What did you expect, eggs and bacon?"

Kurt shook his head in disbelief. It seemed food rations had deteriorated in the 10 months since he'd been away from Germany.

"I'll get some food for tonight," she said.

"It's Sunday."

"I know a farmer close by. Don't worry. We won't starve."

While they ate, Helga resumed her questioning. She asked about his job. How had he become a surveyor?

"It was a good career choice for me once I had my maths degree."

"How does it work?" she said, peering at his theodolite.

"It's complicated," said Kurt, rubbing his eye with a knuckle.

She asked several other questions. What was Mannheim like? Was food rationing any better in the city than in the countryside? What did he have to survey in Haigerloch? Was it for the Wehrmacht?

"Why do you ask that?" he said.

"The castle has been taken over by the Wehrmacht. And there's something strange going on in the cavern at the base of the cliff. We've had a lot of soldiers admitted to the clinic, some with accidental injuries or back problems, but most with lung problems."

"What do these patients say about what's going on there?"

"Not a word, Kurt. Whatever's going on in there is top secret."

Chapter 14

Kurt walked the 5 kilometres into Haigerloch. It was Sunday and all the shops were closed. He spent an hour searching the town for Erika's radioman, Baum the builder, and found two small building sites, both deserted.

He turned his attention to Haigerloch castle, sitting on top of its rock surrounded on three sides by the remnants of an ancient forest. He remembered visiting the castle several times as a boy with his parents. He recalled an open air square, a dining room with a beamed ceiling that must have been 100 metres long and 30 metres wide, and the taste and the smell of the sweet biscuits cooked in the castle kitchens.

The main entrance on the east side of the castle was manned by an armed guard, the hinged barrier in constant use with Wehrmacht vehicles entering and leaving every few minutes.

Kurt followed the perimeter of the castle through the trees and came to the road providing access to the dramatic 10 metre rock face directly beneath the chapel. Another manned barrier barred his way, this one carrying a metal sign *Eingang Verboten* – No Entry. The entrance to the cavern was clearly visible, where a truck was being unloaded onto a forklift.

"Move along!" said the sentry, stepping forward, waving his gun at him.

Hoping to make contact with Pilgrim, he found an open air café in the village square and took a table in the sun, experimenting with various positions until he found one that minimised the ache in his shoulder.

"Were you injured in combat?" the café owner asked, polishing the table top.

"What? Oh, yes. It's well on the mend, now."

"I lost my husband in the advance on Moscow."

"I'm sorry for your loss."

"What would you like?" she said "I can offer you ersatz coffee or wine."

Kurt ordered white wine. The café owner removed two stamps from his ration book as he paid her. It was a bright, warm day. From the peaceful look of the shops in the square, window-boxes everywhere overflowing with early season flowers, it would have been easy to imagine that there was no war at all. He tasted the wine; it was barely drinkable. He ran his eyes over the other patrons of the café. Outside, two old men played chess in the shade of an awning. Inside, a mother battled with a screaming child. A few pedestrians passed by and he scanned them looking for anyone who might be from the secret project in the castle. Several soldiers, an elderly schoolmistress, a pastor, a group of boys in Hitler Youth outfits, a plumber perhaps, a fair-haired electrician-cum-radioman.

His mission companion was heading across the square with a wide grin on his face. Kurt finished his wine and hurried to intercept him.

Walking past Pilgrim, he said, "Follow me," and led him to a discreet laneway near the river where they could talk unobserved.

"What happened to your arm?" Pilgrim asked as they shook hands.

"It's nothing. I dislocated my shoulder on landing. You had no trouble?"

"None. I landed in a field, tucked and rolled, scared the cattle."

Kurt said, "My parachute failed. If I hadn't landed in a tree I would have been killed."

"That's terrible!" Pilgrim's face paled with a shocked expression that was totally genuine; either that or he was the best actor in the world.

They exchanged addresses. Pilgrim was billeted with a widow in the town. Kurt asked about the grenades and Pilgrim assured him that they were well hidden.

Kurt said, "Locate Erika's radioman, Fritz Baum, tomorrow. Get him to send a signal to London. Tell them we've arrived safely." He told Pilgrim where to find the two building sites. "Ask him what he knows about Erika's disappearance. Meet me back here at 1800 hours."

Chapter 15

"I've bought us enough food for a week," said Helga.

"I won't be staying that long."

She pouted. "You're going to have to tell me the real reason why you're here."

"I told you. I have survey work to do."

"Come on, Kurt. I know you too well. You rub your eyes when you lie."

Kurt took a breath before answering. "I am an undercover agent for the Department of Public Health and Racial Hygiene. We suspect the conduct of criminal activities in the cavern and possibly also inside the castle."

"Criminal activities?"

"Deviant activities involving racially impure individuals."

"What? You mean the soldiers are fucking non-Aryan women in there?" Helga was wide-eyed with excitement.

"Don't ask me, Helga. The operation is highly secret."

"Don't you trust me, *Liebchen*?" She clung to his good arm.

Kurt pursed his lips before answering. "We have reports concerning Romany women. I can't say any more. I've probably said too much already."

"That's important work, Kurt. The purity of the Aryan race must be protected at all costs. Is there anything I can do?"

"You must tell no one what you know. You haven't told anyone that I'm staying with you, I hope?"

"I told nobody, but the farmer probably guessed I had a visitor." Before Kurt could ask, she said, "He's a good friend. I'm sure there's no need to worry."

A good friend? Probably a good Nazi friend, thought Kurt

Kurt explained that he couldn't complete his mission without getting inside the cavern.

Helga said, "It's guarded day and night. You'll never get in there."

"I have an idea," he said. "But I'm going to need your help. Can you get me a Wehrmacht uniform from the clinic?"

Her eyes opened wide again – in alarm this time. "You want me to steal a soldier's uniform?"

"I want you to borrow one. I'll need it for one day only. You should be able to remove it and put it back without anyone noticing."

"I don't know, Kurt. What if the soldier goes looking for his uniform and can't find it? There'd be a terrible rumpus. I'd never be able to put it back."

"Pick someone very sick. You must have one or two who are unlikely to be looking for their uniforms in the next 24 hours."

She said, "Well there is a boy in a coma, poor soul. He was injured in a rock fall. His uniform is undamaged but it's not very clean."

Helga made a meal of mashed potato and sauerkraut. After the meal she suggested some physiotherapy on his damaged shoulder. Kurt slipped his shirt off and she worked on him for a half-hour. When she'd finished, he had increased flexibility in his shoulder, but the pain level had increased.

They sat together on the settee listening to the radio for a while. They were treated to a re-run of one of Hitler's speeches and music from a military band. She switched it off and they kissed. Then she reached for him.

"I don't want to do it again," said Kurt. "Not unless you have a fresh rubber."

She smiled at him, her blue eyes hooded. "Don't you want to give me a baby, Kurt, a racially pure baby for the Fatherland?"

"No, I don't," said Kurt, firmly. "We're not married. And how would you manage with a child on your own in the middle of a war?"

She produced a rubber from somewhere and they made love on the settee. Helga led the way again, making allowances for his shoulder injury. It seemed her inventiveness knew no bounds, and Kurt reckoned the risky nature of his mission added spice to her passion. Later, they adjourned to the bedroom and Kurt slept like a stone.

He woke in the early hours of the morning to the sound of Helga sobbing in the bathroom. He found her sitting in the bath, blood running from her nose and down her chest.

When she saw the alarm on Kurt's face, she said, "Go back to bed, Kurt. I'll be fine."

Kurt sat on the bed waiting for her.

She appeared wrapped in a towel and she gave him a rueful smile. "I get nosebleeds from time to time. I'm sure it's nothing to worry about."

"You should tell one of the doctors in the clinic," said Kurt. "How long have you being having them?"

"A few months. Most of the nurses at the clinic have them too. The doctors think it may be caused by our poor diet."

She dried her hair, pulled a packet of cigarettes from the bedside locker and offered them to Kurt.

"You know I don't smoke, Helga. When did you start?"

She lit a cigarette. "In 1935, not long after you left me. I needed all the comfort I could find then."

Kurt immediately regretted asking the question. He knew what was coming next.

"I blamed your father," she said. "He never liked me."

"That's not true."

"Why else would he ship you off to study in Ireland when there are plenty of perfectly good universities in Germany?"

The idea had never occurred to him. Perhaps she was right. The reasons given at the time had been that his father and Professor Hirsch were friends and Professor Hirsch was a famous mathematician. But Kurt had been seriously smitten by this girl between the ages of 16 and 18. All their friends assumed that they would marry some day, but their liaison might have been seen as anathema by his father. A strict Lutheran, he hated the Catholics almost as much as he hated the Nazis.

She drew deeply on her cigarette. "Tell me what happened to us. I thought we were going to be together again when you returned from Ireland, but you broke up with me and moved away with no explanation."

"I explained. I'm sure I told you how I felt." Kurt remembered exactly why he had decided to break up with Helga. What he couldn't remember was the reason he'd given her at the time. "Can't you recall what I said?"

"Every word. You said I was too good for you. You said we should both look for other partners before deciding to settle down, that we had no experience of living with others, only with each other. That was a lie, for a start. You had sexual experiences with Irish girls while you were away. You told me so."

Kurt could feel the ground sliding open beneath him like a silent trapdoor. He said, "But you hadn't met anyone else."

"I waited for you. Weren't we supposed to wait for one another? Wasn't that what we agreed?"

The Nazis were no threat to him, not compared to the onslaught that was heading his way from Helga. "We were young and inexperienced."

"So you keep saying. But I loved you. I never wanted to make love with any other boys. Tell me now, honestly, why we broke up."

Kurt's memories of the break-up had been revived by their two nights together. As a lover, Helga was enthusiastic, athletic, and inventive. He remembered how he'd felt about their intimacy the last time, in 1935. The trouble was that Helga was over-enthusiastic, over-inventive and took the initiative too often. The pressure on him to perform to her standards and her timetable was more than he could live with. And something about the way she continually came up with new ideas suggested that she was thinking about it too much between sessions. She seemed to be trying too hard, obsessively, so that it lost its spontaneity. And there was something creepy about the way she laughed at the sight of his aroused manhood. He couldn't tell her that, not then and certainly not now.

He said, "I suppose I never loved you the way you loved me. I'm sorry, Helga."

"You don't think you should have made that clear at the time?"

He left that one unanswered.

Chapter 16

The following morning Kurt remained in the apartment. The news on the radio was all about Hitler's latest speech. The absence of propaganda from the battle fronts in Europe, Russia and North Africa was an indication that Germany was losing its grip on the war. It was going to take something extraordinary to save her.

There was a knock on the apartment door. Kurt switched off the radio and held his breath.

"It's me. Let me in." It was Pilgrim.

Kurt opened the door and pulled Pilgrim inside.

"God in heaven, Pilgrim, we're not supposed to be seen together," said Kurt.

"I know, but I have news." Pilgrim looked like a cat whose dinner had flown away, his voice no more than a hoarse whisper. "I spoke with Baum. Erika has been taken by the SS."

Pilgrim cast his eyes down and Kurt thought for a moment he saw tears in his eyes, but when Pilgrim faced him again, his eyes were hard.

"Tell me what Herr Baum said, exactly," said Kurt.

"He said Erika was in the town less than a week before she was arrested. The SS have a base in the castle. Baum thinks she was taken there." A picture of desolation, he shook his head. "I can't understand how her cover was broken so soon after she got here. D'you think she could have been betrayed by someone in London?"

Perhaps by the same person who sabotaged my parachute, thought Kurt.

He said, "Did you ask Baum to send a signal?"

"He let me use his radio transmitter. I told London that we had landed safely and that Erika had been captured. They replied that we should get out. Abort the mission, they said."

"This mission is not over," Kurt replied, grimly. "Erika could still be in the castle, and if she is I will get her out. I'm not writing her off yet. See if you can find a way for us to get inside the castle."

That suggestion was all it took to dispel Pilgrim's black mood. He hurried away with a determined look on his face.

#

Helga returned at midday, carrying a Wehrmacht uniform in a bag. Kurt tried it on. The trouser legs barely reached the top of his boots. Helga suppressed a giggle.

He said, "Couldn't you find a soldier more my size?"

She helped him on with the jacket, then stood back and covered her mouth. The sleeves were three centimetres short. He found the soldier's Wehrmacht identity card in the breast pocket. The description on the card was of a man 1 metre 60 tall; Kurt's height was 1 metre 80. The photograph on the card showed a ruddy, unshaven face; Kurt's face was grey and bearded.

Pinned to the jacket was a second card labelled 'Haigerloch Project'. Kurt grinned when he saw it. "It's perfect, Helga. Thank you," he said. "Today I am Heinrich Mutti, private, first class."

#

Kurt walked into Haigerloch and returned to the road leading to the cavern.

He remained out of sight until a Wehrmacht truck drew up at the barrier. Then, while the sentry was dealing with the truck driver, Kurt walked past. The sentry caught sight of the card pinned to Kurt's chest and let him pass without a challenge.

When the driver and his helper climbed down from the cab, Kurt asked to see their consignment papers, hoping to give the driver the idea that he was an official from the cavern. Kurt read the description and origin of the load: 'Iron blocks from Auergesellschaft, Oranienburg.' A forklift emerged from the cavern and the driver positioned it at the rear of the truck. The delivery men lifted the tarpaulin and began to unload, and Kurt directed the operation. As he hoped, those inside the cavern took him as part of the delivery crew while the delivery crew thought he was from the cavern.

The load consisted of 20 heavy wooden crates with rope handles. It took both men to lower each crate from the truck and onto the forklift. Once the forklift had four crates on board, its driver took the load into the cavern. With the papers in his hand, Kurt followed it inside. Nobody challenged him. He scanned the area quickly. The cavern seemed limited in size. There was no indication of any corridors leading deeper underground. Men in white coats walked about, some stood in small groups engaged in animated conversations. Kurt caught a few phrases: 'operating temperature', 'fission temperature', and something about 'heavy water'.

A reinforced door marked *Reaktor* caught his eye. Kurt's pulse rate immediately quickened. He had studied enough theoretical physics at university to know that radioactive materials could sustain extremely high temperatures and had the potential to generate electricity by a process called fission reaction, although no country had built a working reactor yet.

"Who are you?" The question came from a young man wearing horn-rimmed glasses, rubber boots and a white lab coat.

"I'm with the delivery crew," said Kurt, his heart rate increasing again.

The young scientist held out his hand. "Papers."

Kurt handed him Private Heinrich Mutti's identity card.

"This doesn't look anything like you," said the scientist, frowning.

Kurt reached out and took the card back. He shrugged. "That picture was taken a couple of years ago. I was overweight then."

"And clean-shaven?"

"Yes." Kurt returned the identity card to his breast pocket.

Kurt did his best to control his heart rate while he watched the young man going through the puzzle in his mind. How likely was it that he had stumbled across an enemy agent who spoke perfect Germany and was dressed in an ill-fitting Wehrmacht uniform? The security of the project was paramount, but what were the chances he'd make a fool of himself if he said something? Did he really want to start a storm by accusing this innocuous-looking man, or did he want a quiet life?

"Where's your personal monitor?" The young man pointed to a yellow badge pinned to his lapel.

Kurt used his hands to search his chest. "I must have dropped it somewhere."

"Wait here." The young scientist went through a door marked 'Staff' and returned with a spare badge, which he handed to Kurt. "Wear it at all times."

Kurt thanked him and said casually, "How is the research progressing?"

The scientist stiffened. "Why do you ask?"

Kurt shrugged. "We wondered how much more you would be ordering."

The young man relaxed again. "I cannot answer your question. I doubt that any of my colleagues could. What are you delivering today?"

Kurt consulted his paperwork. "Twenty crates."

"That's 300 grams of material." The scientist smiled. "You can expect to make a lot more deliveries of that size."

#

At 6 pm Kurt found Pilgrim waiting for him in the laneway by the river where they'd met before.

Pilgrim laughed at Kurt's uniform before making his report. Casual enquiries about the castle had revealed that local people supplied fresh food – vegetables, meat, and even some fish – for the troops stationed there. Others, repair men and construction workers, were called to the castle to do odd jobs, from time to time. The Wehrmacht maintained a permanent workforce of cooks, but a cleaning crew of locals was admitted every night at 9 pm.

Looking pleased with himself, Pilgrim produced a sketched diagram of the castle. It was crude, but it showed the main buildings. The castle consisted of a six distinct buildings, that Pilgrim had numbered 1 to 6, and a chapel, surrounding an open compound. "I drew this sketch based on what Baum the builder told me. He worked on refurbishments in the castle in 1928-29."

"Do you know what any of these buildings are used for?"

"Building 3 houses the kitchens, Building 2 is the quartermaster's office," said Pilgrim. "The rest, I'm not sure about."

Kurt said, "It's time we paid the castle a visit."

Pilgrim scratched the back of his neck. "And how do you propose we do that?"

"We're going to need a rope."

Chapter 17

Helga lit a cigarette. "Private Mutti has recovered consciousness. I have to put the uniform back, and I have to do it tonight."

"I need to keep it for one more day, Helga," said Kurt. "Then you can take it back, I promise."

Her face drained of blood. She sat down heavily on the bed and swore at him. "Asshole! I wish I'd never met you again. You're nothing but trouble." A single tear rolled down her cheek. She buried her face in her hands. Kurt sat beside her and put his good arm around her shoulders. The single tear became a flood from both eyes.

"Don't cry," he said. "You can have the uniform back tomorrow evening without fail, I promise."

She sobbed. "What do you need it for?"

Kurt said, "My suspicions have been confirmed. The cavern is a den of iniquity. I need to get inside the castle. Chances are the same or worse things are going on there."

"But why do you have to wear the uniform? Why can't you tell them who you are and demand entry?" Her hand shook as she put the cigarette to her lips.

"That's not going to work, Helga. If they get a whiff of who I am, those Romany girls will be smuggled out and I'll have nothing."

"When will the war be over? I'm weary of it," she said.

"I'd give it a year," said Kurt. "Twelve months from now it should be all over."

While they ate, he spoke about Greater Germany, how the war in Italy was turning in Germany's favour and the spring weather was bringing new mobility and new hope to the troops on the Eastern front.

"What about North Africa?"

Kurt laughed. "The Allies have won there. They can have North Africa. They can have all of Africa, and they're welcome to it."

"What about us, Kurt? When it's over will there be room in your future for us? For me?"

And there it was – the question Kurt had been dreading. He swallowed hard and ran through 10 possible responses in his mind. He rejected all of them. What could he say? Sleeping together had been Helga's idea. She had given him no choice. He would never have done it if there was any way to avoid it. Still, he felt like a heel. Rejecting her advances had seemed unthinkable, but perhaps he should have. He never wanted to cause her pain or to give her false hope. And now here she was clinging to the past, dreaming of an impossible future.

She was staring at him, waiting for a reply.

He said, "I have Gudrun waiting for me in Ireland."

"Gudrun! What is she to you? I can't believe she could mean as much to you as I do, or that she loves you as much as I do."

Desperate to stem the tide, Kurt shook his head.

"I knew it! You don't love her. She's an older woman, a mother figure. You feel obliged to her in some way. You know that we were made for each other. Promise me, Kurt. Promise me that when the war is over you will return to me."

Kurt shook his head again. He needed to choose his words carefully. If ever he needed to speak clearly, it was now. "There are three loves in my life, Helga," he said. "Germany, Gudrun and Anna."

She snorted. "*Scheisse!*"

He pressed on. "The Fatherland comes first. If I survive the war, Gudrun and her daughter, Anna, have to come second."

"I see. I come nowhere, not even last."

"I'm trying to be honest, Helga. I won't make a promise that I can't keep. Gudrun and Anna depend on me for a living."

"I hate you," she said, stripping the braids from her hair.

Later, Kurt said, "I found out what they're doing in the cavern."

"The racially deviant sex. You told me."

"Yes, but there was something else."

"I don't want to hear another word," she said.

"Don't you want to know why the clinic has so many patients with lung problems and what's causing your headaches and nosebleeds?"

Helga reached for her cigarettes and lit one. "You're going to tell me, aren't you, whatever I say?"

Kurt took a deep breath. "They're experimenting with radioactive materials."

"God in heaven, Kurt! Are you sure?"

"I'm certain."

"We should tell someone. I should let the doctors know."

"I'm sure they must already know. I can only suppose they haven't released the information for fear of causing panic."

Helga sat on the settee, her face hidden behind her hair. She said nothing for several minutes. When she had finished her cigarette she stubbed it out and stood up, pushing her hair back from her face. "You could be right, Kurt. New general instructions have been issued in the clinic in the past six months. Staff must wash their hands after any contact with the patients."

"Isn't that normal practice?"

"Yes, of course, if a patient has been bleeding, but they're asking us to wash our hands even after contact with the patients' belongings – or their visitors. Some of the nurses think they are taking hygiene to extremes. My hands are raw from washing. And we've all been issued with work shoes, and coloured identity badges." She pointed to the badge on her uniform. "They give us new ones every month."

"That's a radiation monitor," said Kurt. He showed her the one he'd been given in the cavern. The two badges were similar. The only difference was that the film in his badge was freckled with black spots while hers was clear.

Chapter 18

Tuesday, April 13

"Winter will be late arriving this year," said Kurt.

"Ah yes, but the ducks will still fly south in November," the builder replied.

Close enough, thought Kurt.

"Come inside," said Baum, and he opened the door of a garden hut. He was a short, bald man with blond eyebrows that gave him the look of an infant. His clothes were sprinkled with cement powder.

The hut was equipped with a folding table and a blanket box. There was nowhere to sit.

"I use this as my office," said Baum. "It's small enough to move about from job to job. I spoke with a young man yesterday about Fräulein Hoffbauer. I take it you are with him?"

Kurt nodded. "I need information about the castle. How long has it been under Wehrmacht control?"

Baum wiped a spot of powder from his nose, replacing it with a bigger one. "Since August of '41."

He spoke at length about the history of the ancient castle, how he had come to work on it, and the structural renovations that had been necessary in order to preserve the buildings. Kurt produced Pilgrim's rough sketch. Baum laughed when he saw it. He opened the blanket box and pulled out a roll of drawings.

"These were prepared by the architects during the renovations," he said, unrolling them.

Kurt ran his eyes over the drawings. It was clear that the building Pilgrim had labelled Building 6 included extensive cellars.

"These must be wine cellars," said Kurt.

"Once upon a time," said Baum ruefully. "The wines stored in there were a treasure trove. Sadly, no more. The first thing the Nazis did when they arrived was to remove all the paintings from the walls. The second thing they did was to clear those cellars."

"I take it they moved the wine to some other cellars in the castle."

Baum shook his head. "There aren't any. These are the only cellars at the site."

"The building seems to have only one entrance," said Kurt.

"You're right, and the ground floor windows are all barred." said Baum. "It's a fire hazard. It wouldn't pass modern safety standards. But no one thought of things like that in the thirteenth century. But if you're looking for a way in, there is one unbarred window – here." He pointed to a small window at the rear of the building where a single-storey annex had been added that connected the building to the chapel.

#

Kurt slipped through the woods and into the shadow of the castle towering on its rock above. He heard Pilgrim crashing towards him, and cursed under his breath. A half moon hung in the cloudless sky.

He grabbed Pilgrim's arm as soon as he was within reach, and pulled him into the trees. "I asked you to bring a rope." Pilgrim's hands were free and he carried no bag.

"Love your uniform," said Pilgrim with a grin.

"Never mind the uniform. Where's the rope?"

Pilgrim lifted his shirt and revealed what looked like a length of twine wrapped around his torso. Surely this couldn't be the 15-metre rope Kurt asked him to procure?

"That's not strong enough. Where did you get it?"

"I stole it from a flagpole. But look what else I found." Pilgrim ducked into the undergrowth and pointed at a rope ladder hidden behind a bush.

"Where did you find that? No, don't tell me. Tell me it's long enough."

"It's long enough." Pilgrim grinned again. "I'll drop the flag rope down. All you have to do is attach it to the top of the rope ladder and I'll pull it up."

Kurt said, "I take it you've worked out how to get past the guard at the entrance."

"The cleaning crew will be here in the next few minutes. They've agreed to let me join them."

"How did you manage that?"

Pilgrim rubbed index finger and thumb together in the universal sign for cash.

The cleaning crew were a motley group. Armed with mops and brushes, laughing and joking, they filed through the entrance. Kurt watched from the woods as Pilgrim slipped inside with them unchallenged, whistling, and carrying a bucket and mop.

Five minutes later the end of the flag rope slid down the rock from above. Kurt attached it to the rope ladder and watched it rise up the rock face. He gave Pilgrim a couple of minutes to secure the top of the ladder before starting to climb.

At the top Kurt was confronted by the crenellated wall of the castle. He scaled that and found himself behind a troop transport equipped with a pivoting machine gun, the flag rope tied to its back bumper. Pilgrim crouched beside him. People could be seen criss-crossing the square between the buildings, some in civilian clothes others in Wehrmacht uniforms. It could have been daylight, the light from the moon was so strong.

Pilgrim whispered, "How're we going to find Erika? She could be anywhere."

Kurt said, "If she's here, she's in that building." He pointed to Building 6 on the far side of the compound. A gleaming black Mercedes Benz staff car was parked outside.

"How can you tell?" asked Pilgrim.

"Trust me," said Kurt. "Wait here."

Kurt had borrowed a pad and pen from Helga's apartment. Removing these from his breast pocket he strolled across the compound and tried the door. It was locked. He hammered on it and it swung open. He was confronted by a Wehrmacht soldier, his rifle pointed squarely at Kurt's chest. "Stand where you are. No one is permitted to enter this building. Who are you? What do you want?"

"I'm from the quartermaster's office," said Kurt, flipping open his pad. "I'm counting heads. How many in this building?"

The soldier made no move to lower his gun. "Who sent you? Why do you need this information?"

"We have had a directive about waste from Berlin. I expect you've seen it." The soldier shook his head. Kurt looked mildly surprised. "We are directed to eliminate all waste to support the war effort. The quartermaster needs better information about numbers so as to eliminate food waste. Just give me the numbers and I'll be on my way."

The soldier loosened his grip and the gun dropped to a 45 degree angle. It was now pointing at Kurt's knees. "This is the security centre for the area. The number of officers varies from day to day."

"Yes, yes, of course." said Kurt impatiently. "And prisoner numbers?"

The soldier consulted a sheet pinned to a notice board. "There are three."

"Three men," said Kurt, writing on his pad.

"Two men, one woman," said the soldier obligingly.

Kurt gave him a withering look, turned on his heel and left. He waited for the sound of the door closing before returning to where Pilgrim was hiding.

"Is Erika in there?" said Pilgrim.

"I don't know for sure, but they have three prisoners and one of them is a woman."

"That must be Erika," said Pilgrim. "How are we going to get her out?"

"With great difficulty," said Kurt.

Chapter 19

Both Kurt and Pilgrim joined the cleaners' detail 24 hours later, wearing civilian clothes. Kurt carried their precious grenades and the flag rope in Pilgrim's shoulder bag, as well as his theodolite in its canvas bag. Whether their plan was a success or a failure, they would not be returning to their lodgings.

Following an uncomfortable night on Helga's couch, Kurt developed a crick in his neck. She had risen early, and he asked her to apply her healing hands to his neck and shoulder, but she refused, hurrying off to the clinic to return Private Mutti's uniform.

Once inside the castle perimeter Pilgrim went to the kitchens in Building 3 with the bulk of the cleaners while Kurt headed for the chapel with two of them, noting with satisfaction that the SS staff car was still parked outside Building 6.

Inside the chapel Kurt opened the door to the steeple and climbed the stairs. Halfway to the top he found a door leading to a veranda overlooking the annex and used Pilgrim's rope to lower himself onto the annex roof.

The small window at the rear of building 6 was unbarred as Baum had said it would be, but it was nailed shut. Kurt checked his watch. Three minutes to go. The sound of voices warned him of a patrol approaching. He lay flat on the roof and held his breath as two Wehrmacht soldiers strolled past, talking and laughing.

When the three minutes were up, Kurt heard Pilgrim knock loudly on the door to Building 6.

"Hey! Open up in there," Pilgrim shouted.

Kurt waited until he heard the door open and raised voices. Then he put his theodolite through the glass in the window, squeezed through, lowered himself inside, and pulled the theodolite and the bag of grenades after him.

There was an immediate feeling of foreboding, the sharp smell of disinfectant attempting to mask the reek of human waste. There was also a hint of something like rust that Kurt recognised as the smell of blood. Underlying all those were the unmistakeable odours of damp and ancient mould.

Pilgrim was raising a storm at the door. Kurt could hear three voices. He couldn't catch any of the words, but the guards had their hands full with Pilgrim playing the part of a drunken cleaner.

Kurt located the staircase leading to the cellars and hurried down.

Stretching the length and breadth of the building, the cellars had low, vaulted ceilings designed to support the weight of the massive structure above. The whole space had been segmented by the Nazis into individual cells with steel doors, labelled 1 - 20. Only three were locked. He peered into each and found Erika sleeping in cell number 7. He rapped on the door.

"Erika. Erika Cleasby? Wake up."

Erika rolled her head toward him in the bed. "Who's there?"

"London sent me. I'm here to get you out."

She leapt to her feet. "You have a key?"

"No, but I will have in a minute or two."

Kurt hid in one of the empty cells near the bottom of the staircase and waited. Footsteps on the stairs signalled the arrival of one of the guards propelling Pilgrim ahead of him.

"Where are you taking me?" protested Pilgrim.

"I'm locking you up, you drunken bastard. You can sober up in one of our cells. The SS-Sturmbannführer will deal with you out in the morning."

Kurt waited until Pilgrim and his escort had passed by before slipping behind the guard and wrapping an arm around his neck. Within seconds the guard was lying unconscious on the stone floor.

"Pilgrim? Is that you?" whispered Erika.

Pilgrim grabbed the guard's keys and unlocked the door to Erika's cell. And then she was free and they were wrapped in one another's arms.

"I knew you'd come," she said with feeling. "But what kept you – and who's this?"

"This is Kurt," said Pilgrim. "I'll explain later. Come on, we have to get out of here."

Kurt said, "Are you injured? Can you walk?"

"I can walk," Erika replied.

Kurt went to open the doors to free the second prisoner, but the prisoner said, "Please don't open the door. I can't leave. If I do, my family will be killed."

"If you're sure, Wolfgang," Erika said.

"There should be a third prisoner," said Pilgrim.

Erika said, "He's in cell 13, but he's badly injured."

Kurt peered into the cell. The third prisoner lay on his bunk facing the wall. Kurt called out, but the man didn't stir.

Kurt led the way up the stairs. Pilgrim now carried the theodolite, his bag of grenades slung over his shoulder. They almost made it to the end of the corridor leading to the main entrance when a door opened to their right and a guard in uniform emerged, fastening his fly buttons to the sound of a toilet flushing. The guard scrambled to draw his handgun. "Hands in the air! How did you get into the building? This building is off-limits."

None of them raised their hands.

"I found no one at the entrance," said Kurt. "I have orders to transport this prisoner to Berlin, immediately."

"I know nothing of any such order. What about him?" said the guard, jerking his gun toward Pilgrim. "What are you carrying? Put it down."

Pilgrim dropped the theodolite with a clatter.

The guard said, "I sent Helmut to lock him up. Where is Helmut?"

Kurt pointed over his shoulder. "Helmut's downstairs attending to the injured prisoner."

"Why don't we all go down and find him?" said the guard, gesturing with his gun.

"I have no time for this," said Kurt. "I have my orders." He pulled out his pad and waved it toward the guard who took a step closer to look. And then Kurt had a double-handed grip on the guard's gun hand. They wrestled for the gun, Kurt struggling to hold on. A sharp rabbit punch from Erika to the guard's neck ended it, and he crumpled to the floor.

Kurt took the guard's handgun.

Inside the guard's station by the main entrance they searched for keys for the staff car, but found none.

"They've got to be here somewhere," said Pilgrim, ransacking the desk, tossing the contents on the floor.

Kurt tried the pockets of a full-length leather coat hanging on a hook behind the door. He found a pair of black leather gloves, but no car keys.

"Leave it," said Erika, unlocking the main door.

"Halt!" A shot rang out, a bullet pinged off the wall by Pilgrim's ear. Kurt looked back and saw the first guard at the top of the staircase, a wild look in his eyes, a Schmeisser smoking in his hands.

Kurt grabbed the coat, Pilgrim picked up the theodolite, and the three fugitives charged through the door. The driver's window of the staff car shattered under a blow from the butt of Kurt's handgun. Unlocking the back door, he jumped in behind the wheel.

Erika and Pilgrim piled into the back as Kurt reached under the dashboard to grab a handful of wires.

The engine started with a satisfying roar. Kurt put his foot on the accelerator and sent the car hurtling around the compound perimeter toward the gate, gravel spitting from under the wheels. With Helmut firing at them from the security building, Kurt crashed through the gate barrier, demolishing it. The lone sentry leapt for his life, then opened fire with his rifle as the car sped down the road.

They came to a T-junction and Kurt turned right.

"Where are you going?" Erika shouted.

"Switzerland," Kurt shouted back.

Erika leant forward and spoke into Kurt's ear. "Go north."

"My orders are to get you out of Germany," said Kurt.

She said, "Go north. Or stop the car and let me out, now."

Kurt slowed the car.

"You need to get out of Germany," he said. "You have no papers."

She shook her head. "Take me to Leipzig. I have papers there and a mission to complete."

The troop transport appeared in Kurt's rear view mirror, its machine gun spitting bullets.

Kurt floored the accelerator. "Okay, but we'll have to shake off this lot, first. Hold on tight!"

The car bucked under the impact of heavy tracer shells. Then the rear window shattered.

Part 3 - The Factory

Chapter 20

Kurt threw the wheel over and they careered right at full speed onto the main road. "Is anyone injured back there?" he shouted.

"We're both fine, but I wouldn't give much for our chances of staying that way," said Erika.

The troop transport followed, its gun firing furiously. Bullets buzzed by like a swarm of bees, strafing the metal bodywork of the car.

"Keep your heads down," Kurt shouted again.

Gritting his teeth against the pain in his shoulder, Kurt gripped the wheel and put his foot down. The powerful staff car shot forward. They passed a convoy of Wehrmacht trucks trundling along in the slow lane. There was little other traffic on the road. Unable to match the speed of the Mercedes Benz, the troop transport fell back and then disappeared from Kurt's rear view mirror. He kept his foot on the accelerator.

After five kilometres, two military motorcycles joined the road and gave chase, one behind the other, 20 metres apart.

Pilgrim and Erika hoisted the theodolite into the back window.

"Wait until I give the word," said Erika. Then, "Now!"

They dropped the theodolite into the path of the nearest motorcycle. The heavy instrument bounced and rolled across the road behind them, ripping the motorcycle from under the first rider. The second rider swerved around his companion and began to gain on them.

"Can't you go any faster?" Erika hissed. "He's nearly on top of us."

"I won't be able to outrun him. He's too fast for us," Kurt shouted back.

He waited until the motorcycle was within 10 metres. Then he jammed the brakes on. The bike wobbled, managed to avoid colliding with the car, and shot past them. Kurt accelerated again and attempted to hit the bike from behind. To evade Kurt's attack, the bike moved into the slow lane before accelerating again to catch up. The second time that Kurt applied his brakes, the motorcycle rider was ready. He dodged to the side, reduced his speed and drew up alongside the car. For a couple of moments Kurt and the rider locked eyes as they approached a slow-moving truck. The motorcycle rider levelled his handgun and fired a couple of wild shots at them. Kurt waited until they were almost past the truck, then he threw the steering wheel to the right. The dull clunk of the car striking the motorcycle was followed, two beats later, by a squeal of metal on metal as the motorcycle slid under the truck. Driver and motorcycle were shredded in a shower of sparks.

Erika punched the air. Pilgrim cheered.

Kurt tucked the car into the traffic stream. They passed a road sign that read Basel 10 km.

"What's your plan?" said Erika. "You do have a plan?"

Kurt replied, "We need to convince the Nazis that we're heading for Switzerland before turning back."

#

Two kilometres from the Swiss border they topped a hill and saw a long line of traffic ahead. Pilgrim stepped out of the car to see what the hold-up was.

"It's a roadblock," he said, climbing back into the car.

Kurt did a u-turn and drove back a half kilometre the way they'd come. He took a side road and came to the entrance to a farm. He parked the car in front of the farmhouse beside a scruffy old truck that had been constructed from a car by some crude amateur metalwork.

"Wait here," he said. He donned the leather coat and gloves before banging on the farmhouse door.

The response was a lot of wild barking from several dogs inside. After a couple of minutes the door opened a crack, and a man's face appeared.

"Who is it?"

"I need your truck," said Kurt. "My car has broken down."

The door slammed shut. Kurt hammered on it again, and the barking of the dogs grew to a crescendo. "Open up," he shouted. "In the name of the Reich, open this door."

The door opened again, and the farmer stepped outside to face Kurt, taking care to keep his dogs inside.

"What do you want?" said the farmer, the look on his face a mixture of terror and undisguised contempt.

"I need your truck," said Kurt. "Give me the keys."

The farmer shook his head. "I need it to run the farm. Take someone else's truck."

"I am on a mission of national importance," said Kurt. "I am commandeering your truck."

"Where d'you want to go?" said the farmer. "I'll drive you."

Kurt considered this suggestion for a moment before acquiescing. "Very well, fetch the keys."

The farmer went back inside the house, quieted his dogs and re-emerged with his keys.

"Time to use one of your grenades," said Kurt to Pilgrim. "Set it for ten minutes."

Pilgrim fished a grenade from his bag. He set the timer and handed it to Kurt. Kurt tossed it under the rear end of the staff car.

Pilgrim and Erika jumped into the bed of the truck and hid under the tarpaulin. Kurt removed the coat and gloves before joined the farmer up front, dropping the coat at his feet.

An expression of bewilderment passed over the farmer's face, quickly followed by one of anger. "Who are you? Who are those two in the back? I'm not taking you anywhere."

Kurt showed his gun to the farmer. "Take us north."

Muttering under his breath, the farmer selected a gear and set off. "Fucking communists."

Kurt poked his gun in the farmer's ribs. "Do everything I say, get us to our destination safely, and you will live to go back to your dogs."

They went north on the road to Baden-Baden for three kilometres before they hit a roadblock, a massive tailback on the opposite side of the road. All vehicles travelling south were being searched thoroughly by a team of soldiers, while those travelling north were being subject to a cursory inspection only.

The short line of cars and bicycles shuffled forward. They were next in line. Kurt checked his watch. More than 10 minutes had elapsed. The grenade should have gone off by now.

And then all the soldiers were pointing to the sky behind them where a long finger of black smoke was reaching toward the moon. Whistles blew, and the roadblock evaporated as the soldiers jumped into their transports, motorcycle riders started their engines and everyone in uniform rushed toward the source of the explosion.

#

They climbed out of the truck within sight of the railway station at Baden-Baden. Kurt put the coat and gloves back on, and handed the farmer 40 Reichsmarks for his trouble. It was probably more than his truck was worth.

"Go home to your dogs," said Kurt. "Tell no one about us or our friends in the KDP will come calling and burn down your farm."

#

"What now?" said Pilgrim. "None of us has a rail pass."

Kurt said, "The coat should get us onto a train. No one's going to argue with an armed Gestapo man. I can say you are both my prisoners."

Pilgrim grinned. "You're very convincing as a Gestapo man."

"It might get two of us on a train, not all three," said Erika. "We'll have to split up."

They agreed that Kurt and Erika would try to bluff their way onto the train; Pilgrim would find his own way to Leipzig. She gave Pilgrim the address of her apartment, and they embraced. Then Pilgrim handed his bag of grenades to Erika and set off on his own into the city.

"I hope he'll be all right," said Erika, wiping a tear from her eye.

"He'll be fine," said Kurt.

In the railway station Kurt demanded two tickets to Leipzig. The leather coat and gloves and the words, "national emergency" was all the documentation he required.

Finding seats in an empty compartment, Kurt and Erika stretched out their legs and settled in for the five-hour journey.

Erika said, "Thanks for coming to my rescue. How did you find me?"

"I asked an old friend to borrow a uniform for me." Erika's eyebrows shot up at this. "Her name is Helga. She and I were lovers many years ago."

"She was sympathetic to your mission?"

Kurt shook his head. "She's a died-in-the-wool Nazi. I gave her a cock and bull story and she swallowed it."

"I hope you took care of this Helga before you left Haigerloch. You realise she's a danger to us all?"

A tingling sensation in his scalp told Kurt that Erika was right. Helga was the one person in Germany who knew who he really was.

The door opened and two young women came into the compartment, terminating Kurt and Erika's conversation at that point.

As the train was leaving the outskirts of the city, the sound of anti-aircraft batteries signalled the start of an allied bombing raid. Soon the drone of the bombers reached their ears, searchlights punctured the sky, and bombs exploded all around them. The attack lasted less than 30 minutes, by which time the train was out in the countryside, the danger behind them, the wheels beating a comforting rhythm on the rails.

Kurt's thoughts returned to Helga. She had always been a little naïve, but since 1935 her devotion to Hitler and the Nazis had grown in her mind like some monstrous cancer. She was no longer the girl he had loved in his youth. His elaborate fiction about his purpose in gaining access to the castle was beyond ridiculous. It was only her blind faith in Nazi propaganda that made her swallow it. Still, he regretted deceiving her. Could he rely on her to keep his identity secret? He wasn't sure.

Approaching Erfurt, the last stop before Leipzig Central, a ticket inspector opened the compartment door. He checked the two women's tickets and their travel documents before asking for Erika's.

"She's my prisoner," said Kurt, handing over the two tickets. The two young women gasped.

"You have travel documents?" said the ticket man.

Kurt looked up at him. "Do you doubt it?"

"No, but I'd like to see them."

Kurt got to his feet. First, he fastened the buttons of his leather coat. Then he fixed the ticket inspector with his eyes, pulled his leather gloves from his pocket and put them on with much ceremony, all the time holding the rail-man's gaze.

"Now what did you say?" said Kurt quietly.

The ticket inspector broke eye contact. "I'm sorry, sir." He punched both tickets and handed them back. "Have a pleasant journey."

#

In Building 6, Haigerloch Castle, SS-Sturmbannführer Necker moistened a finger and ran it down his duelling scar.

The prisoner was seated, bleeding from the mouth. A soldier stood over him, his tunic discarded, shirtsleeves rolled up to the elbows.

Necker said, "You say the woman offered to release you from your cell, but you refused?"

The prisoner nodded weakly.

"Why would she offer if you didn't know her? And why refuse? It makes no sense."

The prisoner shook his head.

The SS man checked his watch. It was 2 am. "I admire your loyalty to your friends, Wolfgang. Really, I do, but I don't have time for this." He nodded to the soldier who delivered a roundhouse fist to the prisoner's belly.

The prisoner groaned. "I've told you all I know. There were two men."

"Give me their names."

"I don't know their names."

"Give me one of their names and you can return to your cell. Maybe you overheard them talking."

"No, I swear."

"You're lying. Why are you lying to me?"

"I'm not, I swear–"

The soldier delivered another blow that drove the air from Wolfgang's lungs.

"Tell me again what happened, exactly."

The prisoner croaked, "Two men..."

"What did they look like?"

"It was dark. There's not much light..."

"Go on."

"They attacked the guard. They took his keys and freed the woman."

"Yes, yes. And then what?"

"I told you, they offered to let me out, but I refused."

"Why? Why refuse?"

"I was afraid..."

"You must have heard them talking. What did they say to the woman?"

"Nothing. I don't know. I can't remember."

"You can't remember. So you did hear something."

"No, I heard nothing."

Necker nodded to the soldier again...

#

The SS man returned to his office, and made a call to the ORPO station in Stuttgart.

"A prisoner has escaped from lawful detention in Haigerloch Castle. She is using the name Porsche Hoffbauer–"

"A *woman* prisoner?" said the duty sergeant in amazement.

"Yes, a woman prisoner. She is accompanied by two subversives, both male. I will require your office to keep a lookout for them. They made their escape in a staff car. If you see them, arrest them immediately and call me at this number."

"Ach! We have a report of a burnt-out staff car in a forest to the south, near the Swiss border," said the duty sergeant.

"That must be them," said Necker. "Find out how they continued their journey. Call me the instant you have any news."

"Very well, sir. Should I alert the State Police?"

"No!" Necker shouted into the telephone. "If I wanted the help of the Gestapo, don't you think I would have called them?"

"Very good, sir," said the sergeant.

Necker terminated the call.

Chapter 21

5 am Thursday April 15

Alighting from the train at Leipzig Central, Erika set off on foot across the vast concourse, the rising sun casting strange shadows from the roof, denuded of glass. Kurt followed thirty metres behind her.

Erika's apartment on the second floor of a three-storey building was small but homely, with charming paintings hung on the walls. Kurt sank down on the stuffed sofa with a sigh and looked out. The front windows overlooked the river; a barge hooted sadly as it passed.

While she made tea, she suggested to Kurt that it might be time for a wash and change of underwear, directing him to the bathroom and a closet full of men's clothing in the bedroom. When Kurt asked whose clothes they were she said, "They were my fiancé's." She handed him a framed photograph of a Kriegsmarine officer. "He went down with the Bismarck."

"I'm sorry for your loss," said Kurt.

With a sigh she replaced the picture on the mantel. "It's been nearly two years now."

Kurt stripped off in the bathroom and used a pitcher of cold water and a bar of hard soap to wash from head to toe. Then with a towel around his waist, he picked out some clothes in the bedroom. He emerged smelling of the cheap soap and dressed in a dark blazer and loose-fitting pants.

"Very fetching," said Erika with a grim smile. "Thank you for rescuing me, by the way. You did a fine job."

"I would agree with you if we weren't having this conversation in Leipzig," said Kurt. "Tell me why we aren't safely across the border in Switzerland."

"I have resources here, and a mission that I must complete."

"Does that mission relate in any way to the cavern under the castle at Haigerloch?"

"I can't discuss it," she said, and she disappeared into her bedroom without another word.

Kurt was puzzled by Erika's reaction. It seemed she didn't trust him. He wondered what he would have to do to earn her trust; obviously, rescuing her from the Gestapo wasn't enough. When she emerged from her bedroom, an hour later, he said, "I suppose you know that the Nazis have been stockpiling fissionable material in the cavern, and that they are experimenting with an atomic fission reactor."

Erika did nothing to hide her surprise at this. "How do you know this?"

"I was inside the cavern. I saw the work *reaktor* on a door and I heard some of what the scientists were discussing."

"You have some knowledge of physics?" Her lip curled in a sneer.

"I studied mathematics at university," said Kurt. "But I have enough understanding of atomic physics to know the potential of atomic fission for generating power."

"Well, bully for you!" she said, placing the backs of her wrists on her hips. "You'd better tell me exactly what you discovered."

Feeling his blood pressure rise, Kurt ignored the put down. Why did all scientists believe they were more clever and better educated than anyone else, and why did they all despise mathematics and mathematicians? Calmly he related the story of his visit to the cavern while the truck was off-loading crates of iron containing fissionable material.

"You discovered where this material was coming from?" It was clear from her leery expression that Erika hadn't succeeded in penetrating the cavern's security.

"Auergesellschaft in Oranienburg," Kurt replied.

"I know this company," said Erika, frowning. "They work with metal alloys. I had no idea they were producing fissionable material."

Erika opened a tin of beans and heated them up on her stove. The food disappeared quickly; they were both ravenous. As they ate Kurt explored various topics of conversation, but Erika remained cold and aloof. It wasn't until he mentioned Pilgrim that she became animated.

"I'm sure he'll be all right," she said. "He's usually pretty good at looking after himself."

After that Kurt was in no doubt that Pilgrim and Erika had been lovers in London, and that theirs was an ongoing affair.

As she cleared the table she said, "I will arrange new papers for you in the morning. You should have no trouble making your way back to London through Switzerland."

Kurt shook his head. "I'm not leaving without you, Erika. My job is to get you out of Germany."

"I still have a mission to complete," said Erika. "I have resources here that I can call on to help me, but it wouldn't be safe for you to remain."

"What is this mission?" said Kurt, quietly.

"I can't discuss it," said Erika.

Kurt's blood pressure rose another notch. "I think you're going to have to. I'm certainly not leaving the country until I know more about the Nazis' atomic reactor. I assume you intend to check out the industrial plant at Oranienburg? We should do that together, and I'd like to know where the raw materials are coming from."

"None of that is your concern," she said.

"If the Reich is developing atomic fission power, London needs to be informed."

"They know that much already," she snapped.

"London will need much more detail," said Kurt. "Like what materials they're using, how far advanced are they, who's working on it and is it a Wehrmacht project."

The argument continued for another 15 minutes before Erika had to agree that she could use Kurt's help to complete her mission.

"We need a plan," she said. "Let me think about it."

At 10 am she left to find them new travel permits, giving Kurt strict instructions to stay indoors and out of sight. While she was gone, Kurt played solitaire and listened to *The Girl Under the Lantern* over and over on Erika's gramophone. It was the only record she had. By noon he was starving and rustled up a Spanish omelette using the one remaining egg and limp vegetables in Erika's pantry.

Erika returned mid-afternoon with the travel permits and carrying supplies of eggs and fresh vegetables.

"I'll rustle up a Spanish omelette," she said. "You must be hungry."

Kurt groaned silently.

#

Kurt was given the settee to sleep on that night, and in the morning Erika went out early for fresh bread. Kurt was in his underwear when she came rushing back. Clutching his healing shoulder she waved a newspaper in his face. Kurt's picture was on the front page under a stark headline:

ATTENTION! KLAUS RANDAU
WANTED DEAD OR ALIVE.

The article gave a description of Klaus Randau, an enemy agent sought by the authorities. "Randau is armed and dangerous. He should not be approached. If seen, notify any office of the ORPO."

Underneath were two smaller pictures. One showed the burnt-out staff car, the other was a picture of Erika captioned 'Porsche Hoffbauer, enemy of the state.' The article said that the two fugitives were travelling together with another unidentified man. All three were armed and dangerous. If seen, the police should be informed immediately. Under no circumstance should they be approached.

"What are we going to do?" said Erika. "The minute anyone sees either of us, we will be turned in to the police. My neighbours will recognize my picture."

Kurt said, "We'll have to move on as fast as we can. You'll need to dye your hair." He scratched his beard. "Do you have a razor I could use?"

Kurt began hacking at this beard with a blunt pair of scissors. Erika's ex-fiancé from the Kriegsmarine had left a serviceable razor and a few rusty blades and Kurt used these to remove the remaining stubble. By 10 am his beard had vanished, his face a raw, angry red.

Erika emerged from her room wearing a blonde wig and bright red lipstick. She grinned at Kurt's new look. "You'll have to get your photograph taken so that I can arrange a new set of papers for you."

"That won't be necessary," said Kurt. He showed her his secret back-up identity card and ration book that he had carried with him from Ireland. The clean-shaven Frederick von Schönholtz was back in circulation!

Obviously pleased with her new look, Erika left the apartment to organise fresh travel papers under the name von Schönholtz. She promised to return within the hour. Kurt pulled the last two bottles of beer from the pantry and put Erika's lone record on the gramophone again. He was finishing his tenth game of solitaire and the second beer when his senses told him something was wrong.

He turned the music off and tuned his ears to the street below, where an unnatural silence gave him instant goose bumps on his arms. He peered through the lace curtain of the window. The street was deserted. He opened the window and stuck his head out to get a better view. A police car straddled the street at one end. As he watched, a second police car entered and blocked the other end.

He closed the window. And then there was a crash as the front door of the building disintegrated, followed by boots pounding up the stairs.

Kurt grabbed Pilgrim's bag of grenades and the handgun, left the apartment and took the stairs to the roof.

A door led onto a severely slanting roof with a parapet. He slid down to the parapet, ran along that, found a fire escape ladder and used it to descend onto the roof of the adjoining building. That roof was pitched too, although not so severely, but it had no parapet. Clinging to the tiles he edged his way to the far end of the roof, where he was faced with a two metre gap to the next building along. Weighed down by the grenades, and with memories of his parachute jump fresh in his mind, Kurt balked at the prospect of making the leap. Then there was shouting from behind and above him. Planting his feet firmly on the guttering, he braced his legs. Then, bending his knees like a frog, he leapt across the gap and landed safely, the guttering and downpipe clattering to the ground from the roof behind him.

He reached the far end of the parapet on that roof before the police saw him. He heard a shout and shots. Bullets whistled past him as he scrambled down the fire-escape to the ground. Emerging in a deserted alleyway, he ran toward the city centre. Once out of immediate danger, he slowed his pace and disappeared among the crowds.

Kurt regretted leaving the leather coat behind. It had proved useful, but if he'd been wearing it he could never have made that leap. He worried about Erika. Would she return to the apartment and be captured or would she see the police cars and steer clear? He had to assume that she would turn up at the railway station sooner or later, and made his way there.

The giant clock dominating the railway station concourse showed 1 pm while the notice boards and public address announced trains for Berlin leaving at 10 minutes past the hour, every hour from Platform 12.

Kurt's picture was on the front page of newspapers everywhere, and yet he passed unrecognized among the crowds. Mingling with the hundreds of people that thronged the station's vast concourse, he marvelled that the simple removal of facial hair had made him invisible. He wondered if Erika's disguise would work as well. Her broad face and full lips were strikingly beautiful and instantly recognizable. Would the simple transformation from brunette to blonde be enough?

There was still no sign of Erika by the time the giant clock was showing 2 pm. Not daring to sit down, Kurt had to keep moving endlessly through the crowd, as if walking to or from a train.

Somehow he would have to find his way to Berlin and from there to Oranienburg without a travel permit and without the leather coat.

The crowd became skittish and anxious, like a flock of sheep that has sighted a dog. Half a dozen armed SchuPo municipal police had entered the concourse. Fanning out to encircle the crowd, they began to shepherd them together.

Kurt slipped away, vaulted the barrier at the end of an unoccupied platform and jumped down onto the tracks. Keeping his head low, he followed the tracks beyond the reach of the concourse and out into the sunlight.

He came upon a rail workers' hut at the side of the tracks, smashed the padlock off with the butt of the gun and slipped inside. The hut was no more than three metres square, packed with sledgehammers and rail spikes. A rail worker's uniform, cap, and leather bag hung on a hook on the wall. Quickly, Kurt tried it on. It was a loose fit, but close enough.

He was fastening the last buttons on the jacket when a voice from outside the hut called out, "Police! I know you're in there, Randau. Come out with your hands in the air."

Chapter 22

Kurt undid the buttons on the trousers. He put the peaked cap on, slipped a heavy rail spike up the sleeve of the jacket, opened the door of the hut, and raised his hands. Blinded by the low sun, all he could see was the silhouette of a uniformed SchuPo man with his gun drawn.

Kurt said, "I'm not Randau, sir. I'm sorry I fell asleep. Please don't shoot me."

"What are you doing here?" the policeman shouted. "The padlock on the door is broken. Show me your papers."

"That padlock gets broken all the time, officer. Vandals!" said Kurt wearily. "My papers are in the hut." He gestured to the policeman to come inside.

"Step outside!"

Kurt stepped out of the hut, hands on his head.

The policeman gestured at Kurt's crotch with his gun. "The piglet's out of its pen," he said, smirking.

"My papers are inside the hut," said Kurt again.

The policeman grinned. "Didn't you hear what I said? There's a snake in the long grass."

"Where?" said Kurt, peering into the grass embankment.

The SchuPo man burst into laughter. "You're credentials are showing!" He pointed his gun at Kurt's crotch again.

Kurt looked down. "Oh, sorry," he said with a cheesy grin, buttoning his trousers.

Still laughing, the policeman lowered his gun and stepped past Kurt into the hut. "We can't be too careful. There's an armed and dangerous fugitive on the loose. And I don't mean the one in your pants."

The policeman bounced like a sack of flour when he hit the wooden floor, raising a cloud of dust. Kurt checked and found a steady pulse.

He removed the policeman's uniform. Then he used the rail worker's belt to tie his hands securely around a leg of the bench. The rail worker's cap made an effective gag.

He removed the rail worker's clothes and put on the green uniform. The conical hat carried the insignia of the Schutzpolizei, the municipal police for the city. Apart from the hat which was small and the knee-high boots which were over-large, the uniform was a good fit, and the handgun had a full clip.

He checked the SchuPo man's police identity card. The policeman was older, but he was clean-shaven and his height was close enough. He could use it in a casual check.

Inside the rail worker's leather shoulder bag Kurt found a sandwich – sausage and sauerkraut in rye bread, and an apple. He ate the food. Stuffing his own clothes and boots inside Pilgrim's bag with the grenades, he left the hut. He used the spike to wedge the hut door closed and headed off in search of the Berlin train on platform 12.

Approaching the platform from the wrong side, Kurt opened a door and climbed aboard near the rear of the train, found an empty compartment, and took a seat.

Within five minutes a whistle sounded and the train began to move. Kurt hid Pilgrim's bag under his seat and setting off toward the front of the train.

"Papers." Kurt frowned as he scrutinized the passenger's identity papers and travel permits. He smiled as he fielded questions from the passengers. Thank you, madam, but I don't need to see your ticket. Transfer to Lichtenberg Bahnhof in Berlin for trains to the north. There are several empty seats in smoking compartments near the rear of the train, sir.

Fifteen minutes out from Leipzig, the train's ticket inspector caught up with Kurt, gave him a look of disdain and went on past him without a word.

Thirty-two minutes later the train stopped at Lutherstadt Wittenberg and two uniformed ORPO officers came on board. These policemen worked the train from the front. Kurt met them half-way up the train.

They demanded to see Kurt's papers. He handed them the SchuPo man's identity card.

"Where did you get on?" asked one of the ORPO men, barely glancing at the card.

"At Leipzig," said Kurt. "I started at the rear of the train, and I've checked everyone to this point."

"We'll check them all again, if you don't mind," said the policemen. He handed back the identity card with a sneer.

Kurt shrugged and stood aside to let them pass. He continued to the front of the train, checking papers as he went. Several of the passengers complained that they'd already had their identity cards and travel papers scrutinized by the other two ORPO men.

Leaving the train at the Berlin terminus, Kurt had to change trains twice before catching a suburban shuttle to Oranienburg. Wearing his municipal police uniform he sailed through all barriers unchallenged.

The first order of business at Oranienburg was to change back into his own clothes in a public toilet. He was sorry to lose the uniform, but he disposed of it and the gun in the canal.

Oranienburg was a pretty, suburban town, the shops in the main street painted in bright colours. Belching steam, the Auergesellschaft factory squatted like a giant carbuncle to the west of the town. To gauge its size Kurt attempted to walk around it, but found his way blocked at the rear of the plant by an offshoot of the canal system. He estimated the size of the site at five hectares. Parallel to the canal a single rail track ran into the rear of the site. As Kurt watched, a freight train with 20 open-top wagons emerged from the site and rattled down the track, heading south.

He found a house in a working-class area that rented rooms by the week and paid for a week in advance. When the landlady had gone off, taking her eager smile with her, he checked all the escape routes. The door to the roof was padlocked. Like a good citizen he picked the lock and slid out. Leaving the bag of grenades hidden behind a chimney, he came back in and replaced the padlock.

He bought some sauerkraut and black bread and ate in his room. He slept poorly that night, as his mind ran through all the problems he now faced. His main concern was with Erika and Pilgrim, whether they were safe and whether he would make contact with either of them again.

#

Kurt went back to the factory gate the following day. It was Saturday but workers were streaming in. "Who do I ask about work?" he asked one. She pointed at a notice on the gate. "Wanted Skilled and General Labourers and Kitchen Staff. Apply to the Foreman in Room 39."

The foreman looked him up and down and examined Kurt's hands. "You don't look much like a general labourer. Where have you worked before?"

"I was in the Wehrmacht," Kurt replied. "I was wounded in Belgium. Shot in the shoulder."

The foreman grinned. "Doesn't surprise me. Must have been a German bullet. Those Tommies had hardly any ammunition left at the end."

Kurt laughed. "And our men couldn't shoot straight."

The foreman frowned at that. "How's your shoulder now? How strong are you? There's a lot of lifting in this job. What do they call you?"

"Strong enough," said Kurt. "And my name's Frederick."

The foreman agreed to give Kurt a couple of days' trial. He led him to a railway siding inside a gigantic warehouse where three men were shovelling coal from a mountain of the stuff into wheelbarrows, and handed him a shovel.

#

SS-Sturmbannführer Necker's telephone rang.

"Sir, I have news." It was the ORPO police sergeant in Stuttgart. "The municipal police in Leipzig have discovered one of their men in a workman's hut at Leipzig railway station. He was unconscious, tied up, and his uniform stolen."

Necker's pencil snapped in his hand. "You fool! That was the work of our three fugitives. No question about it. Keep the force in Leipzig informed and make sure you keep up the search to the south, but be careful. They are ruthless killers."

"The State Police could help us, sir," said the sergeant. "They have resources–"

"I've told you before: I don't want the Gestapo involved. Just do your job and locate these three subversives. The rewards will be great when you get the job done."

#

After two hours the factory foreman returned and spoke to Kurt.

"How's your shoulder holding up? Show me your hands."

Kurt's hands were blistered. His shoulder was throbbing.

The foreman shook his head. "Your hands won't last a day. Is there anything else you're good at?"

"I'm good with numbers."

By midday, armed with a clipboard and pen, Kurt was busy checking quantities of raw materials entering the warehouse and processed metals leaving. Running his eyes over the figures from the previous days, he spotted a simple arithmetical error, and pointed this out to the foreman.

At 1 pm the foreman led him inside the factory. "The canteen food's a bit rough and ready," he said, "but you won't starve and you can keep your money and your ration book in your pocket."

Special rations! This was the first indication that the factory was engaged in work that was important to the Reich and the war effort.

Kurt took a tray. As the queue shuffled forward, he eyed the food on offer. There was some grey-looking meat and vegetables. Nine out of ten of the other workers chose the meat. When it was his turn, Kurt said to the serving girl behind the counter, "What meat is that?"

"It's meat. What d'you care where it comes from?"

Kurt looked up at the girl. She wore a filthy apron that did nothing to inspire confidence in the food. Her blonde hair was wrapped in a scarf, but the eyes were unmistakeable.

"Make your mind up, mister," said Erika. "You're holding up the line."

Chapter 23

𝑓rom the moment he sat down until he finished the meal Kurt's heart was pounding. He'd found Erika! Was Pilgrim somewhere nearby?

He reckoned the meat was horsemeat.

The foreman was talking. "...all new workers. He'll see you this afternoon."

"Excuse me? What did you say?" said Kurt.

"Otto Staerling, the recruitment manager will see you as soon as you've finished eating," said the foreman. "He'll want to check your papers. There are enemy agents everywhere, you know."

After the meal, the foreman took Kurt further inside the factory. It was Saturday, and there were few people about, but any that Kurt saw were dressed in smart suits or white coats. Some wore radiation monitors like the ones he'd seen in the cavern at Haigerloch.

The foreman knocked on Staerling's office, and when a terse "Komm!" was barked, opened the door and let Kurt slide past.

Staerling looked up from the papers scattered over his military-style steel desk. When he saw Kurt, he stood up, a comfortable belly bulging out of his Hugo Boss suit, and said, "Ah, the bookkeeper, Herr *von* Schönholtz." He shot his cuffs. "We don't get a lot of aristocrats applying for factory work."

Staerling's voice was deep, like dark honey rolling about in a bowl. Kurt detected something odd in his accent and filed it away for later scrutiny. "I'm not–"

Staerling held up a hand. "Of course not. I jest. Where are you from?"

"I've lived all over Germany. Mannheim, most recently."

"And how did you come to this part of the Fatherland?"

There it was again. Just a hint of something in Staerling's accent, and the word 'Fatherland' seemed to stick in his throat.

Kurt lifted a shoulder. "I was in Berlin for a while, needed a change. I heard there was work here, work that will help the war effort."

"You served in the Wehrmacht?"

"Yes. I was wounded in the shoulder in Belgium."

"From a German bullet, I expect." The same joke that the foreman had made. It must have been a stock joke in the factory.

Staerling opened a file on his desk. "I hear you have been counting inventory. The dispatch foreman tells me you picked up an error in the count."

"It was nothing," said Kurt.

"You obviously have a talent with numbers," said Staerling. "I think we can find you something better to do than inventory tally. What level of education do you have?"

"I finished school at eighteen, if that's what you mean," said Kurt.

Staerling handed Kurt's identity card back. "Report to me at 9 am Monday morning. I'll tell the guards to expect you."

#

At the end of the working day, Kurt waited at the factory gate for Erika, and when she emerged he followed her. She walked briskly beyond the northern edge of the town and climbed a stile into a wooded area.

They embraced quickly. "I thought I'd lost you," said Kurt.

"I thought you'd been arrested," she replied. "Do you have the grenades?"

"I have them. I've hidden them at my lodgings, although I'm not happy about the hiding place."

"Better let me have them, so. Bring them along the next time we meet."

Kurt nodded. "I liked your dirty apron," he said. "Very fetching."

She punched his good arm. "It's an effective disguise. Not everyone can grow and shed facial hair like you."

"Has Pilgrim appeared yet?"

The pained expression on Erika's face gave him his answer. "Not yet. Where are you staying?"

They exchanged addresses and agreed to meet at her lodgings the following evening.

He slept well that night. Pilgrim was still unaccounted for, but Erika was safe, and on Monday morning Otto Staerling would find him a better position where he might discover some of the secrets of the Nazis' atomic reactor programme.

#

In the OSS offices in London the US marine handed a sheet of paper to Captain Johnson. "That British agent has turned up in Oranienburg, sir."

The captain ran his eyes over it and handed it back. "I knew he'd surface sooner or later. Do we know if he's operating alone?"

The marine shook his head. "No, sir, but I've asked Musicman to tail him, see where he's staying, where he goes, who his contacts are."

"Cancel those orders, soldier," said the captain. "We don't want to spook him or his contacts, and Musicman has more important things to do. See if you can set up a meeting with Bertie Weir. I don't want the Limeys trampling all over our operation in their hobnail boots."

#

At 6 pm the following day, Sunday, Kurt made his way to Erika's lodgings and handed over Pilgrim's bag of grenades. He was glad to be rid of them.

Kurt asked her, "How did you get here, and how did you get a job in the factory?"

Erika replied that she had seen the police cars at the apartment and made her way directly to the railway station at Leipzig. She waited for Kurt for an hour before catching a train to Oranienburg.

The recruitment manager at the Auergesellschaft factory had found her work in the kitchen when she caught his eye.

"By 'caught his eye' you mean what, exactly?" said Kurt.

"Certainly not what you're thinking," she said.

Her new cover name was Marta Maynard.

Kurt told Erika what Otto Staerling had said about finding him better employment.

"That's excellent," she said. "You may get to see what method they're using to enrich the uranium. You should be able to work out how quickly they can produce the stuff."

"You're sure it's uranium they are working with?"

"Yes. I'd like to know how much they have stockpiled already and where they have it stored. Oh, and the quality of the product."

"Is that all?" said Kurt, sarcastically. "Don't you want to know where the raw uranium is being mined?"

"That's pitchblende. And yes, that would be useful to know."

Erika had a gas ring and some rudimentary pots and pans in her room. As darkness fell, she offered to make a Spanish omelette. Kurt declined politely.

They found a crowded beer cellar serving a locally brewed Helle beer, and spent a couple of hours there before returning to Erika's room.

Erika lit a cigarette, and, for the first time, Kurt noticed a tremor in her hands.

"You were treated badly in Haigerloch castle?" Kurt asked her.

"Oh, they acted like perfect gentlemen at all times. There was an SS man called Necker…" She shuddered.

"Have you any thoughts on who betrayed you?" said Kurt.

"You think I was betrayed? By someone in London, you mean?"

"It seems likely, given how quickly you were arrested in Haigerloch. And how they knew where to find you in Leipzig."

She shrugged. "I've been working for the British for a year. I assumed my past simply caught up with me."

"And it was just a coincidence that it happened where the Nazi scientists are working on a secret fission reactor?"

She said, "You're being neurotic."

"Am I? Did I tell you that my parachute was sabotaged? Someone in London tried to kill me before I could even start my mission. I would have died, too, if I hadn't landed in a tree."

"Maybe your parachute was defective."

Kurt shook his head. "One of the cords was cut through with a knife. Also, that photograph of me in the newspapers could only have come from London."

Erika said, "If you're right, Kurt, why hasn't Pilgrim been betrayed?"

Good question, thought Kurt. He said nothing.

Erika took a few moments to organise her thoughts. Then she said, "I've considered everyone in 'The Cage' in London, and it's ridiculous to suggest that any one of them could be a traitor."

"Major Weir would be my choice," said Kurt. "His German was too perfect for an Englishman."

She shook her head. "Scott and Weir are old British army. They both served in the last war, and have to be beyond suspicion."

"That leaves General Anderton," said Kurt, and they both laughed.

Chapter 24

Monday April 19

Otto Staerling fiddled with his tie, a tasteful affair in several shades of grey that set off his light blue Hugo Boss suit.

"I've set up a meeting with Rickard Blaue," he said, his eyes darting to the door. The honey in his voice was lighter, today. "Blaue is the general manger in charge of 'Special Operations'. You have your identity card?"

Again, Kurt picked up something strange in Staerling's accent, but he still couldn't put a finger on what it was.

"Blaue is a scientist?" Kurt asked, handing his identity card across the table.

"He's an engineer." Staerling ran an eye over the card. "I knew a well-to-do family Schönholtz in Saxony. No relation, I suppose?"

"None." Clearly, Staerling was still struggling with Kurt's alias – Frederick von Schönholtz.

Rickard Blaue came storming into Staerling's office without knocking. He was a tall, heavy man with a permanent frown. His black hair, greying about the ears, swept back from a high forehead. He addressed himself to Staerling. "This is the worker you told me about?" And before Staerling could respond, he said to Kurt, "Otto here tells me you have a way with numbers. Is that correct?"

"Yes, Herr Blaue," said Kurt, rising from his chair. He noticed a radiation monitor, speckled with black marks, pinned to Blaue's jacket.

Blaue turned to Staerling again. "I hope this isn't going to be another waste of my time, Otto. That last man you sent me was less than useless."

"I assure you, Rickard..." Staerling ran a finger under his collar. "I think you'll be pleasantly—"

Blaue snapped at Kurt, "Have you used a comptometer?"

"Of course, Herr Blaue." This was a barefaced lie, but Kurt was confident that he could find his way around any mechanical adding machine.

"Very well, come with me."

Blaue led the way into the factory to a massive metal door marked *Eingang Verboten* – No Entry. A persistent hum emanated from behind the door. Using all his weight, the engineer pushed the door open. The noise increased a hundredfold. Kurt followed him up a flight of metal stairs and onto an open metal walkway suspended six metres above the factory floor. Kurt looked down and suffered an instant attack of vertigo. The workers on the floor were engaged in a multitude of tasks. All were dressed in white protective suits, complete with glass-fronted helmets. Some worked at a smelting furnace pouring molten metal from a giant vat into moulds; others used cranes to move slabs of cold metal from place to place. Twelve large centrifuges took up a quarter of the available floor space.

Directly below the walkway was a vat, five metres in diameter, filled with a sinister yellow liquid that bubbled seductively. Fumes from the vat wafted up Kurt's nose and made him choke.

"Don't you like the smell of our soup?" said Blaue with a grin.

The racket from the factory floor was a deafening cacophony that would quickly drive a person out of his mind. Kurt thought maybe that was why he was feeling an inexplicable impulse to leap over the guard rail and plunge to his death in the foul-smelling vat. He clung to the rail and closed his eyes.

"This way, Schönholtz," Bachman shouted. Kurt shook himself back to reality and followed the engineer to a glass-fronted office overlooking the factory floor. Blaue closed the door, and the noise abated to an acceptable drone.

"Sit there," said Blaue. Kurt sat at a table where a comptometer with two handles crouched, its columns of buttons eyeing him contemptuously.

Blaue placed a wide, leather-bound ledger on the table and opened it. "Don't worry about what the columns mean for the moment. Turn to the page for January. For today I need you to resolve an arithmetic anomaly. See these two totals here?" He pointed to two figures at the bottom of the right-hand column. "They should agree. I'll give you the morning. If you resolve the problem by noon, I can use you. Otherwise, you can go back wherever you came from. I'll be in my private office next door if you need anything."

Blaue left, and Kurt looked around him. The room had an uninterrupted view of the factory floor, and vice versa, giving Kurt the feeling that he was sitting in a goldfish bowl.

He got to work. First, he scanned the pages quickly. There were columns full of numbers, rows annotated with dates. He had a little over 90 minutes to solve the puzzle. Sorting out how to operate the comptometer consumed the best part of 10 minutes. The discrepancy in the figures was 198 units, and the units he guessed were milligrams weight.

Kurt was soon satisfied that the January page contained no intrinsic errors; the problem had been carried forward from an earlier page. He flipped back a page and began to check the figures for the earlier months. He found the problem with 15 minutes to spare. Two digits had been transposed in July, and the anomaly carried forward from there.

He examined the column headings: The first four looked like shortened place names: Joh, Ronne, Freit and Schl. Others read: Sheets, Blocks, Crumbs, Scrap, AR7, Fe23, STS. There were columns labelled H-sheets, H-blocks, KWIP-sheets, KWIP-blocks, BA-sheets, BA-blocks and so on. He thought 'H' might stand for the Haigerloch reactor project, but what 'KWIP' and 'BA' stood for he couldn't guess. He made a mental note of the totals for the month. The BA total was over 30,000, the H total was 2,500, the KWIP total less than 2.

Rickard Blaue returned at 11:55 pm. Kurt showed him the source of the anomaly and how he had corrected it through from July to date. Blaue said, "All right. Put this on and report back here in the morning." He produced a radiation monitor and Kurt pinned it to his jacket.

The monitor was showing blue.

"If it turns to grey let me know immediately," said Blaue.

#

When Kurt described what he'd seen on the factory floor in 'Special Operations', Erika's pupils dilated, she tucked both hands between her legs and her mouth hung open. She looked as though she was having an erotic moment. She lit a cigarette with trembling hands.

"It is as I thought," she said. "Those centrifuges are enriching uranium. And 'H' must stand for the Haigerloch Reactor as you suspected."

"What d'you think BA stands for? And what the hell is 'KWIP'?"

"BA could be anything, but KWIP must be the Kaiser Wilhelm Institute for Physics in Berlin," said Erika. "That's where Werner Heisenberg and his cronies hang out."

"The place names could be mines," said Kurt. "I could check the figures and see if they represent raw material quantities."

"You didn't think to do that today?" Erika said, rolling her eyes.

Kurt ignored the barb, but Erika's superior attitude was beginning to get under his skin. "I had a job to do, Erika."

She sneered. "Helping the enemy by adding up their numbers."

Kurt asked Erika if she had met Rickard Blaue.

Erika said, "We've never met, but I know of him. He's an engineer. Not in Heisenberg's league, but he has a solid reputation. I've even seen him at a convention."

"Shit!" said Kurt. "He might recognize you."

"We have a bigger problem than that," said Erika. "Manfred Necker, the SS man from Haigerloch, was in the canteen today. I managed to duck out of sight, but it's only a matter of time until he recognizes me. The guy knows every mole on my body. He has seen me naked."

Chapter 25

The next day, Tuesday April 20, was Hitler's 54th birthday. The people of Oranienburg were in celebratory mood and many of the shops in the town were closed. In the factory, however, it was just another work day.

Blaue handed Kurt a bundle of new consignment notes for raw materials inventory received. He explained that the first four columns on the ledger, Joh, Ronne, Freit and Schl were indeed mines: Johanngeorgenstadt, Ronneburg, Freital and Schlema.

When Kurt asked what the column marked 'BA' stood for, the engineer replied, "That need not concern you."

Kurt began the tedious work of entering the details into the ledger. Blaue went about his business, leaving Kurt alone in the room.

At 12:30 pm Blaue invited Kurt to join him for lunch. Kurt had an inkling that the invitation was some small compliment to his skill with the numbers, an undeclared vote of confidence or thanks for the work he'd done. He was also acutely aware of the dangers of casual conversation. He was living a lie under an assumed name and a badly constructed lie, at that; one verbal slip and the whole house of cards could collapse around him.

Erika, or 'Marta Maynard' was in her usual place behind the counter. Her apron was spotlessly clean.

The line seemed to be moving slower than usual. When Kurt looked ahead he could see that it was stalled by a Wagnerian giant of a man two metres tall and broad as a barrel. He was wearing the uniform of a factory guard, a ceremonial axe dangling on a leather strap from his belt.

Blaue examined the meat on offer. "Looks like rat," he said.

"It's rabbit," said Erika. "Rat is a delicacy in this canteen." She gave a nervous laugh, and Blaue looked up at her sharply.

"I had the meat yesterday, Herr Blaue," Kurt said hastily. "It was excellent."

Blaue ordered a plate of vegetables. Kurt went for the rabbit, raising a chastising eyebrow at Erika as she served him. Kurt selected a table and sat down.

Blaue excused himself and took his tray to another table where he joined a nondescript man in his forties wearing a three-piece suit. An animated conversation between Blaue and the stranger ensued.

Kurt was ravenous and pitched in to his food with enthusiasm.

A man, thin as a pikestaff, placed his food tray on the table and sat opposite Kurt. "Good day, Frederick. My name's Gutkind."

Gutkind was of indeterminate age. First impressions suggested he was young, but his hair was almost all gone, and the few strands that remained were grey.

"I hear you're working in Blaue's office. I was the last one in there. I'm afraid I failed to solve the mystery of the ledgers."

"So, who do you report to now?" said Kurt.

"I still report to Blaue," said Gutkind, "I'm in the accounts department."

Kurt finished his food, excused himself from Gutkind's company, and hurried back to his desk in Special Operations.

#

That evening, when Kurt mentioned the man in the three-piece suit, Erika said, "Didn't you recognize him, Kurt? That was Professor Werner Heisenberg, head of the Kaiser Wilhelm Institute for Physics."

"I've heard of his Uncertainty Principle," Kurt muttered tentatively.

Erika's eyes were wide with excitement. "He won the Nobel Prize in 1932. I was covered in goose-bumps just serving his food. I'd love to have been able to speak to him about his work. And I'd give my right arm to sit in on a meeting between Blaue and Heisenberg."

When Kurt asked about the giant with the axe, Erika said that he regularly stalled the line in the canteen, demanding double helpings. She had no name for him.

There was still no sign of Pilgrim. Kurt suggested that he might have been captured, but Erika refused to believe that. "He's a resourceful chap," she said. "He'll catch up with us eventually."

Then Erika said, "I'd like you to help me smuggle the grenades into the factory and use them to destroy the uranium enrichment plant."

Kurt snorted. "That's out of the question, Erika. An explosion in Special Operations would do terrible damage to the countryside all around."

"I have my orders," she said.

"What orders?"

"I have to do everything I can to stop or delay the Nazis' atomic programme."

Through gritted teeth, Kurt said, "Tell me, what is the half-life of enriched uranium?" He expected an answer of perhaps 200 years.

Erika replied, "There are two main isotopes of uranium, 235 and 238. Uranium 235 has a half-life of seven hundred million years. The half-life of U238 is longer, something like four billion years."

Kurt's jaw fell. His voice rose two notches. "And you want me to contaminate the area and the water table for four billion years? You're crazy, Erika!"

"I have my orders," she repeated. "I must carry them out."

"I won't be a party to such lunacy," said Kurt, "And I won't stand by and watch you do it either."

Erika scowled. "Have you forgotten why we're here?"

"I know why we're here, and it's not to contaminate the German countryside for the rest of time. You're not even German. You're Swedish or Canadian."

Erika responded, "Keep your voice down, Kurt. We're not playing games here. Has it occurred to you that the Reich may have other plans for this enriched uranium?"

"What the hell are you talking about?"

"I'm talking about a weapon, a weapon of unimaginable power."

"That's ridiculous," said Kurt. "The atomic bomb is a myth, a crazy idea, a mad scientist's dream."

"Are you sure about that?" she said.

"Everybody knows that if they ever succeeded in pulling it off it would kill all life on the planet."

"How?"

"A hundred possible ways. The radiation released would spread on the wind and contaminate the soil. Or the debris from the explosion would blot out the sun for a thousand years. At worst it might set off an immediate chain reaction that would destroy the earth's atmosphere in minutes."

Erika curled her lip in contempt. "Schoolboy theories! Have you any idea how pathetic you sound? The sky will fall on our heads!"

"Maybe so, Erika," said Kurt. "But do we want to run the risk? I say, let's stay well away from the atomic bomb."

Erika did not respond. She began to prepare some vegetable soup.

During the meal, Kurt said, "It's not as if mankind doesn't have weapons enough to kill one another already."

"I agree with that sentiment," said Erika. "But you know as well as I do that the Nazis will go ahead and develop the bomb if there's the slightest chance that it can be done. And if they do manage to build one, you know they will use it."

Chapter 26

Mid-morning the following day, Blaue led Kurt from the goldfish bowl to the office next door. This was Blaue's private office, as evidenced by his name painted on the door's glass panel. There were three chairs and a desk in the office, and a blackboard on the wall covered in a jumble of mathematical symbols and figures.

"Take a seat," said Blaue.

Kurt had barely sat down when the door opened and in stepped a tall man in an SS uniform. Kurt guessed that this must be Manfred Necker.

"This is he?" said Necker.

"Frederick von Schönholtz from Mannheim," said Blaue.

The SS man snapped his fingers and held out a hand to Kurt. Kurt handed over his identity card, which Necker scrutinized.

Kurt glanced at the blackboard. He recognized some of the symbols from the meagre amount of theoretical physics he'd covered at university, but he was out of his depth.

"Your date of birth?" said the SS man.

"July the first 1913."

"You are from Mannheim, I see. I know Mannheim, well. What is the main square called?"

Kurt had no more than a passing acquaintance with Mannheim. He had been there with his parents in his youth, but he had no knowledge of the names of any of the streets. The main square was an easy one, though. Most big towns and cities in Germany had a square or a main thoroughfare named after the Grand Duke.

"Friedrichsplatz," said Kurt.

"Named after the Grand Duke of Prussia." Necker's smile was like a death rigour. "The old aristocracy are irrelevant in today's Fatherland, of course. Anyone with a 'von' in their names will find life in Germany more than difficult when the war is won. They will all be swept away by modern democracy. The new Germans will have no time for baronial titles and inherited wealth." He looked to Blaue for confirmation.

Blaue nodded solemnly.

"History will scorn such people. The Third Reich is rewriting the history of our great nation, even as the Führer is building the greater Germany."

Kurt bit his tongue.

"Who is your father?" said Necker, returning to the matter at hand.

"My father is dead," said Kurt

"What was his name?"

This was shaky ground. Any solid information that Kurt supplied about his fictional father, old man von Schönholtz, could be checked.

"Joseph."

"And what did he do?"

"He was a carpenter."

Necker's face betrayed a mixture of disbelief and disappointment. "Joseph the carpenter. When did he die?"

"Father died when I was a child – in the first war. At Verdun"

"Ah, he was an officer! Where is he buried?"

"He was a footsoldier. We never got his body back for burial." Kurt shook his head in sorrow.

"Ah, so the aristocrat lacked the intelligence for the officer corps?" Necker tapped his front teeth with the edge of Kurt's identity card. "Why does your face look familiar to me? Have we met before today?"

"I don't think so."

"Hmm," said the SS man. "I know of a family Schönholtz in Saxony, although they have dropped the 'von' affectation. Are you related to them?"

"Not as far as I know."

Necker handed back the identity card. "Herr Blaue tells me you have a way with numbers. Do you have any formal education?"

Kurt shrugged. "I have always been good with numbers."

"Otto Staerling, the recruitment manager, tells me you were wounded in Belgium."

"In the shoulder, yes," said Kurt.

"One of a very few," said Necker.

Kurt expected the stock joke that the bullet must have been a German one, but instead, he got a shock, "I'll need to see your Wehrmacht discharge papers."

"I have those at home," said Kurt. "I'll have to send for them."

"Do that. Tell Herr Blaue when you have them and he will notify me."

Again, he looked to Blaue who nodded his confirmation.

Necker prepared to leave. He paused at the door, frowned, and said, "I'm sure we have we met somewhere before. I never forget a face."

#

In London, Major Weir sat on a bench facing the river. He opened his brown bag and checked his sandwiches. Captain Johnson of the OSS sat beside him on the bench, a rolled-up newspaper and a brown bag on his knees. Weir raised an enquiring eyebrow and Johnson said, "Beef jerky on rye. How about you?"

"Cucumber and egg." The same as yesterday.

A thick fog rolling off the Thames obscured their view of the opposite bank. Everything was coated with moisture: the path, the trees, evenly spaced along the embankment, even the bench they were sitting on. Both men wore waterproof coats. Weir's was a mackintosh, Johnson's a stylish trench coat.

There was nobody about.

Johnson said, "We've had reports of a car chase near the Swiss border, involving an SS staff car."

Weir bit into one of his sandwiches. The bread was cut thin as paper. "Any details? Were any arrests made?"

"Not as far as we know. Shots were fired, and two motorcycle riders were killed or badly injured. And we have this." Johnson handed Weir the newspaper.

Weir wiped his hands before taking it. It was a copy of the Nazi daily *Völkischer Beobachter* dated Thursday April 15. The front page headline read:

ATTENTION! KLAUS RANDAU
WANTED DEAD OR ALIVE.

There was a picture of Kurt, who was described as 'armed and dangerous'. A smaller picture of Erika Cleasby was captioned Porsche Hoffbauer, and there was a picture of a burnt-out car.

Weir scanned the article quickly. Erika was alive, which was good news, but she was on the run with Kurt. He was pretty sure they hadn't made it across the border, as he had heard nothing from Switzerland. There was no mention of Pilgrim.

Weir folded the newspaper and offered it back.

"Keep it," said Johnson fishing his lunch out of the bag. It was a sandwich as thick as a doorstep, but it looked delicious. He said, "Our man on the ground reckons it was a prison break. I take it this was one of your operations?"

"I couldn't possibly comment." Weir offered his American counterpart a sandwich. "Try one of mine. They're really rather good."

The OSS man declined and began to devour his food.

The two men finished their lunch in relative silence. When they had finished, they each brushed crumbs from their knees. As if by magic four fat pigeons appeared at their feet and began to tidy up.

Johnson said, "One of our men in Oranienburg has made contact with your team there."

"Oranienburg? That's near Berlin, isn't it?" said Weir.

"Yeah, right. Look, Major, we have an active operation in that factory. I'd be grateful if your team kept out of it, okay?"

They both stood up. Weir said, "Thank you for the newspaper."

"Do we have an understanding?"

Major Weir bestowed his most avuncular expression on the younger man. "I think it's worth reminding ourselves that we're both on the same side, eh, Captain?"

Chapter 27

Wednesday April 21, evening

"If Necker remembers where he's seen my face, I'm a dead man," Kurt said to Erika that evening. They were in the open air, walking by the canal, but Kurt felt as if there were walls closing in around him.

"Where has he seen your face?" she asked.

"My picture must be posted on every police notice board in the country. I'm a Wehrmacht deserter and a traitor to the Reich with a price on my head."

"But you're clean shaven now," she said. "That should help."

"Why d'you think I grew the beard in the first place?" said Kurt. "I had no beard ten months ago when I escaped from Germany. And even if, by some miracle, Necker doesn't remember who I am, I probably have four days – a week at most – before he comes looking for discharge papers that I don't have."

"Tell me what you saw on the blackboard," said Erika.

Kurt shook his head. "I recognized some of the symbols. There were several tensor equations and lots of figures."

"You must write down what you remember," she said.

"I don't remember anything. I told you, I was out of my depth."

"I thought you said you studied physics at university." She clicked her tongue and rolled her eyes.

#

The next day, Thursday, as major parts of the factory were winding down for the night, Kurt waited for Erika at the entrance to the canteen and led her through the factory to the Special Operations area. The furnace was idle, the factory floor abandoned. The noise level from the machinery had reduced to a tolerable level, and now consisted mainly of the whine from the centrifuges.

"Those are uranium enrichment centrifuges. They will run uninterrupted for weeks," Erika said as they crossed the walkway. She peered down at the vat of yellow malodorous liquid directly below them and shuddered. "And that's some sort of radioactive yellowcake sludge."

When they reached Blaue's office, Kurt tried the door. It was locked. Signalling Erika to stand back, he poked his elbow through the glass panel. The racket from the factory floor swallowed the sound of the shattering glass. Kurt reached in and unlocked the door from the inside. Erika stepped over the broken glass into the room, and Kurt switched on the light.

Erika's eyes opened wide when she saw the blackboard. "It *is* a bomb!" she whispered. "Those are Einstein's field equations and you can see here where they have calculated the critical mass of enriched material needed to create a chain reaction, and over here the energy yield expected from the atomic blast. That's close to 1,000 tons of a conventional explosive. I need to get to the Institute as soon as possible. That's where Heisenberg and his team are doing all the real work. Find me something to write with." She seemed incapable of tearing her gaze from the board.

Kurt searched Blaue's desk and came up with a pen and notebook "Be quick, Erika," he said.

Erika sat at the desk and began transcribing the figures from the blackboard. Kurt stood at the door watching the walkway. Within a couple of minutes he noticed a new sound layered on top of the noise from the factory floor: Heavy footsteps on the metal staircase. "Someone's coming!" There were two of them. The first was a young Wehrmacht soldier armed with a Schmeisser submachine gun; the second was the factory guard, the Wagnerian giant from the canteen, his axe now dangling on its leather strap from his wrist.

Kurt stepped out to meet them. "Don't shoot. We've had an intruder, but he got away."

"Hands up," said the soldier, levelling his gun at Kurt's midriff.

Kurt raised his hands and felt a sharp reminder from his damaged left shoulder.

"Back inside Herr Blaue's office," said the giant, his gravely voice like milled pyrite.

Kurt placed his hands on the top of his head and turned back the way he'd come. All three men entered Blaue's office, their feet crunching over the broken glass. Erika had vanished. Kurt guessed that she was under the desk. It was the only place she could have been hiding.

"What were you doing in here?" said the giant, wrapping his fingers around the handle of the axe.

"I heard glass breaking. I was looking for the intruder, but he must have got away."

"We saw no one," said the soldier. "Keep you hands on your head." He moved around the desk and began opening the drawers.

The soldier disappeared behind the desk suddenly with a loud groan. His Schmeisser clattered to the floor and Kurt dived across the desk for it. The giant lurched forward, the first blow from his axe missing Kurt by 20 centimetres. The second missed him by a hair's breadth and split the desk in two. Kurt backed against a wall and the giant advanced, lifting the axe in preparation for the final blow.

Like a jack-in-the-box, Erika popped out of the shattered desk holding the Schmeisser. She pointed it at the big guard. "Halt or I'll shoot!"

The axeman spun around to face her, and Kurt stuck him between the shoulder blades with both fists. The blow had little effect, Kurt rebounding as if he'd struck a brick wall.

Erika waved the gun at the guard and pointed to the door. "Move!" She handed the gun to Kurt and bent down to retrieve her notes.

The security man gave a massive sigh and moved toward the door. The expression on his face showed how little he thought of the threat posed by Erika or Kurt, but he wasn't prepared to argue with a Schmeisser. He crunched over the broken glass back onto the walkway, followed by Kurt with the gun and Erika. Half-way across the walkway an alarm klaxon sounded. Then the soldier appeared behind them. There were tears in his eyes. Tears of pain or tears of humiliation from Erika's assault on his wedding tackle, Kurt could only guess, but the soldier was angry. He leaped on Erika's back, knocking her down and scattering her notes.

Erika regained her feet quickly and tussled with her attacker. Kurt marvelled at her skill in unarmed combat, the way she turned the limited space available in the narrow walkway to her advantage

A downward blow from the giant's axe knocked the gun from Kurt's hands, clattering onto the walkway. Kurt cursed himself for his momentary loss of concentration, and took a step backward. The axe whistled by his left side and struck the metal guardrail with a clang, creating a shower of sparks. The giant stepped closer, pinning the Schmeisser to the walkway under his foot, swinging the axe for a third murderous blow.

Chapter 28

The ear-splitting wail of the klaxon continued. Using both hands, and ignoring the stabbing pain in his shoulder, Kurt caught the giant's descending arm and hung on. The giant delivered a finger jab with his free hand to Kurt's right kidney. Kurt roared. The giant grinned and jabbed again.

The pain was worse than anything Kurt had ever felt. The pain in his shoulder seemed almost a pleasure in comparison. One thought filled his mind: his kidney could not take another jab like that – he must do whatever necessary to prevent it. He twisted the hand holding the axe out over the guardrail and held it there, keeping the giant off balance, his back against the railing.

For one long moment everything froze. They were in stalemate. The giant was immobilized. But so was Kurt. He couldn't loosen his grip; if he did, the axe would surely finish him. Above the wail of the klaxon the factory clocks all struck 10 pm. Then Erika appeared at Kurt's side and swept the giant's feet from under him. Now the giant lay across the guardrail like a huge insect on its back, his legs dangling above the metal of the walkway, his upper and lower body perfectly balanced. The bug-eyed look of alarm on his face reinforced the impression.

Directly below him bubbled the vat of radioactive sludge.

With the touch of a feather to his heels she tipped him over, and the weight of the axe did the rest. His high-pitched scream became a gurgle as the giant hit the bubbling surface of the foul yellow liquid, and slid under.

Erika went back to gather up her notes, but more than half of them had fallen from the walkway to the factory floor below.

"Leave it, Erika," said Kurt, and they ran to the end of the walkway and down the staircase. At the bottom, Erika went left toward the canteen. Kurt headed in the direction of the main plant and the warehousing at the rear of the site.

A shot from behind sent a bullet whistling past Kurt's head. "Halt!"

Kurt ran through the factory, the hue and cry intensifying behind him. A second shot, and a third, rang out.

He reached a warehouse as big as a cathedral, and began to search for somewhere to hide. Six or eight men with guns followed, fanning out among the shelves. Behind the last row of shelving he came to a staircase and climbed as high as he could. He looked down and a wave of vertigo swept over him; he was 10 metres up.

Frantically, he cast his gaze around. There was nowhere to hide, nowhere left to run.

Then he heard a train whistle. Below, an empty goods train was starting to move along the tracks out of the factory site. Without a second thought he climbed onto the guardrail.

"God protect me," he whispered and dropped into one of the open-top wagons.

Part 4 - The mine

Chapter 29

The SS-Standartenführer stood in the centre of Lange's office, a riding crop in his left hand. His field grey uniform was immaculately laundered, the edges on his trousers sharp as knives.

Lange spoke with exaggerated enthusiasm. "...measurable progress. We have infiltrated several dissident groups..."

The SS-Standartenführer suppressed a yawn. He could smell Lange's sweat. The man was disgusting, overweight and unhygienic. Visiting these minor factotums was not something the SS-Standartenführer enjoyed, but it had to be done from time to time, and right now – largely thanks to Lange's incompetence – he was under pressure to produce results.

"... one significant student revolt has been put down with uncompromising force."

"You are referring to the White Rose students of the University of Munich?"

"Indeed, Herr Standartenführer."

Lange's office was a mess. His desk was covered in papers and dog-eared files. The noticeboard on the wall was a riot of official notices, all bearing the eagle standard of the Third Reich, each one screaming for attention. The condition of a man's office reflected that man's state of mind, and Lange's mind was clearly disorganised. He was a dummkopf who would benefit from a swift kick up the backside.

"The White Rose business is ancient history, Lange. What have you been doing more recently? Tell me how many members of the Black Orchestra have been detained."

"I assure you, sir, we are making every effort–"

"Your assurance is not what I require," said the SS-Standartenführer. "What I require is some indication that progress is being made."

"I have a unit permanently assigned to that task, sir. Their mission is to seek out the ringleader, Kurt Müller, the Abwehr deserter."

The SS-Standartenführer suspected that this was a barefaced lie, but he let it pass. He ran his eyes around the room. "I don't see Müller's photograph anywhere."

Lange sprang from his chair and removed some notices from his congested noticeboard to reveal Kurt's picture.

"You should keep that picture on view as a constant reminder, Lange. Capturing this subversive must be your only concern." He slapped his boot with his riding crop once for emphasis. "Everything else is of minor importance."

"Yes, sir. Of course, Herr Standartenführer, but we believe that Müller may have left the country."

"I have received reports of a staff car burned out in a forest near the Swiss border. What do you know about this?"

"I am aware of that incident," said Lange. "I have a unit down there investigating it as we speak."

The SS-Standartenführer suspected this was another lie. He said, "You must be aware that your performance over the past six months has left a lot to be desired. Questions are being asked. Our masters are not convinced that your section is pulling its weight. And your poor performance reflects badly on those above you."

"I'm sorry, sir. We have been given some difficult–"

"From now on, you will submit a written report to my office on Monday morning each week. And I expect you to bring these subversives and traitors to account without further delay. Do I make myself clear?"

Chapter 30

Kurt woke from a dream where Pilgrim was shaking him by the shoulders while a giant with a huge axe was pressing on his kidney. Pilgrim and the giant evaporated with the dream, but the ache in his side remained. His shoulder was aching too, and there was a sizeable lump on his head, tender to touch, where he had hit it upon landing in the wagon.

All four sides of the wagon were made of wood. The timber floor was covered in coal dust that was in constant motion as the wagon rattled and rocked along the tracks. Kurt's whole body shook. Even his teeth rattled, and he found it difficult to remain on his feet. Kurt thought he might lose his mind if he had to endure the shaking – and the noise that went with it – for any length of time. He dusted himself off as best he could, but the coal dust was ingrained into his clothes and hair.

A sliver of moon showing through broken cloud gave him just enough light to check his watch: 1:35 am. Assuming the train was heading south to the mines in the Ore Mountains – a distance of between 300 and 350 kilometres – and assuming an average speed of 50 kph, he calculated it was a journey of six or seven hours. He had been on the train for about 30 minutes. He should arrive at the mine at 8 am at the latest.

He wondered whether Erika had made it out of the factory safely. She was an experienced agent, strong-willed and resourceful and well able to look after herself. The memory of the dispassionate way that she had tipped the giant security man into the vat of radioactive sludge made him shudder. He was confident that she was safe. In hand-to-hand combat, Erika Cleasby was a match for any man.

Holding on to two protruding bolts, he put an eye to a crack in the side of the wagon. He could see very little – shadows of trees, countryside, hills in the distance.

He thought about jumping from the train, but to try that while the train was in motion and shaking would be suicidal, and the distance from the rim of the wagon to the ground was probably more than he could jump in safety. He would have to wait and hope the train stopped soon.

Grit got into his eyes, and rubbing them with his grit-encrusted fingers made them worse. With both eyes tightly closed, he lifted his shirt and pulled out the bottom of his vest. Taking care not to contaminate it with grit, he spat on it and used it to clean his eyes. He wiped his hands clean on the vest before tucking it back under his shirt. Finally, he used his hands and some more spittle to clear the remaining grit from around his eyes.

Recalling what Helga had said – that he rubbed his eyes with his knuckles when he told a lie – gave him a moment of amusement. A long time ago, Gudrun had said the same thing and he was sure it was the truth.

He wedged himself in a corner and tried to sleep, but now the grit was on his vest and the slightest movement irritated his skin.

A stray thought popped into his head in a moment of supreme lucidity. London must have known, or suspected, that the Third Reich was engaged in atomic research. Why else would they have assigned a physicist like Erika to the mission? And if this was true, why had he not been properly briefed?

It took an hour of determined effort before he finally dozed off. About 30 minutes after that the wheels squealed like a pack of love-crazed banshees for two minutes and the train came to a juddering halt.

He debated whether or not to climb out. Would he gain anything? There might be a more comfortable wagon somewhere on the train.

Listening to the sounds from the front of the train, he guessed that they had stopped to take on water. That thought was enough to drive him crazy with thirst, and he made up his mind. Using the protruding bolts as a ladder, he climbed the front of the wagon and lowered himself onto the couplings. From there he dropped onto the ground and looked around.

As he suspected, the locomotive was taking on water from a water tower. He gave some serious thought to sneaking to the front of the train in hopes of catching a few stray drops of water, before dismissing the idea. Crossing to the other side of the train where the driver and the engineer were less likely to see him, Kurt spotted a wagon with a roof and a side door near the rear of the train.

The train began to move.

He waited until the last wagon reached him, but when it did he was disappointed to find it locked with chain and padlock. He had to run to get back on board the last open-top wagon.

Standing on the couplings was seriously frightening, as each jolt threatened to throw him off. He began to climb the wall of the wagon. The bolts that protruded inside were nothing but studs on the outside, and climbing these while the wagon was shaking proved difficult and dangerous. One slip and he would be thrown under the wheels.

The train was descending a long gradient, the shaking getting worse as the speed increased. It took several minutes to reach the rim of the wagon, by which time the wagons were shaking violently; climbing down the inside was no longer an option. Kurt leapt from the rim, using his parachute training to tuck and roll as he hit the floor. He was unhurt, but covered in coal dust again from the top of his head to the soles of his feet.

Wedging himself into a corner, gritting his teeth to contain the chattering, he did his best to divert his mind from his dry mouth and extreme thirst. Thoughts of Gudrun and Anna and fleeting memories of his childhood helped to pass a half hour. He dozed, slipping in and out of sleep for another hour until fatigue overtook him.

He awoke in darkness, strange and unexpected. After a moment he realised that the rattling and shaking had stopped; the train had come to a halt. As his eyes adjusted to the dark, he could make out a roof glistening overhead. There were sounds – clanking noises and coughing – and the air was thick with coal dust. He was in the mine.

He climbed the protruding bolts, reached the rim of the wagon and looked around him.

There was no one in sight. Dropping to the ground, he headed toward the sounds, and came upon a gang of men working the coal face in a side tunnel. He took a step backward intending to go to the rear of the train in search of an exit, but one of the guards spotted him. Levelling his gun at Kurt he ordered him, "Back to work."

Kurt picked up a shovel.

Chapter 31

Friday April 23

There were roughly 30 men in the gang. Ten with pickaxes worked the coal seam in the walls, five broke up the larger lumps with sledgehammers, and five with shovels filled small iron wagons with the coal. Some of the remaining men looked after the wagons, pushing them down the tunnel when they were full and replacing them with empty ones, while others were kept busy shoring up the walls and ceiling of the tunnel. The workers were indistinguishable one from the other. All were caked in coal dust, head to toe, the whites of their eyes the only sign that any of them was human.

The man beside Kurt shuffled his feet to make room for Kurt's shovel.

"I'm Frederick," said Kurt.

The man replied with a single word in Russian that Kurt recognized as "Shut up!"

Within an hour Kurt's shoulder was aching. Two hours after that his back went into spasm. Dropping his shovel, he put his hands on the small of his back and tried to straighten.

"My back's broken," he said to his companion.

Kurt's companion put down his shovel and gestured for Kurt to follow. He led Kurt to a water barrel with a tin cup on a length of twine. Kurt filled a cup and slaked his thirst here before the man took him to a side tunnel. Here five men where busy pushing the wagons along a narrow-gauge rail track, taking them away full, and returning them empty.

Two of the men stood aside to allow Kurt and his companion to take their places. Kurt put his shoulder to the rear of the wagon. At a spoken signal all five men pushed and the wagon began to roll.

The track ascended a slight incline. Constant pressure was required to keep it moving until they reached the end of the track and one of the men put the brake on.

To the side of the tunnel was an opening. Kurt looked down and saw a half-filled open-topped railcar in a tunnel below them. The bed of the wagon was pivoted with circular handles attached, front and back. It took four men turning these handles to tip the small wagon onto its side, emptying the load into the railcar below with a roar, raising a choking cloud of dust.

Kurt was exhausted. Leaning against the wall of the tunnel he sought relief from the pain in his back. He closed his eyes for a moment.

One of the men said something in Russian. Kurt opened his eyes again to find all four men facing him, grim expressions on their faces, one of them holding a hand out, palm upward.

"What d'you want?" said Kurt.

The man grabbed Kurt's arm and removed his watch. Two of them examined it. Then one of the men spoke in halting German. "You are German?"

"Yes, I shouldn't be here–" Kurt replied.

With that all four men began a murderous assault on Kurt. Blows rained on his body from three sides as they scrapped among themselves for the privilege. Only the constricted nature of the tunnel saved him from serious harm as they struck him with their fists and their boots. Fighting back would have been futile. He tried to remain on his feet as long as possible. If their boots made contact with his head they would kill him for sure. As the battering continued Kurt sank to his knees, using his arms to shield his head.

The assault stopped abruptly. The four men stood back. Kurt looked up to see by two armed soldiers towering over him.

"On your feet," said a soldier, grabbing Kurt by his collar.

"Look at his clothes," said the second soldier.

Kurt said, "Thank God!"

"You are German? What are you doing among the Russians? And why are you dressed like that?"

The soldiers dragged Kurt to his feet and pushed him out of the tunnel, staggering. At the entrance to the tunnel a tuck was waiting, engine running. They hauled him into the bed of the truck, and one leaped in to sit beside him. Kurt coughed painfully, and wiped the blood from his coal-blackened lips. As the truck bounced over the rough ground, the guard leaned over Kurt, staring into his face and Kurt saw that he was wearing a radiation monitor.

"Where are you taking me?" said Kurt.

There was no answer.

The journey lasted 20 minutes, their destination a wide compound laid out on a level piece of ground, containing row after row of low huts. The entire compound was enclosed by a barbed wire fence three metres high punctuated with lookout posts.

The guard marched Kurt through a gate into an inner compound. They entered a room in a hut with several chairs along the walls, like a doctor's waiting room. Guard and prisoner sat.

After a few minutes a door opened and they were admitted to an office. Behind a desk sat a man dressed in an SS uniform with the insignia of an SS-Obersturmbannführer.

Kurt stood swaying before the desk.

The guard gave his report: The prisoner was a German. He was found in the mine fighting with a group of Russian workers. He was not wearing camp workers' clothing.

Narrowing his eyes, the commandant leaned forward across his desk. "Who are you? Where did you come from?"

"My name is Frederick von Schönholtz," said Kurt. "Until yesterday I was working at Auergesellschaft in Oranienburg. I fell into an empty rail wagon and was transported here."

The commandant clicked his fingers and Kurt handed him his identity card.

"You fell? How? Some sort of industrial accident?"

"Yes, Herr Commandant. I was working in a warehouse high above the train. I lost my footing..."

"And you remained there in the rail wagon all the way from the factory to the mine?"

"I hit my head when I fell and lost consciousness for a time. I couldn't leave the wagon while it was moving."

The commandant handed Kurt's identity card to the guard. "Find him a place with his compatriots."

The guard led Kurt to another area within the inner compound. He was ordered to remove his clothes. As he took off his jacket he noticed the display on his radiation monitor. It was black. Kurt was unsure how worried he should be, but clearly he had received a heavy dose of radiation.

They hosed him down and gave him a camp uniform. They allowed him to keep his boots, but not his identity card and other papers. The Reichsmarks the British had given him were divided up between the guards.

The guards took him to a hut in the main compound, opened the door, and pushed him inside.

Immediately, Kurt found himself surrounded. A verbal barrage began. Two of the men laid hands on him.

"You're not from this hut."

"He's a spy."

One of the men stepped forward. He was frail, with sunken cheeks, hollow eyes and few teeth in his head, but it was clear that he was their leader. He waved everyone back and held up a hand for silence. "Who are you?"

"My name's Frederick Schönholtz," said Kurt, dropping the 'von'.

"Who sent you? Where did you come from?"

"I came from the Auergesellschaft factory on the train."

A murmur ran around the hut.

"That's not possible," shouted someone.

Kurt was in a tight spot. He looked at the tense faces of the men around him. If his story didn't satisfy them they would surely tear him limb from limb.

"I was working in the warehouse. I slipped and fell into one of the rail wagons," he said.

This was greeted with a cacophony of voices.

An old man stepped forward. "What is the name of the recruitment manager at Oranienburg?"

"Otto Staerling."

"What section did you work in?"

"Special Operations."

"Who's the head of that section?"

"Rickard Blaue."

The old man nodded affirmation to the leader.

The leader spoke to the men in the hut. "For the moment we will take this man at his word. He is under my protection. Anyone who does him harm must answer to me. Is that clear?"

The men dispersed slowly. Kurt staggered to an empty bunk and lay down. His ribs were bruised and sore, but none seemed to be broken. His legs had taken some punishment, and his hands had borne the brunt of the blows aimed at his face and head. He closed his eyes and took a moment to review his situation. In leaving the factory he had avoided almost certain death from rifle fire, but he was under no illusion about his prospects of survival in this camp. Dressed in the camp clothing he had little prospect of escape and with the loss of his own clothes had gone the suicide capsule that the British had given him.

Later, a watery gruel was served in the compound. The hut leader stayed close to Kurt. He said, "You must be the only man in history to break *into* a Nazi labour camp."

Kurt responded with a hollow laugh. "What's your name?"

"Call me Peter."

After the meal Peter took Kurt on a tour of the compound. Peter was reluctant to talk about his past, but from the fragments that he let slip Kurt gathered he had been a teacher before the Nazis came to power. His crime had been the distribution of leaflets containing the doctrine of Calvinism and the homilies of John Calvin's disciples. Someone in the security establishment must have decided that predestination was a subversive doctrine.

The camp housed tens of thousands of men. Most were German citizens that had fallen foul of the Nazis one way or another. Some were part-Jewish. There were Czechs, Poles, Russians, Bulgarians and other East Europeans, Greeks and Armenians. All of the men worked in the mines. They worked in shifts, three weeks on, one week off. When Kurt asked why this was, he received the chilling reply, "Working in the mines is a death sentence. Everyone in the camp has bad lungs and many have other health problems, nosebleeds, eye problems. And Old Man Cancer stalks the camp. The life expectancy here is about seven months. We call it heaven's waiting room."

"How long have you been here?" said Kurt.

Peter replied, "Six months and seventeen days."

Kurt ran his eyes over the lookout towers spaced 30 metres apart all around the compound. Each one was manned by armed soldiers. "I need to get out. My work is important."

Peter shook his head. "You'll never get out. It's impossible. The camp and the mine are too well guarded. All that have tried to escape in the past have been caught and punished. Some were shot. I'm afraid you must resign yourself to spending the rest of the war here."

"I have to get out," said Kurt.

They were standing at the entrance to a hut that looked deserted. It had a large "F" painted on the door.

Peter said, "The man who asked you those questions about Auergesellschaft, how old do you think he is?"

"Fifty? Fifty-five, maybe?"

"He's thirty-two." He pointed to the hut. "That's hut 'F', the punishment hut. He tried to escape and spent 24 hours in there, in the standing cells." Kurt raised a questioning eyebrow and Peter explained, "The punishment cells are so narrow that it is impossible to lie down, or even to sit. Twenty four hours in one of those with no food or water is enough to break any man."

Kurt tried to imagine standing for 24 hours without a break. "Is it always 24 hours?"

"Sometimes it's 48. And sometimes they let men out early. Those are the lucky ones. They get a bullet in the head."

Chapter 32

The following morning the inhabitants of the hut were transported back to the mine. They were given nothing to eat and Kurt's stomach complained loudly in the truck.

When they returned from the mine in the evening a standing tap outside the hut was used for washing. Kurt stripped off and joined the line, using his allotted two minutes to remove most of the grime from his skin and hair. As he was putting his clothes on he developed a sudden nosebleed. The sight of blood on his fingers gave him a moment of panic, quickly followed by a curious feeling of serenity. He might be sick – he might even be dying – but he didn't care. If he could find a way to get out of the camp and stop the Nazis from building the atomic bomb he would die happy.

He went in search of the man who had asked about Auergesellschaft and found him sitting at the back of the hut, basking in the evening sun. He was thin as a needle, the sunshine like a Röntgen-ray lighting up the shadows of the bones in his arms and legs.

Kurt sat beside him. "How long have you been in the camp?"

The man said nothing for a full minute. Then this: "Did you really come here from the metal works in Oranienburg? And did you really ride the freight train?"

"Yes."

Flashing his few remaining teeth in what Kurt took to be a smile, the man said, "What did you think of Werner Heisenberg?"

"I didn't have any dealings with him," said Kurt. "He looked young for one so famous."

"He's older than he looks. What about Otto Staerling?"

Kurt was aware that he was being interrogated again. It seemed the inhabitants of the hut needed assurance that he really was who he said he was.

"Staerling seemed friendly enough. Why do you ask?"

"You know he works closely with the security service. There was an SD man in charge of security at the factory. What was his name?"

Kurt flinched. "SS-Sturmbannführer Necker."

"How is Manfred Necker?"

"Look, this is pointless," said Kurt. "How many more stupid questions will I have to answer before you accept that I worked in the Special Operations section of the factory?"

"Tell me what work you did there," said the man.

"I worked with an engineer called Blaue entering figures into a ledger."

A faint smile passed over the man's thin lips. "Ah, that ledger!"

"You worked in Special Operations? You are a physicist?"

"I was an engineer. I worked for Blaue." He closed his eyes, luxuriating in the weak sunshine.

Kurt waited, but got nothing more. Then he tried again. "I don't believe you. I think you have no idea what the Special Operations section is working on."

There was no response.

"I've seen the uranium enrichment processes, and I know what the Nazis intend to do when they have amassed enough of it."

The engineer opened one eye. "Have a care what you say. The atomic energy programme is highly secret."

"I'm not talking about electricity generation," said Kurt. "You must know what the Nazis are working on."

"Shut your mouth!" said the engineer, his eyes wide open, now. "Do you want to get us both executed for treason?"

"Too many Germans have turned a blind eye to the Nazis," said Kurt. "Someone has to take a stand."

"Fine speech. What can you do?"

"If I can get out of here, I'll do what I can to stop them."

The engineer closed his eyes again and shook his head. "You'll never get out of the camp. And even if, by some miracle, you did, there's nothing you can do. There's nothing anyone can do. We're all dead anyway. The Nazis will blow up the whole world."

Kurt said, "You're wrong. The Nazis will fail."

"How do you know this?" said the engineer without opening his eyes.

Kurt was encouraged by this response. He made something up to keep the conversation going. "I've seen their calculations. They have no idea how much fissionable material they need to start a chain reaction, and their uranium enrichment methods are crude and inefficient. They will never succeed."

The engineer's eyes sprang open again. He fixed Kurt with an intense stare. "What if I told you they have already successfully tested an atomic bomb?"

"I'd say you were a liar."

"No word of a lie," said the engineer, spittle running from his mouth. "I worked on the payload delivery system, and I was there when they tested it."

"Where was this?" said Kurt. He waited a full two minutes without a response. Finally he stood up. "I don't believe you. You're talking nonsense."

Using an arm to shade his eyes from the sun, the engineer looked up at Kurt and said, "The test was carried out in an underground cavern at a secret base."

"And this test was successful?" Kurt's tone was sarcastic.

"The explosion created a seismic wave that was felt as far away as Leningrad. I'd say that was a success, wouldn't you?"

The expression of dismay on Kurt's face prompted the engineer to add, "There were problems with it, though. The delivery mechanism was unreliable, and the yield from the blast was less than the physicists had hoped for. We all knew that a second test would be needed before the weapon could be used."

"And was there a second test?"

"Not while I was there," said the engineer. "This camp is my reward for the failure of the test. Others were less fortunate." After a pause he continued, "I should never have left the farm and gone to university, should never have taken up engineering. I joined the project the day after graduation and from that moment my fate was sealed."

"The farm?"

"My father has a sheep farm. I should have been content with that. He... I thought a good university degree would keep me out of the war. And now I will surely die here."

Kurt sought words of reassurance, but could find none. The engineer already looked like a talking skeleton. "Where is the base?" he asked.

The engineer squinted at Kurt in the weak sunshine. "Let me have your boots and I'll tell you."

"I need my boots," said Kurt.

"You can have mine. They're about the same size."

Kurt sat down again and they exchanged boots. The engineer's boots had seen better days, but they were a good enough fit.

The engineer smiled at his new boots. "I won't survive much longer. The workload and the poor food will finish me soon, but these boots will make my last few months more tolerable." He coughed, a racking, painful cough that left him gasping.

Affected deeply by the engineer's words, Kurt shook his head, but before he could protest, the engineer said, "You could do me one more favour. You're young and fit. If anybody can make it out of here, it's you." He reached inside his shirt and pulled out a grubby piece of paper. "Take this letter and deliver it to my father at that address."

Kurt examined the letter. It was addressed to Dieter Khall in Carpin, near Neusterlitz.

Kurt said, "What if your father is not there?"

"Just deliver the letter to that address."

Kurt put the letter inside the left boot before lacing it up. "I will do my best, I promise."

"That's all I can ask. When you see my father, tell him you knew me."

"And the location of the base?"

He lowered his voice. "It's on the Baltic island of Rügen. Base Alpha they call it. But you'll never get inside. It's heavily guarded. There's only one entrance and that's locked up tighter than a lizard's arse in a sandstorm. And the Kriegsmarine patrols the sea around the island."

Chapter 33

Three days passed, three days of toiling in the mine, sleeping, trying to survive on the miserable food. Kurt's back became stronger and the spasms eased. On the second day he took a turn with a pick axe, aggravated his damaged shoulder and discovered a whole new level of back pain. As he worked, Kurt watched the guards' routine for any lapse that would allow him to escape. He had to tell London that the Nazis had completed one successful test detonation and where they test base was located. London's order to destroy the uranium enrichment plant at Oranienburg made sense, now. The spread of radiation over a small area of the country would have been an acceptable consequence, given the unthinkable alternative. The engineer's pronouncement that the Nazis would "blow up the world" was a real possibility. In the hands of fanatical and power-hungry Nazis a weapon like that could easily bring about the destruction of the entire planet.

The boots that the engineer had given him had seen better days, and Kurt regretted the exchange. In the hopes of getting his own boots back and maybe learning more about the Nazi's atomic bomb programme, he searched the camp for the engineer, only to learn that the man had died in his sleep.

He followed Peter, and when they were alone, told him, "I must get out of the camp and resume my work."

Peter replied as if speaking to a child. "You told me that already. And, as I said, it's impossible. If you try you'll be captured and punished – or shot."

"You don't understand," said Kurt. "I have information that could shorten the war. If I can't get it into the right hands the Nazis will be able to turn the war in their favour and millions more will die."

"What is this information?"

"I can't tell you that, but it is imperative that I get out of here to do what I can."

Peter said. "I wish you luck with that, friend." He hesitated before adding, "Come with me."

Peter led Kurt to an area near the rear of the camp where twenty or thirty bodies lay in a jumbled heap on the ground. A foul odour assailed Kurt's nostrils. The bodies were all clothed, although most lacked footwear. Half a dozen black birds – ravens and carrion crows – were feeding on the corpses, and flies swarmed everywhere. A sole camp inmate was busy competing with the birds among the bodies.

Kurt covered his mouth and nose with the tail of his shirt. He gagged.

"I told you, this place is heaven's waiting room" said Peter. "You might escape by lying among the bodies when they're taken outside the camp for disposal."

Kurt shook his head. "I couldn't..."

"It's your only chance."

Kurt ran his eyes over the nearest corpses and recognized the body of the engineer, now barefoot. The scavenger had a pair of boots hanging around his neck that looked suspiciously like the ones Kurt had given to the engineer. He turned to say something to Peter, but the hut leader had vanished.

Kurt spoke to the scavenger. He was Armenian, without a word of German. Resorting to sign language, Kurt indicated that he was interested in the boots around the man's neck.

The Armenian gave Kurt a toothy grin untied the left boot and handed it to Kurt. Kurt squeezed the leather as if he were checking a loaf of bread. Looking inside he identified the boots. They were definitely his own.

Using sign language again, Kurt offered the boots he was wearing in exchange, but the man scowled at him and shook his head. Kurt racked his brain. If only he hadn't lost his watch!

There was nobody else around in what must have been the least popular area of the entire camp. Kurt was desperate. Determined to get his boots back, he hid by one of the huts and waited. Soon, the Armenian came to the end of his evening's work, and set out toward the Armenian quarter. In a deserted area between two windowless huts, Kurt barred his way.

Kurt's intention was clear. The scavenger's responded by clearing his throat and spitting in the dust. Then he dropped the boots on the ground between them and, with a finger-flicking gesture from his upturned palms, challenged Kurt to attempt to take them from him if he could.

Kurt advanced, the Armenian stood his ground, and they wrestled. Kurt had judged this no contest. His opponent was shorter by 10 cm, thin as a knife, the shape of his bones visible through his skin. His toxic body odour suggested that he was probably weakened by dysentery, and yet, no matter what Kurt tried, the Armenian remained on his feet.

Kurt recalled something his father had taught him when he was a boy. When a rabbit is chased by a dog, the rabbit will nearly always get away. The dog is running for a meal; the rabbit is running for its life. This man fought as if his life depended on the outcome. Perhaps it did.

Kurt untangled himself from the Armenian and stepped back, holding up his palms in a submissive gesture. "I yield," he said. "You're a better man than me. Keep the boots."

The Armenian showed his teeth again and pointed to Kurt's boots.

"I'm not giving you my boots," said Kurt. "Forget it friend. I'll be on my way."

A flash of metal told him that the Armenian was now wielding a short knife, and meant to relieve Kurt of the boots on his feet.

Kurt took a couple of steps backwards. The Armenian stepped after him. And then the knife was swinging across in front of Kurt's stomach with frightening speed, threatening to rip him open. Keeping his eyes on the Armenian's face to try anticipating his moves, Kurt continued to move backwards, one step at a time. Then his rear made contact with the side of a hut and he had to skip sideways to avoid instant evisceration.

"Enough!" shouted Kurt, but his opponent kept advancing.

Kurt turned and ran. The Armenian retreated to collect the contested boots, and Kurt made good his escape. Once he was out of range, Kurt looked back. The Armenian waved his knife and flashed his broken and blackened teeth at him in what could only have been a primitive display of feral dominance.

Afterwards, Kurt thought it might have been a smile.

Chapter 34

Kurt walked the length and breadth of the compound in search of a way out. He avoided the Armenian quarter. An urgent call of nature forced him to use the nearest latrine – in the Polish section. The Poles made it plain that he was not welcome. Their hostile reaction surprised him. Even in this most miserable corner of the universe it seemed man's territorial instinct was alive and well.

The wire fence and lookout posts were impassable. During the day the fence was patrolled by armed guards with dogs and at night it was swept by powerful searchlights; cutting his way out was not an option. It seemed only the dead could escape from the camp, and Kurt decided to try Peter's suggestion.

"You'll have to act quickly," said Peter. "The burial detail is tomorrow night. If you miss that you'll have to wait a week before the next one."

Kurt thanked him for his help.

"I wish you luck with it," said Peter. "You only have one go at this. If you fail you'll never get another chance."

The following night, shivering from hunger and excitement, Kurt slipped out of the hut and, dodging the searchlights, ran to where the bodies were piled. He was relieved to see that the only scavengers at work were the feathered kind, but a light drizzle falling from a blanket of cloud was an unwelcome complication. Removing his precious boots, he tucked them inside his jacket and hid behind the nearest hut.

Within minutes an open truck drew up. Two guards, their faces protected by scarves, jumped out and began to manhandle the bodies into the truck. Kurt was close enough to hear their grunts and occasional curses. The birds barely moved as they worked.

As soon as the last body was in the back of the truck, the guards got into the cab and started the engine. Kurt dashed from his hiding place, climbed aboard the back of the truck and lay down with the bodies.

Kurt lay face to face with a dead man. The eye sockets were empty, the nose half-gone and distorted, the open-mouthed grimace a caricature of a broken-toothed grin. An endless procession of well-fed black flies came and went through all four orifices, and the weightless body bounced about with the rattling of the truck over the uneven ground.

An evil-looking raven that had come aboard with the cadavers ran its beady eye over Kurt. Kurt swiped at it. It hopped out of range and continued to feed.

The reek of the bodies was overpowering. Kurt held his breath and tried not to gag.

The truck stopped at the main gate. Kurt heard a short conversation between the guards at the gate and those in the truck. One of the gate guards shone a torch on the bodies. Kurt kept his head down, his eyes closed.

"Go ahead," said the gate guard.

The truck moved forward. And then they were outside the compound, rocking and lurching over a rutted track. With each lurch the bodies around him moved, giving a macabre impression that they were all alive. He felt his own body slipping down among them, as if they were trying to gather him to them, to make him one of their own. After a half kilometre, the truck reached a paved road. The rocking stopped and they picked up speed. Another kilometre further on, they left the road again and entered a forested area.

Kurt sat up and looked around him. He could taste freedom. He would have no difficulty hiding among the trees. Quickly, he put his boots on. He was just about to jump from the truck when disaster struck. A fly shot up his nose, and Kurt sneezed violently.

The driver of the truck applied the brakes. Kurt fell back among the bodies and closed his eyes. He heard booted feet jump down from the cab and then the click of rifles being cocked.

"Come out of there with your hands high!"

Chapter 35

Kurt stood in the commandant's office sandwiched between the two guards as if he might make a dash for freedom at any moment. A small part of Kurt's mind saw the comedy in the image; the larger part saw the menace.

"Name?" the commandant barked.

"Frederick von Schönholtz. I'm here by mistake, sir," said Kurt.

"You're here because you attempted to escape. You will be punished." The commandant waved his hand, and the guards turned to leave, taking Kurt between them.

Kurt shouted over his shoulder, "I shouldn't be in the camp. I work for Rickard Blaue in Oranienburg."

They frogmarched him into the punishment hut – hut F. The hut had rows of normal cells on either side, numbered F1-F16 and, at the end farthest from the entrance, four narrow cast iron doors, numbered F17-F20. Kurt was pushed inside the first of these.

The cell was just wide enough for his body. Behind him a wall, ahead another, 15 centimetres from his face.

"When you're ready to come out, just bang on the door," said one of the guards.

They both laughed and the door slammed shut.

Kurt was in the dark.

He couldn't sit or stretch his arms. He could barely bend his knees. All he could do was stand there. It was like being buried alive in a vertical coffin.

He fought rising nausea as an overpowering smell of body wastes mingled with the smell of death still rising from his damp clothing.

With his eyes open, wave after wave of anxiety swept over him. He tried closing them, and his anxiety immediately turned to panic. He left them open, even though he could see nothing.

Gradually, his mind began to work again. He hated himself for his failure to escape. He had probably ruined any chance of ever making it out of the camp now. It would be up to Erika and Pilgrim to stop the Nazis from building the atomic bomb. He would play no further part in that struggle.

He hated the commandant and the guards who had put him in here. And he despised the twisted mind that had conceived of this inhuman punishment.

He had the urge to pee and managed to open his fly and relieve himself against the wall. The warm steam from the urine wafted up around him, and he dry-retched. He shuddered at the thought of throwing up in such a confined space. He managed to fasten most of the buttons on his fly, but gave up the struggle when his arms began to cramp.

In an attempt to maintain some measure of control over his situation, he began to count seconds and minutes. At 16 minutes and a few seconds, his mind went into a spin and he lost count. He started again, but soon abandoned that idea. Counting seconds for 24 hours was a sure route to insanity.

His isolation pierced him like a sword through the chest. He roared at the wall and the sound echoed around him. He could not have felt more alone if he had been the last and only man alive on the planet.

His stomach grumbled and a thought came to him that froze the blood in his veins. What happen if he needed the latrines and they didn't let him out in time?

He had been sure that the guards were toying with him when they locked him in, but after a while he began to wonder. Little by little he began to believe that it might be true. What if they were waiting outside with orders to release him when he banged on the door? Perhaps it was a test. They would judge his worth by how long he endured the punishment. The more he thought about it, the more he became convinced that he was being tested. He would show them what he was made of! He would hold out as long as he could.

Forcing himself to remain calm, he turned his mind to Gudrun and Anna waiting for him back in Ireland. They would be sleeping, but when Anna awoke she would spend all her free time playing with her doll's house. Hopefully Gudrun would have found a job by now with the help of Professor Hirsch at the university. These thoughts did nothing but increase his discomfort and aggravate his feelings of despair.

He tried shifting his weight onto one leg and then the other to ease a growing pain creeping up his back. Peter had said that he would have to endure this place for 24 hours. His mind spiralled back into panic at that thought. How could anyone survive that long in such an uncomfortable position?

#

Time slowed to a crawl. Each minute felt like an hour, each hour a lifetime. Cramping pains seized his calves, spreading to his upper legs and from there into his back. He longed for a moment's relief from the pain.

Exhaustion overcame him and he slipped into unconsciousness, only to wake up in a blind panic and in agony from his wedged knees and lower back. It took all his strength to straighten his knees. Obviously, sleep was not an option. He needed to remain awake to support his upper body.

He peed again, but this time he couldn't undo his fly, having lost the feeling in his fingers. He swore at himself for fastening his fly the previous time.

Then his stomach gave a lurch. He needed to get out now, to get to the latrine!

It was already too late, but he banged on the door. He yelled. He screamed. He beat his fist on the door as hard as he could. No one opened it.

Listening for sounds from beyond the door, all he could hear was his own harsh breathing.

And then his bowels opened.

He fell into a pit of despair.

He felt like a child. Not just because he had soiled himself, but because he had been taken in by the guard's cruel joke.

His life ran through his mind like a film in reverse, as he tried to work out why he was where he was. What could he have done differently? The Black Orchestra was the root of all his problems. He should never have joined. He should never have tried to stand against the Nazis. What difference had he hoped to make, one man against the might of the Third Reich?

He felt shame. The shame of the whole German race seemed to weigh him down and threatened to crush him, so he replaced shame with hate. It was the Nazis who had brought this shame on the people of Germany. The Nazis were the only Germans who should bear the blame, and he hated them for it. He fed his hatred. Hatred was good; hatred would keep him alive. Hatred became anger, and he fed that. But then his mind wandered and he forgot what had made him angry.

He tried unsuccessfully to recall Gudrun's face and his thoughts moved on to Melissa in London, to Helga, and then to Erika.

A moment of lucidity accompanied his thoughts about Erika. She was a strong-willed woman whom he admired, but he realised that his feelings for her went well beyond admiration. She was a beautiful woman.

He allowed that notion to grow and with it came arousal. This was something he could use to take his mind off his predicament, and he fed it with crazy images of Erika slipping out of her clothes, laughing seductively, reaching into his pants, doing things to him that his frozen fingers couldn't do.

His erection died, and he roared, his roar one of frustration and pain and self-loathing. Most of all it was a roar of anger that he had been placed in such a dehumanising position where there was nothing he could do to relieve his suffering – not even masturbation.

After that he simply felt foolish. The erotic thoughts had helped to pass some time, five minutes, perhaps. But now he felt like a fool.

He was hungry, but he had been hungry from the first day in the camp; the camp food wasn't enough to feed a bird. He was thirsty, too, but he decided not to dwell on that for fear of losing his sanity.

He tried to work out how much time had passed. His mental clock suggested he had been incarcerated no more than a couple of hours, perhaps 3 or 4 at most, but there was a part of his mind insisting that at least 12 hours must have passed. Hadn't Peter said that people were sometimes allowed out early? The circumstances eluded him. And then he remembered: Those were the lucky ones.

Chapter 36

In Gestapo headquarters in Berlin the runner was breathless with excitement. "He's back in the country, sir!"

"Take your time," said Lange. "Take a breath, then tell me who you're talking about. Who is back in the country?"

"We've just had word from one of our informers," the runner gasped. "The Abwehr spy, Kurt Müller has been spotted."

SS-Hauptsturmführer Lange ground his teeth in irritation. This was not the first time he'd heard those words, and on every other occasion they had raised false hopes and sent him chasing shadows that led nowhere.

"Who is this informant?"

"We received the information from one of our regular sources in Stuttgart, but I believe the information originated from someone called Helga."

"Tell me exactly what this Helga had to say."

The runner took a deep breath. "The ORPO have been chasing a runaway female suspect who broke out of lawful detention in Haigerloch Castle."

"Yes, yes, I know all about that," said Lange.

"The female suspect was freed by two men. One of the men was called Klaus Randau. They stole an SS staff car and burned it out on their way to the Swiss border."

"Yes. And?"

"Klaus Randau is Kurt Müller!"

Lange shot to his feet. Flipping through the pile of newspapers on his desk, he found the copy of *Völkischer Beobachter* containing Klaus Randau's photograph. The runner ripped Kurt's picture from the notice board and placed it on Lange's desk. A quick glance at Kurt Müller's picture was all Lange needed to confirm the truth. The bearded Randau was indeed the Abwehr deserter and murderer Kurt Müller.

Lange's next thought caused him to slump back into his seat. "Tell me Müller hasn't escaped into Switzerland."

The runner shook his head. "Nobody knows where he is, sir. All the border crossing posts have been told to keep on the lookout. If he tries to leave the country he will be captured."

#

Kurt slept on and off, and each time he woke to fear and pain, his legs excruciatingly cramped, the soiled clothing stinking and chafing. His feet were so swollen that the boots crushed them. Hot tears rolled down his cheeks as he discovered anew the cramps in his legs and the chafing from his soiled clothing.

Again, he hammered on the door. He wept. No one came.

Silently, he prayed to a God he only half believed in. He prayed for a miracle to save him.

Keep the faith, boy.

Father? Is that you?

Remember what Martin Luther said: 'It is only by good deeds and mortifications of the flesh that sins may be forgiven.'

Where are you Father? I can't see you.

Think, boy. How many of the ninety-five Theses can you recall?

The 95 Theses of Martin Luther! He learned to recite them at school. They were drilled into him. He tried to dredge them up. '1. Our Lord Jesus Christ willed all men to repentance. 2. Repentance does not mean sacramental confession and absolution. 3. It means inward repentance by outward mortifications of the flesh...' Kurt's memory failed him. He recalled that there was a sequence, starting at 42, that listed what Christians should be taught, and he remembered how the Theses ended: 'Christians must be diligent in following Jesus, for he will lead them through death and purgatory to the kingdom of heaven.'

Keep going, son. Number four...

Leave me be, Father.

Number four. Think, boy.

Something about self-hatred. Leave me be.

After that his thoughts began to drift randomly, swinging wildly from childhood memories to present fears, from his physical pains to mental anxieties, from fears for his future to episodes from his recent past. Dying of thirst now, his emotions stripped to the essentials, he lost his capacity to feel anything, not shame or hate or rage or love. Not even fear.

He was in hell, his sanity slipping away from him in a jumble of thoughts. And then one idea shone bright in his head: If he had that British suicide pill in his possession he would have used it. He prayed again. This time he prayed that they would come and take him out early to put a bullet in the head.

Part 5 - The Institute

JJ Toner

Chapter 37

"He's coming round."

He was lying down. An illusion, obviously. There was light around him, although his eyes were closed. He was afraid to open them. Would he be greeted by the angels?

"Frederick, how are you feeling?" This voice was deep and sounded like honey rolling about in a bowl. Kurt had heard it before, but he couldn't remember where. He kept his eyes firmly closed. It was some sort of trick, obviously.

"Give him time," said the first voice. "He's been through a lot."

It was a woman's voice, and Kurt could smell antiseptic. Was he in a hospital?

He opened his eyes. He was lying on a bed, his head on a pillow, bright lights everywhere, above him a white ceiling. To his left stood a woman in a nurse's uniform. She was taking his pulse. To his right stood Otto Staerling, the Auergesellschaft recruitment manager, in his dark blue suit, his hands clasped in front of his bulging stomach like a schoolboy awaiting punishment.

"How are you, Frederick?" said Staerling.

Kurt tried to speak, but couldn't find his voice. He tried a second time, and managed, "How long...?"

"You've been unconscious for two hours," said the nurse.

"How long?" said Kurt again.

"I think he means how long was he in the punishment cell," said Staerling. "They tell me you were in there eleven hours."

A feeling of dread crept over Kurt. Hadn't Peter said that the ones that got out early are shot?

Staerling said, "The doctor tells me you've no broken bones. We can leave whenever you feel up to it. How do you feel?"

Kurt's mind went into freefall. Had he dreamt the past week? The labour camp, the mine, losing his watch and shoes, his attempted escape? What did Staerling mean 'we can leave' – leave and go where? How had Staerling found him, and why?

He wriggled his toes and fingers. Then he explored the rest of his body. He had aches in his back, his kidney, his knees and his shoulder, but otherwise he seemed fine.

The nurse helped him to sit up. She handed him a glass of water. He gulped it down.

"Take your time," said Staerling, making a show of looking at his watch. "It's close to lunchtime. I'd like to get started back as soon as possible."

Back? Back to Oranienburg, presumably.

Kurt was still not convinced that this was not all an elaborate hallucination, but the nurse's breast felt good against his shoulder.

"We managed to save your boots, but we had to burn the rest," said the nurse. "You'll find fresh clothes in the closet."

Kurt climbed out of the bed. Otto Staerling opened the closet and passed him a camp uniform, freshly laundered. The nurse left the room while he dressed. And that was when Kurt noticed the Wehrmacht soldier standing by the door.

As he was putting on his boots he checked inside for Khall's letter. It was still there, scrunched up and jammed into the toe.

When Kurt was dressed Staerling handed him his identity papers and led him from the room down the stairs and outside to the car park. Kurt was unsteady on his feet. Staerling reached out a hand and steadied him when he stumbled.

A blanket of dark clouds covered the sky overhead.

To the sound of distant thunder, Staerling opened the passenger door of a black Horch and Kurt got in. Then Staerling got behind the wheel and started the engine.

"I don't understand," said Kurt. "Where are you taking me?"

Chapter 38

They headed north. Kurt said nothing. Staerling would take him back to the factory to face the music. He would be shot as a spy and a murderer. He didn't care. Anything was better than being locked up in the dark in that cell.

A flash of lightning and a clap of thunder signalled the arrival of the storm.

"What should I call you?" said Staerling, keeping his eyes on the road ahead. "Frederick von Schönholtz is a bit of a mouthful, wouldn't you say?"

Kurt said nothing.

The rain began to fall. Staerling switched on his windscreen wipers. Several minutes passed before he spoke again.

"Give me your papers and leave the talking to me," said Staerling.

Peering through the rain Kurt saw that they were approaching a roadblock. He gave Staerling his papers, and Staerling wound down his window.

When their turn came, Staerling handed his own and Kurt's papers to the policeman.

Rain dripped from the ORPO man's cap as he checked the papers. "The Wings of the Eagle? What is that?"

"Take a look at the signature on the letter," Staerling replied stiffly.

The ORPO man handed the papers back and waved them on.

"Your papers are excellent forgeries, I'll grant you," said Staerling to Kurt once they were back on the road. "But we know the name is an alias. Who are you, really?"

'We' meaning who? Kurt wondered. The car was every centimetre a Gestapo staff car. "Go to hell!" he said.

"Just as you like, Herr von Schönholtz. I'm sure SS-Sturmbannführer Necker will be happy to beat the truth out of you when I tell him who you are."

The prospect of interrogation by the SS turned Kurt's stomach. It would take them no time at all to find out who he was – Kurt Müller, notorious Abwehr deserter and member of the subversive Black Orchestra. Once they had him, they would use the most extreme torture methods to get him to talk. The only question was whether Necker would conduct the interrogations himself or hand him over to the experts – the Gestapo.

"How did you find me?" said Kurt.

"The camp commandant called."

"You could have left me at the camp. You know the mine is a death trap."

"You were enjoying your punishment?" Staerling glanced at his passenger. "I've seen what 24 hours in those cells can do to a man. Not many survive the experience."

Kurt said nothing.

"Don't bother to thank me," said Staerling, peering through the rain.

Kurt knew that he would almost certainly crumble under interrogation. That would be the ultimate humiliation. He was resigned to the prospect of his own death, even under torture, but to give the Nazis the names of other members of the resistance, that was something he could not countenance. If that happened he would never forgive himself. He would die broken in spirit as well as in body. Better never to have been born than to die betraying his friends.

They had passed several road signs showing Berlin straight ahead. They passed another.

"Where are you taking me?" said Kurt.

For the first time Staerling smiled. "This road leads to the factory or to Berlin. Where we go depends on you."

Kurt ran through a number of possibilities in his mind. Staerling could be toying with him, or he might be looking for a bribe.

"I can get money, if that's what you want," said Kurt.

Staerling shook his head. "You think you can buy your way out of a double murder?"

So Erika had killed that soldier on the walkway. Mercifully, Staerling seemed unaware of her involvement. Kurt said, "I have no idea what you mean."

"There wasn't much left of Reckendorfer when we fished him out of the vat of yellowcake. His axe was still attached to his arm, by the way. And that young soldier, Trautfeld, had a wife and a mother in Munich."

Kurt said, "I don't know either of those names."

"There's a school of thought that Reckendorfer killed Trautfeld. The giant had a fondness for other men's wives. It's quite likely that they fought and the younger man died. Reckendorfer's death might have been an unfortunate accident. I couldn't count the number of times I've warned him of the dangers of carrying that heavy axe around the factory. I think he must have slipped on the wet walkway and the axe pulled him over the rail and into the vat."

The thunder and lightning continued all around them. Staerling's wipers weren't coping too well with the downpour.

Kurt was confused. This was an unlikely explanation for the two deaths. Did the recruitment manager have enough influence to persuade others to accept such a bizarre story? And why would he?

"What do you want?" said Kurt.

"I want you to understand who your friends are, Frederick."

Kurt's heart leapt in his chest. Could Staerling be a member of the resistance? Surely this was an elaborate trick to get him to talk.

Staerling's eyes were fixed on the road, what he could see of it. He said, "We know you are working for the British. We've been watching you since you left Ireland."

"We?"

"I'm with the American OSS. We are on the same side, you and I."

This hit Kurt like a bolt of lightning. If the Office of Strategic Services knew who he was there was only one explanation: Professor Hirsch had told them.

Staerling switched to English. "My friends call me Rocky." His honey-in-a-bowl voice suited his American accent perfectly.

"How did you get me out of the camp?" Kurt stuck with German.

"I pulled rank on the camp commandant. I told him I wanted you back."

"You say you've been watching me since I left Ireland. How did you find me after I arrived in Germany? Does the OSS have a mole in British Intelligence?"

"We knew your alias. All we had to do was wait for Frederick von Schönholtz to surface in Germany. We have agents scattered all over the country. I guess I drew the short straw." He laughed.

Kurt recalled the man in the library in London who had removed the mathematical reference book from the shelf. That man must have been OSS, and he must have taken the ticket to the left luggage office, opened the parcel, and discovered Kurt's secret alias.

Staerling gave up the struggle against the storm. He pulled over to the side of the road, leaving the engine running.

"How do I know you're telling me the truth?" said Kurt.

"I guess you don't," said Staerling. "You're just going to have to take my word for it. I know the British are interested in the Nazis' atomic programme. Well, so are we. I'm prepared to do a deal with you, Freddy. I'll find a position for you in the Institute in Berlin where Heisenberg and his buddies are doing all the real work, but only if you agree to let me eyeball everything you find before you send it to London."

"What makes you think I could hold down a job in the Institute? I'm not a physicist."

"I know that, but you've a degree in advanced mathematics, right?"

He was definitely getting his information from Professor Hirsch in Dublin.

Kurt said, "What d'you think I might find?"

"I don't know – schematics, drawings, plans, calculations, Heisenberg's notes, rough sketches – anything."

"If, as you say, I'm working for the British, why would I want to hand over such material to you?"

Staerling's eyes narrowed. "Play the game my way or I hand you over to Necker. The choice is yours."

Kurt mulled it over. It could all be an elaborate plot to get him to incriminate himself, but that seemed unlikely. Staerling was right: Kurt had no option but to accept the American's offer. "I'll need clothes and somewhere to stay in Berlin," he said, switching to English.

"Not a problem," said Staerling. He put the car in gear and they resumed their journey. The rain had eased and a brightness appeared in the sky ahead.

Kurt was acutely aware that without a radio he had no way of contacting London. But he wasn't about to share that with Otto 'Rocky' Staerling.

Staerling surprised him: "I can arrange access to a transmitter if and when you need one."

Staerling had said nothing about Erika or Pilgrim. It was a relief to know that they were both under the Americans' radar.

"That's generous of you," said Kurt.

"I've told you," Staerling replied. "We're on the same side. Play the game by my rules and we'll get on fine."

Chapter 39

As they approached Berlin, Kurt sank lower and lower in his seat. Ten months had passed since he'd fled the country, but he was a wanted man, his face well known in Berlin. The Nazis had long memories. And according to Professor Hirsch there was a price on his head.

The doubts that had plagued him in the standing cell still lingered. He had chosen a difficult path, working with Germany's enemies to help bring about the end of the Third Reich. Operating as a spy outside Berlin was risky enough; inside the capital it would be suicidal.

They came to another roadblock at the southern city limits. Once again, Staerling produced his pass, and once again they were waved on without hesitation.

"Whose is that signature?" asked Kurt.

"The pass is signed by the Reichsführer-SS."

Heinrich Himmler himself!

"And The Wings of the Eagle?"

"That's Professor Heisenberg's name for his atomic project."

Staerling crossed to the west side of the city, parked the car, and led Kurt into an apartment block. They took the elevator to the third floor and Staerling opened the door to one of the apartments.

"Where are we?" said Kurt.

"Dahlem, The Institute is a couple of streets to the north. You won't be disturbed here. The apartment is secure."

He showed Kurt into a bedroom. "Feel free to use the bath. You'll find clothes in the closet."

There was plenty of hot water. As Kurt sank into the water, he relaxed. For the first time since he'd left Ireland, his muscles unclenched. The water soothed his aching body, and the soap overcame the ugly smells of death and human waste clinging to his skin. The sound of sweet music wafting through the bathroom door refreshed his tortured soul.

Memories of his recent ordeal lay hidden in a special place in his mind, but he couldn't leave them there to fester. Closing his eyes, he lifted the veil and allowed the horrors of darkness and isolation to visit him again. He felt again the humiliation of the punishment, the misery of soiling himself, and the fingers of insanity that had touched his mind. Hatred filled him for those that had placed him in the cell. For those that had devised such a cruel punishment, he felt shame, shame that they were his own countrymen.

His father's voice came to him once more, before fading to silence.

Remember, boy, the greatest evil is the evil in our own hearts.

Thirty minutes later he emerged from the bath, every square centimetre of his skin scrubbed clean. He picked out some clothes from the closet – a light pair of trousers, a clean white shirt and a dark jacket. Retrieving Khall's letter from the toe of his boot, he smoothed it out as best he could and put it back.

Staerling placed a plate of spaghetti in front of Kurt, and Kurt devoured it without another word.

"I'll have to see where I can place you," said Staerling. "How good a mathematician are you?"

"I'm an excellent mathematician. But you never explained why you need my help to get the information you want. Why can't you do it yourself?"

"Good question," said Staerling. "I don't have the requisite skills. I'm no scientist."

"Doesn't the OSS have scientists?"

"We do have an engineer at the factory, but his math skills couldn't cut the mustard with Blaue."

"Who is he, this engineer?" said Kurt.

"His name's Gutkind."

Kurt remembered the thin balding individual he'd met in the factory canteen.

"I'm sure we could place someone else in there with the required skills, but not within the available timeframe. Your arrival was just the lucky break I was hoping for." Staerling beamed. "Washington suspects that the Nazis are close to achieving a viable atomic bomb."

"How close?" said Kurt.

"That's difficult to say, but their first test detonation could be weeks, or maybe even days, away."

According to the engineer at the labour camp the first test had been conducted several months earlier. If that was true, thought Kurt, then the American's information was seriously out of date.

Warning Kurt to keep out of sight, Staerling went out in search of supplies. Kurt immediately began a search of the apartment. It took him 30 minutes to unearth the American's shortwave radio hidden in a false compartment under the shoe rack in a wardrobe. Kurt admired the device. It was the most compact he had ever seen and it carried markings that showed it was made in the USA.

Continuing his search, he uncovered no signs to indicate that Staerling could be working for the Reich security services.

#

Kurt slept badly. Every time he began to drift off, his mind wandered to the 95 Theses of Martin Luther and from there back to the terrifying confines of the standing cell, and he woke up yelling, his father's face imprinted on the back of his eyelids.

Finally, Staerling appeared, dressed in striped flannel pyjamas, and gave Kurt a sleeping draught. The drug-induced sleep was deep but haunted by nightmares, mostly about incontinence, and Kurt woke early, bathed in sweat.

Staerling made breakfast. This consisted of two apples and the remains of an overripe melon, washed down with water that tasted of rust.

"I have picked out a position that I feel will suit your skills," said Staerling. "You will be working with an engineer and mathematician called Franz Zingler. Zingler works directly with Professor

Heisenberg – and, get this – his main responsibility is coordinating the technical drawings for the project."

The walk to the Institute took seven minutes. The Kaiser Wilhelm Institute for Physics was a solid four-storey building with a strange white tower attached at one end.

"That's the 'lightning tower', where they run a particle accelerator," said Otto Staerling.

Two soldiers stood guard at the main door of the Institute, rifles slung over their shoulders. It seemed the Institute was under the control of the Wehrmacht as both the factory in Oranienburg and the pitchblende mine in the Ore Mountains had been.

They paid a quick visit to Staerling's office on the ground floor, where he gave Kurt an access pass for the building. Then he led Kurt to a room – also on the ground floor – knocked and entered. A tall, curly-haired man sat at a table operating a comptometer like the one Kurt had used in the factory. He looked up as they entered.

Staerling said, "Franz, here is the help I promised you. This is Frederick von Schönholtz."

Zingler's sharp nose and recessed cheekbones gave his face the look of the keel of a capsized ship. The small eye sockets like the holes for the propeller shafts.

"Otto tells me you are a mathematician," said Zingler to Kurt.

"I studied under Professor Stephan Hirsch."

"Good, good," said Zingler. "Take a seat." He pointed to a chair. "You are familiar with the calculus of von Leibniz?"

"Yes," said Kurt. The sole attribution to the 18th-century German mathematician was a debatable point, as Isaac Newton had at least equal claim to the calculus, but he let that slide.

"Mostly what we do here is a succession of complex integrations."

"I'll leave you to it," said Staerling, rolling his eyes as he headed for the door.

Zingler ignored him. He handed Kurt a sheet of paper and a notebook. "Take a look at this one and tell me how you would go about solving it."

Ten minutes later, Kurt had run through all the strategies he had learnt in university for solving complex integrals. None was up to the task. He said, "I think you'd have to use numerical analysis for this. I can't see any other way of solving it."

"Good, good," said Zingler again, pushing the comptometer across the table. "Let me know when you have the answer."

#

By midday Kurt had solved half a dozen integrals. Zingler checked each one. He said, "Your solutions need to be accurate to four decimal places, but you do seem to know what you're doing."

Kurt asked what the integrals were used for.

"You don't need to know that."

"But where do they come from?"

Zingler fixed Kurt with his pinhole eyes. "Your job is to solve the things. You don't need to know anything about them."

"What is your job title?" Kurt asked.

"I don't have one."

"What is the project called? What is it for?"

"It's called The Wings of the Eagle. You have no need to know its purpose."

They adjourned to the canteen for an early lunch. "I like to come here ahead of the crowd," said Zingler. "I can't afford to waste too much time away from my desk."

The canteen was similar to the one in the factory. The food was similar, too, and just like the factory, the food was free and ration books were not needed. Kurt took this as further indication of Wehrmacht involvement in the work of the Institute.

He checked the catering staff for familiar faces. There were none.

As they ate, Kurt attempted to make friends with his new supervisor. He began by asking where Zingler had studied.

Zingler gave him a withering look. "I don't see that as any of your business, but I studied for my doctorate under Professor Heisenberg at the University of Leipzig."

"You studied physics?"

"Physics, advanced mathematics and some physical chemistry. My thesis was on the field of refractive spectrometry. I demonstrated how the technique could be used to measure the relative strengths of covalent bonds in certain radioactive isotopes of radium."

Kurt was way out of depth. He'd never heard of refractive spectrometry, and he had no notion what a covalent bond might be. "Have you worked here long, Herr Zingler?" he said.

"Long enough."

"You live locally?"

"What possible reason could you have to know where I live?" Zingler frowned at him.

"I'm new in this part of the city. I was hoping to find somebody who could show me the night life," said Kurt.

"I know nothing of the social life of the city. You'll have to ask someone else," said Zingler. "Now, if you've finished your meal we should get back to work."

On the way back to the office, they passed the foot of the staircase.

Kurt said, "What's upstairs?"

Zingler replied, "The director and senior physicists work on the upper floors. Access to that part of the building is restricted."

"Can you go upstairs?" said Kurt.

"That's not something that should concern you, but yes, I report directly to Professor Heisenberg."

When they were back at their table, Kurt asked about the lightning tower. "Herr Staerling tells me there's a particle accelerator in there."

"And?"

"I wondered what it is used for."

"Accelerating particles, obviously."

"Yes, but why accelerate particles? What are they used for?"

Zingler stared at Kurt. "I can't answer your questions. Now can we please return to your work."

Chapter 40

As Kurt was leaving the Institute late that evening, he saw a prostitute hanging about at the end of the street to the south. She was dressed in gaudy colours with a skirt that barely covered the essentials. She was too far away to make out her face.

Heading north toward Staerling's apartment, he became aware that the woman was following him. He ducked around a corner, ran 20 metres and slipped into a shop front. When she drew level with him he stepped out, grabbed her arm and drew her into the shelter of the shop.

Standing behind her, he locked an arm around her shoulders. "Why are you following me?" he whispered into her ear.

She turned her face to him and replied with a broad grin, "I thought you might like a little company, *liebling.*"

It was Erika.

"I knew you'd turn up sooner or later, like bad money," she said, kissing him lightly on the cheek.

A strong westerly wind had arisen, ahead of one of the early summer storms which were common in Berlin. Erika had a room in a boarding house to the south of the Institute. The first drops of rain began to fall as they headed there.

The rain came in a torrent then, and they ran.

"Where have you been?" said Erika as she closed the door of her room. "I thought I'd never see you again."

"I paid a visit to heaven's waiting room," said Kurt, and he sketched his experiences in the pitchblende mine and the punishment cell.

"How did you escape?"

"I was rescued by a friend," Kurt replied cryptically. "You haven't seen Pilgrim, have you?"

Erika's smile vanished. "Not yet. I've placed a small notice in the *Völkischer Beobachter*. If he's still alive and free he will find me."

While Kurt did what he could to dry his clothes, Erika cooked a simple meal of potatoes mixed with a little turnip, and they exchanged stories. Erika had escaped from the factory without difficulty, walking out in her catering outfit while the guards were all racing around looking for Kurt. She had collected the grenades from her apartment and taken a train to Berlin. "It was easy!" she said. Gaining employment in the Institute proved impossible, however: she had heard that the interviews were being conducted by an unpleasant SS man, and couldn't take the risk that this might be Necker.

She ground her teeth. "It's ridiculous that I can't get a job as a physicist in the Institute. I have the necessary qualifications. In fact, I would probably outshine many of the men in there."

Kurt gave Erika a shortened version of his adventures on the train, the camp, and the mine. He said very little about his time in the punishment cell, but he could see from the look on Erika's face that she sensed at least some of the horrors of his experience. Erika became animated when he told her what the engineer at the camp had said: that the Nazis had already completed a test firing of an atomic bomb, a test that had been partially successful.

"Did he say where the test was carried out?" she asked.

"At an underground base on Rügen Island, called Base Alpha."

"There were reports of an earth tremor in the western Soviet Union some months ago that London scientists were suspicious about," said Erika. "They were right to be suspicious. What we need to know now is the date of the next test."

Outside, the storm grew in intensity. The wind rose, driving the rain against the window. Kurt's clothes continued to steam in the warmth of the small room.

"Who was this friend that got you out?" said Erika as they ate.

Kurt told her how Otto Staerling had come to his rescue, Staerling's story that he worked for the OSS, American Military Intelligence, and how he had given Kurt a room in his apartment.

Erika laughed at this. "And you believed him? The guy's built like a barrel."

"I'm pretty sure he is who he says he is," Kurt replied. "I've seen his radio transmitter, and it's US-made. But I don't trust him. He's too oily for my taste."

Erika showed Kurt where she had hidden Pilgrim's bag of grenades. "I was worried that I might have to use them myself. I think it's time you showed me how they work."

Kurt opened the bag and pulled out one of the small, matchbox-sized grenades. He showed Erika how it could be set and primed. "We have four of these. All you have to do is set the time on this dial, then pull the tab, place the grenade and retire to a safe distance."

He pulled the last grenade from the bag, about twice the size of the others. "This one contains a radio receiver. It is programmed to detonate when it receives a short Morse code signal. If we place it carefully we may be able to cut the electricity supply to the entire base."

"If we can get in there." She picked up the grenade and examined it, turning it over in her hands. "How are you going to send it a signal? Are you sure it'll work?"

"I'll use the radio at the base. There's bound to be one," said Kurt. "And they demonstrated the device in London. It will work."

"You do know the Morse code – the one that detonates it?"

"No, Pilgrim never told me what it was."

"Don't you think that was a bit stupid? What you're saying is the thing is useless without Pilgrim, and we've lost contact with him."

"I'm sure he'll find us," said Kurt.

"And what if he doesn't?"

"In that case we'll have to make do with the four smaller grenades," said Kurt.

He went on to elaborate on the job Staerling had arranged for him in the Institute, working out complex integrals for Werner Heisenberg.

When he mentioned the name of his supervisor, Erika stopped him. "Franz Zingler?" she said. "I know him. He's had a couple of minor papers published. Could he be any help to us?"

"I'm not sure," said Kurt. "He reports directly to Heisenberg, but he's told me nothing of value so far."

"Let me get close to him," she said. "I'll soon get him to talk."

#

The following day was Saturday. Kurt and Franz Zingler were obliged to work as normal, but they were allowed to leave the Institute at 4 pm. At the gate, Kurt invited Zingler for a beer.

"I don't think so," said Zingler.

"I have a friend who has read your academic papers and is dying to meet you," said Kurt.

That swung it. Kurt and Zingler made their way to a beer cellar not far from the Institute. Erika was waiting for them at the bar wearing a tight-fitting dress in a floral pattern. Kurt made the introductions.

"I very much admire your work, Herr Doctor Zingler," Erika gushed. "How long have you worked with Professor Heisenberg?"

"A year." Obviously unused to discussing his work with a woman, Zingler showed little or no signs of relaxing.

"Everyone knows your paper on planar mechanics must have influenced the professor's formulation of the quantum model," she said, gazing at him through fluttering eyelashes.

Zingler melted. "You're a very clever little girl," he said, revealing long, pointed teeth in a coy smile.

Kurt slipped away.

Chapter 41

Sunday evening.

Erika dabbed a little vanilla essence on her neck and throat. She knew of old that its warm, maternal scent would excite any man as much as the most expensive perfume. She was wearing a blue dress that she'd picked up at a market stall a few days earlier – not a perfect fit by any means.

A rat-a-tat on the door signalled Zingler's arrival.

She threw her bag across her shoulder, checked her wig one last time in the mirror, and opened the door. Zingler stood there like a teenager on a first date, dressed in a pinstriped suit, a miserable bunch of flowers clutched in his hand. She took the flowers from him, tossed them inside the room, tucked a hand around his arm, and steered him toward the staircase.

Arm in arm they walked two kilometres under a crescent moon to a restaurant in Pückler Strasse. Zingler's conversation skills during the meal were abysmal, apart from when they were discussing his favourite subject. He didn't seem surprised to be dining with a woman who could listen to him drone on about particle physics without yawning. He explained everything to her in layman's terms, and Erika made sure to pitch her questions at a level that disguised the depth of her knowledge. Much of what he told her was general knowledge about nuclear fission and electricity generation, or speculative theories about the nature of matter and the origins of the Universe – first year university stuff.

Wide-eyed with admiration, she pushed him on and on, and gradually he began to stray into areas of his more recent work, but by the end of the meal he still had made no mention of an atomic bomb.

As they were putting their coats on in the restaurant, Zingler invited her back to his apartment.

He turned the key, whirled her in and pressed his lips to hers. Erika broke away after a moment.

"What an elegant apartment!" She waved a hand around the brown tartan wallpaper and torn linoleum. "A man like you is certain to make fine cocktails, yes?"

Zingler put on his phonograph and reduced the lighting. He took out a bottle of schnapps and two grubby glasses, and filled them to the brim.

"Heil Hitler!" he cried, wrapping his arm around hers so that they gazed into each other's eyes as they drank.

Erika knocked back the schnapps, slipped off her shoes, and draped herself across the settee in what she hoped was an alluring pose.

"You seem well versed in physics," said Zingler, handing her a cocktail. "For a girl, I mean."

"It's all far too complicated for me, really," she replied, "but you explain it so clearly, and with such energy. I wondered if you might have been a teacher at some time in the past?"

"I was never a teacher," said Zingler, "but perhaps it's something I should think of doing after the war. I do enjoy explaining things to people."

"Tell me again how something so small could contain so much power." She smiled and flapped her eyelashes at him.

Zingler sat beside her and ran an exploratory hand up her skirt. "We don't want to talk about physics all night."

She stopped his hand half-way up her thigh. "Slow down, Franz. What sort of girl d'you think I am?"

"I know what sort of girl you are," said Zingler with emphasis, a sinister glint in his eyes. "I just hope you're not a tease."

"We need to be better acquainted," she said. "Fetch me another drink."

While Zingler poured the drinks he said, "Are you married?"

"I was married once upon a time," she replied, "but not any more." A tease. Most men find experienced women more exciting.

"What happened?"

"I don't want to talk about that. It was a long time ago."

He handed her a fresh drink. "Your turn. Ask me anything," he said.

"I'd like to hear your opinion about the war," she said. "Do you believe the Führer will lead us to victory?"

"Yes, of course. It may take another year, but the Fatherland will prevail in the end."

"You don't think the Americans have tipped the conflict against us?"

"That's two questions," he said. "It's my turn."

"All right, what would you like to know?"

"I want to know what you're wearing under that dress." He lunged for her, but she slipped from the settee and got to her feet.

"You're not leaving." said Zingler. It wasn't a question, but Erika answered as if it was.

"No, but those sort of questions are not allowed. Maybe later. Ask me something else."

Zingler's colour had deepened. Erika wasn't sure if this was due to the schnapps or the frustrated swelling in his pants.

"Tell me why you accepted my invitation tonight. Tell me what you want from me."

"I like you, Franz. I find clever men fascinating."

"How, fascinating? Attractive?"

"Of course. I find clever men irresistible."

And then his arms were around her, his leering hatchet face in hers, his eager hands everywhere.

#

Erika arrived back at the lodgings in the small hours of Monday morning to find a message pinned to the wall by the telephone. She called the number and Pilgrim answered.

"Where are you? How are you?" she said.

"I'm fine. I'm in a small hotel in the city centre. Give me your address."

When Pilgrim arrived, he had a tale to tell. He had found work on a Rhine barge and travelled north as far as Weisbaden. From there to Berlin overland was more difficult, but he took rides from several supply trucks. The drivers were happy to help a soldier on leave.

Erika brought Pilgrim up to date on her time at the factory, how she'd lost contact with Kurt when he was transported to the pitchblende mine and how she'd found him again working at the Institute. When she told him about Zingler, Pilgrim clenched his fists. "You didn't... You didn't let him...?"

"I did enough, no more and no less," said Erika. "Now, let me get to bed. I'm exhausted."

Pilgrim watched her undress. When he saw the friction marks on her wrists and the bruising on her buttocks, he grabbed her arm.

"As I told you, Pilgrim, I gave Herr Doctor Zingler a little of what he wanted and he gave me some information in exchange. Don't worry about it."

"Tell me what you let him do to you."

"You don't want to know. Really, you don't."

"Just tell me."

Erika took a moment to consider her response. Pilgrim was an adult, fully acquainted with the ways of the world. But he was also a hothead, and he loved her with a passion. If she revealed too much about Zingler's strange sexual preferences and what she'd allowed him to do to her, Pilgrim could act irrationally and do something to put her whole mission at risk.

"Some nudity. A little bit of spanking."

"The man's a depraved monster! How much nudity?"

"Just leave it please, Pilgrim. I don't want to talk about it. I'll tell you when the mission is over and we're safely back in London."

"You'll tell me everything then?"

"Yes, everything. I promise."

He seemed satisfied with this. He said, "What information did you get from him?"

"He gave me various details about the project. How long it's been in operation, who's working on it – that sort of thing."

"Is that all?"

"The project is called The Wings of the Eagle."

Pilgrim snorted. "Didn't he give you anything useful?"

"I have to take it slowly, Pilgrim. Otherwise he might smell a rat. I'll get the rest of it from him the next time."

"You mean you're going to see him again?" He grabbed her around the waist and forced her to look him in the eyes. "Promise me, Erika" he said. "Promise me you won't let him do anything..."

She put two long fingers across his lips. "Hush, my love. You know what I have to do. It is for the Allies, for the war effort. It means nothing."

"But I love you Erika. I can't bear to think of another man's hands on you."

She kissed him lightly. "I love you too, Pilgrim. Be assured Franz Zingler is going to have to work for anything I give him."

Chapter 42

Professor Heisenberg and Franz Zingler met in Heisenberg's office for their weekly meeting. Running through the work that Zingler and had completed during the previous week, the professor was pleased with Zingler's increased productivity.

"How's your new assistant working out?" said Heisenberg. "Holtz was it?"

"Von Schönholtz. He's a first rate mathematician, and an excellent worker, but..."

The professor looked up sharply. "But? But what?"

Zingler shrugged. "He asks an awful lot of questions."

"What sort of questions?"

"All sorts, Professor. Personal questions..."

"That's normal, Franz," said the professor. "People ask one another personal questions. Not everyone's a dry stick like you."

"He asked about the integrals, what they were used for..."

"That's just natural curiosity. I'd be surprised if he showed no interest in the purpose of the work."

"He wanted to know about the particle accelerator, what it's used for and so on."

"More natural curiosity. Was there anything else?"

"He asked about the upper floors. I told him you were here."

The professor took a moment to consider this. Curiosity again, but taking all that curiosity together it did seem rather too much. He said, "Otto Staerling has given von Schönholtz full security clearance, but if you're really concerned I could have him replaced. The decision is yours, Zingler."

Zingler said, "I'd like to keep him. He's a good worker."

"So, what you're asking for is a new check on his background – by the SS?"

Zingler nodded.

"Have you thought this through, Franz?" said the professor quietly. "You know what will happen if we involve the SS directly. God knows where their investigations may take them. Your own position could come under scrutiny. Are you sure every aspect of your private life is beyond reproach and above suspicion?"

Zingler's normally pallid countenance was suddenly suffused with a blush. He shook his head. "Better leave it, Professor. I'll keep an extra vigilant eye on Schönholtz, make sure he has sight of nothing important."

The professor nodded. "Very well, Franz. Keep me informed."

Professor Heisenberg waited 15 seconds after Zingler had left the office before lifting his telephone. "Put me through to SS-Sturmbannführer Necker."

#

SS-Hauptsturmführer Lange sat at his desk in Prinz Albrecht Strasse 8, Berlin, staring at a typewriter containing a blank sheet of paper, and chewing his nails. It was Monday. His superior the SS-Standartenführer would be here by mid-afternoon, and Lange had precious little to put in his weekly report. The news that Müller had been seen in the south and was probably yodelling and eating Swiss cheese by now was not something he could share with his superiors.

The telephone rang. He picked it up on the second ring.

"Lange?" Lange's bowels roiled as he heard the voice of the man he hated most, the SD man SS-Sturmbannführer Manfred Necker. "I need a security check on a Frederick von Schönholtz."

"Why, what has he done, this Frederick von Schönholtz?" Lange wrote the name on his notepad.

"Nothing that I'm aware of. He's a recent arrival at the Institute in Berlin, and he worked in Oranienburg before that. I just need a background check, and I need it done quickly."

"What do we know about him?"

"He's from Mannheim, date of birth July the first, 1913. His father was a carpenter called Joseph. He served in the Wehrmacht, and was discharged wounded."

Lange wrote all these details on his notepad. "I take it you have seen his discharge papers?"

"Not yet. No."

Lange thought that reply sounded a little sheepish.

"So you don't know what unit he served in, or where he was wounded?"

"He was wounded in the shoulder," said Necker.

Idiot! thought Lange. He said, "That's not what I meant. I meant whereabouts was he stationed when he was wounded."

"That was a small joke, Lange. He was wounded in Belgium."

Lange was slightly unnerved by this, but he completed the standard joke reply, "By a German bullet, I imagine." One joke deserved another.

Lange and Necker had been working together for close to a year. In all that time Lange had never seen Necker laugh or make a joke of any kind.

"What are you talking about?" said Necker.

"Haven't you heard that one? It was Belgium. The British had run out of bullets..."

"What are you jabbering about? You're making no sense, man."

"Never mind," said Lange. "Leave it with me." He replaced the telephone in its cradle, shaking his head.

Pressing a button on his intercom, he said, "Get in here. I have an urgent job for you."

He checked his watch. He had a couple of hours. If his men could complete the task quickly he might still have something meaty to put in his weekly report.

Chapter 43

Monday evening, May 3

Kurt had the feeling that he was intruding on a fraught domestic scene. Erika and Pilgrim were reunited, but the atmosphere in Erika's lodgings was thick with tension.

She reported on what she had found out. Zingler was custodian of all the schematics for the project.

"I've struck pay dirt! This is why I was sent to Haigerloch. My mission was to get copies of those schematics back to London."

Kurt said, "I hope you've given some thought to why the British want those, and what they will do with them."

"Of course I have," she replied. "The Americans want them for the same reason – and the Soviets. The greatest danger comes from one side having an atomic bomb. If both the Allies and the Germans have one, they will be reluctant to use them."

"You should think about what you are doing, that's all I'm saying, Erika. This weapon has terrible potential. If it were used it could wipe all life from the face of the Earth."

Erika reported that Franz Zingler had confirmed with pride the first test of the bomb, partially successful. And he had hinted that a second test was imminent.

"When?"

"I didn't press him for a date," she said.

"Why not?" said Kurt.

"These things can't be rushed. I'll get the date from him, tonight, I promise."

Pilgrim gave a muted moan and left the room.

#

"I knew you'd come," said Zingler, his eyes shining in anticipation.

Erika was wearing a white blouse and a pleated skirt that was rather too short for comfort. Zingler had torn the blue dress at their last encounter.

He made her a glass of schnapps with a wolfish smile, and patted the settee, inviting her to join him. Erika remained standing. She sipped her drink and considered her next move. Zingler was a depraved monster – Pilgrim was right about that – but he was a clever depraved monster. He must have realised by now that she wanted something from him, and she fully expected that he would string her along until she satisfied his latest fantasy, whatever that might be, and then kick her out, empty-handed.

He sat cross-legged on the settee holding a bottle of schnapps, his pin eyes watching her the way a cat watches a canary, the expression on his face somewhere midway between comical and terrifying. He said, "You enjoyed our last encounter, I think?"

"Of course. What woman could resist your sharp mind, an imagination as rich as yours?"

"Women are all the same in my experience," he said. "They love a strong man, and once they get a taste of that they can't resist."

"I like strong men, that is true," she replied, "but I love a man with a brain, and yours is a supreme intellect, Franz."

"What about your husband? Was he clever?"

She dropped her eyes. "Not as clever as you, Franz."

"Was he strong?"

"Not as strong as you, Franz."

"Finish your drink and we can start." He stood, emptying his glass down his throat.

"Tell me about your project," she said. "Why is it called the Wings of the Eagle? What a beautiful name!"

The look he gave her was like an owl contemplating its prey. "You know how the war has been progressing?"

"Yes, of course, Germany has been victorious on all fronts. Soon, it will be over."

He shook his head. "Sadly, that is not entirely true, Marta. The Reich has suffered some losses. The final outcome is no longer certain."

She fixed a look of horror on her face. "It's not serious, though. Say it is not serious."

"Germany is like an eagle with broken wings. Our project will restore those wings."

"That makes perfect sense. You explain it beautifully," she said.

He stepped closer. She let him.

"You find me attractive?" she said.

"Yes, yes, of course. Why else would I have invited you here?" He placed a single paw on her left breast. "We should get undressed. I don't have much time."

She persisted. "What is it that you find attractive about me?"

"These are wonderful," he said, both hands on her breasts now.

"You think I'm good-looking?"

"And these." He leered at her and grabbed a buttock in each hand. "Come, it's time."

She gave him a smile. "But you must talk to me about your work while we make love."

He sprang to the bedroom door and opened it. Looking into the bedroom, she could see a leather thong hanging from each of the four brass posts of the bed. He had used only two the last time. A slight shudder ran up her spine. She stepped toward the bed. As she passed him Zingler made his move, twisting her arm behind her back, forcing her onto the bed, face down.

"You're hurting me," she protested.

"Whore! Shut your mouth."

He attached her right wrist to one of the thongs. Then he tore off her blouse. When he reached for her left wrist, she sprang into action.

Turning on him, she caught him with her arm around his neck in a choke hold. He struggled and fought to break free, but she increased the pressure. He kicked and bucked. She held on grimly, like a rodeo rider, tightening her grip to block the flow of arterial blood to his brain.

He slumped to the ground, unconscious. She heaved him onto the bed, stripped him naked, and secured his hands and feet to the bedposts. She stood back to admire her work. Franz Zingler looked like a pink starfish with a half-eaten grey worm in its mouth.

She removed her skirt. Then she slapped him awake.

Zingler yelled and swore at her. He strained at the leather thongs holding him down.

"You bitch!" he hissed. "What are you doing?"

"Isn't this what you had in mind, Herr Zingler?" she said.

"Let me loose, you devil's whore!"

Smiling at him, standing to his left where he could view her half naked body, her long legs, she waited for the inevitable reaction. When there was none, she ducked out of his sight at the end of the bed.

"Where are you going?" he cried. "Cut me loose. What are you doing?"

She reappeared on the other side of the bed. "Isn't this what you wanted?" she said. A riding crop appeared in her hand. She ran her eyes down his torso. His shaft was stirring. "I see it is. Let me know when you're ready."

Soon, he had a raging erection. "What are you going to do to me?" he stammered.

"That depends on you," she said. "I need some information. And if I'm satisfied with what you tell me, then I will give you what you want."

His eyes opened wide in alarm.

"I want the date and time of the second test," she said, resting the riding crop on his stomach.

He groaned. "You're a madwoman! Why do you want to know that?"

"That is not your concern. Answer the question, and don't lie to me." She slid the tip of the crop down his quivering penis. "I'll know if you're not telling me the truth."

Chapter 44

Tuesday 4 May

Professor Heisenberg had been at his desk for over an hour when his telephone rang at 6:15 am.

"Professor?" It was the SS man, Manfred Necker. "I have completed my checks on Frederick von Schönholtz, and it looks likely that your suspicions are confirmed. Hold him for me. I'm on my way."

"What's the problem, Manfred? He's a superb mathematician, one of our best workers."

"I could find no records for Frederick von Schönholtz in Mannheim or in the Wehrmacht, and when I interviewed him in Oranienburg, I asked to see his Wehrmacht discharge papers. He never produced them."

"Probably a simple oversight. I don't think you realise how busy we are here–"

"Listen to me, Professor, Schönholtz is not who he says he is. Hold him for interrogation."

"But he passed all of Otto Staerling's security checks."

Necker grunted. "That just proves how useless those checks are. His papers are almost certainly forgeries. Hold him for me. I'll be there in less than an hour."

"But I have to leave here before seven–"

Necker had terminated the call.

#

"I need to send a signal to London," said Kurt. "Where's your radio?"

Dressed in his flannel pyjamas, Staerling was an unlikely-looking OSS agent. "You have some intelligence to transmit?"

"You did say you had a radio and that I could use it."

"Sure, but if you have something to tell London, I'd like to keep our boys up to date as well."

Kurt decided to accede to Staerling's request. There wasn't a lot of choice, really. Staerling was with the OSS; Kurt had seen nothing to suggest otherwise. And Staerling was the one with the radio. "I have the date and time of the test. It's tomorrow morning, early."

Staerling gave a low whistle. "Have you managed to get your hands on any documents? My people will need sight of those documents. And I'm sure London will too."

"Agreed, but I have none. I expect all the technical drawings are locked up in a safe somewhere in the Institute, but I'm sure we'll find them at the test site."

"You reckon?"

"Certainly. They won't be locked away there, that's for sure."

"You know where Base Alpha is located?" said Staerling. "It's on Rügen Island, about 300 kilometres north. We'll have to get our skates on if we're to get there in time."

"Any ideas how to get there?"

Staerling replied, "We'll have to take my car."

He fished his radio from its hiding place and switched it on. Pilgrim had encoded a short signal that Kurt had composed. Kurt set the frequency and transmitted the signal:

WEAPON TEST TWO AM WEDNESDAY MAY FIVE RUGEN ISLAND REQUEST RAF

There was a long pause before London responded. Kurt quickly decoded the return signal using Pilgrim's codebook.

BEACON REQUIRED FOR DROP ONE AM. CONFIRM

Kurt replied with the confirmation code before transmitting one more encoded signal:

NIGHT FLIGHT MALMO SWEDEN TO LONDON REQUIRED THREE PASSENGERS MAY SIX

London responded with the short confirmation code, and Kurt switched the radio off. Then he headed for the bathroom, leaving Staerling fiddling with the frequency dial.

Staerling was waiting for Kurt when he re-emerged from the bathroom. "We should leave immediately."

"Agreed," said Kurt. "You'll have three passengers in total."

They drove to Erika's lodgings where Pilgrim was waiting. He introduced himself to Staerling using his alias, Willi Pfaltz. When Staerling saw who the third passenger was he insisted she sit beside him, patting the front passenger seat and smiling at her.

Erika was dressed in dark slacks and tunic. She threw her eyes to heaven. "What is it with men? You all think you're God's gift to women."

"Just get in, Marta, or we'll never get started," said Staerling.

#

Professor Heisenberg was waiting at the door of the Institute when Necker arrived at 7 am.

"Where is he?" said the SS man.

"He's not here yet," the professor replied. "Mathematicians as good as von Schönholtz are hard to find. Are you sure of your facts?"

"There's every likelihood that he may be an enemy spy," Professor Heisenberg blanched at that word. Necker continued, "There's no record of the man anywhere. If Otto Staerling were doing his job properly he would never have allowed him into the building. A certain Klaus Randau broke into the SS building at Haigerloch and freed a female prisoner. I believe von Schönholtz and this Randau are one and the same, and he may still be travelling with the female. There was a second man involved in the breakout, too, but we have no information on him, as yet."

"A female prisoner?" said the professor, with slight tilt of a disapproving eyebrow.

"Her name is Erika Cleasby. She has been using the alias Marta Maynard. We know she works for British intelligence."

"Oh my god! I hope I don't need to stress the sensitive nature of the work we do here, Manfred. It is imperative for the war effort that this threat be eliminated. Imperative."

"Which is why I need you to hand over the suspect without further delay. Where is he?"

"I haven't seen him this morning," said the professor.

Necker raised his voice a couple of notches. "Who was the last person to see Schönholtz?"

"I saw him leaving with Franz Zingler last night," the professor replied.

"Send for Zingler immediately."

The professor shook his head. "He should be halfway to the island by now. You do realise that we will be conducting an important test firing tomorrow morning, and how important that is to the Führer?" Necker gave the professor a withering look, and the professor's tone changed. "You don't think Zingler could be involved? Surely not Franz Zingler. He's one of Germany's best physicists and one of my closest helpers."

"What we have here is a nest of spies, Professor. Your whole project is under threat."

"But Otto Staerling cleared everybody," said the professor, spreading his palms.

"We're wasting time, Professor. Get me Zingler's home address."

"Staerling keeps all those details in his personnel files," said the professor, and when Necker scowled at him, the professor scurried inside to fetch them.

#

SS-Sturmbannführer Necker hammered on the door of Zingler's apartment. "In the name of the Führer, open this door!"

He waited 15 seconds before putting a boot through the door and charging inside. He found Zingler strapped to his bed by four leather thongs, his underwear stuffed into his mouth. There were streaks of dried blood on his lower torso. Necker took a moment to register the scene before removing the gag.

"Who did this to you?"

"A woman. A devil-spawn whore bitch!" Zingler croaked.

Necker showed him a picture of Erika. "Is this the woman?"

"That's her! Do you have her? Tell me you have her."

Necker spotted a riding crop on the floor by the bed. He picked it up. "Tell me what happened. There's not a minute to spare."

"Cut me loose," said Zingler. "I'm needed at the island."

Zingler saw the movement of the riding crop as a blur. He felt it, though, as the tip caught his upper legs like a knife. His involuntary yell was one of alarm; the blow had been delivered uncomfortably close to his wedding tackle.

"Tell me," said Necker.

Zingler painted a picture of a romantic evening with soft music and candlelight in his apartment, he an innocent man tricked and seduced and then rendered unconscious by a scheming harlot. He left the end of the tale untold.

"And the rest? What did she want?"

"There's nothing more to tell," Zingler screamed. "She took advantage of my hospitality–"

Necker cut him off with a second blow. This one caught him squarely on the gonads. Zingler screamed.

"Tell me. Tell me the truth or, so help me, you'll never father a child."

"I've told you the truth." Zingler sobbed with pain.

"She asked you for information," said Necker.

"No–"

"I know this woman is a British spy. Don't lie to me. What did she ask you?"

"I swear on my mother's grave, I told her nothing."

The riding crop struck him again. Zingler screamed.

"You're a miserable little pervert, and a bad liar, Zingler. I know your mother's not dead. Now tell me the truth. What information did the British spy ask for?"

It was a few moments before Zingler could speak. "I swear, there was nothing."

Necker beat him about the head with the switch. "Tell me the truth, you miserable pile of excrement, or so help me, I'll beat you to a pulp before I have you strung up as a traitor."

Zingler shrank away from the rain of blows. He shouted, "She knew about the planned test of the bomb. She wanted the date."

"And you gave it to her!"

"I'm sorry, Herr Necker."

"She must have asked for the location of Base Alpha. Did you give her that, too?"

"No, I think she knew it already, I swear."

"So, you betrayed your country," said Necker. He threw down the riding crop and drew his pistol. "I hope it was worth it."

"No!" Zingler screamed. "I can help you."

"I don't think so." Necker cocked the gun and pointed it at Zingler's head.

"Don't shoot me. Professor Heisenberg needs me on the island!"

Part 6 - The Island

Chapter 45

Necker roared into the telephone, veins bulging in his jaw. "Lange, I want you to intercept a black Horch staff car, driving north toward Rügen Island. There are three subversives on board. They must be stopped at all cost."

At the other end of the line SS-Hauptsturmführer Lange took a deep breath before answering. "When you say subversives, what do you mean? Are these Communists or foreigners, or members of a dissident group?"

Necker licked his lips. Even though he outranked the man, he was going to have to play along with Lange's charade. Necker was in a hole. He needed cooperation from the Gestapo. And Lange would provide it, but first he would extract the pound of flesh that he was fully entitled to. "I believe they may be enemy spies."

"That is a serious matter. How long have you been aware of this nest of spies?"

"Since yesterday when I asked you for that background check on Frederick von Schönholtz."

"This Frederick von Schönholtz is one of the spies?"

"He is. He also uses the alias Klaus Randau."

There was a strange sound at the end of the telephone, as if Lange had dropped the instrument.

"Lange, are you still there?"

Lange replied, "You didn't think to alert me before now?"

"There is not a moment to lose. As I said, they are heading north. They left here approximately one hour ago. I will give chase. What I'd like you to do—"

"I hope it is not your intention to tell me my job, Herr Sturmbannführer. We have been aware for some time that you had a *situation*, as you call it, and that your situation was steadily worsening. You have seen fit to act on your own until this moment. You'll need to explain why you feel you need our assistance now."

"My resources are limited, as you know, Lange. It should be a simple matter for you to mobilize a unit and set up a roadblock to intercept these fugitives. There is much at stake. Capture of these enemy agents will be a major achievement for national security."

"For the Gestapo?"

"For the Gestapo."

Lange said, "You don't have a roadblock on the bridge at Stralsund?"

"We have a permanent roadblock on the bridge, of course, but civilian traffic to and from the island is heavy and the directors of the Institute prefer not to draw too much attention to the base. I'd like you to set up another one somewhere south of the island."

"Very well, Herr Necker," said Lange. "I will divert one of our units in the north and have them set up a roadblock at Neubrandenburg. It will be in place within the hour. But be aware that I will be withdrawing resources from other work of national importance. If this turns out to be a waste of time you will answer fully for the consequences."

Chapter 46

For the first 30 kilometres Staerling kept up a constant chatter in English. He seemed nervous. He told them the story of his life growing up in suburban Chicago with a drunken German mother and an absent father. Erika did her best to be polite until he began to repeat a story about the black sheep of his family, an uncle who'd run away to join a circus.

In English, Erika said, "Tell me what you know about the test site."

"I know very little," Staerling replied. "I know it's big and well-guarded."

"You do know where it is? Rügen Island is the size of Berlin."

"We're looking for an underground cavern. How difficult can it be to find that?" said Staerling.

Erika snorted. "The whole island is made of limestone. That means it's almost certainly riddled with caves and underground caverns. Kurt, do you have an exact location for the Base Alpha test site on the Island?"

"Who's Kurt?" said Staerling.

Kurt replied, "No, but how difficult will it be to find? Wake me up when we get near Neusterlitz. We need to take a detour, there, to Carpin."

She said, "What's in Carpin? This is the first you've said about any detour."

"I have a letter to deliver," said Kurt. "It won't take long. An hour at most."

"We don't have time for detours, Kurt."

"I made a solemn promise, Erika."

"Who's Erika?" said Staerling. "I thought your name was Marta."

"We don't have time for personal matters," she said, ignoring Staerling. "Be realistic, Kurt."

Pilgrim, who had been sleeping in the back seat, woke up, rubbed his eyes and said, "What's going on? Where are we?"

Erika adjusted the rear view mirror so that she could see Kurt's face. "Tell me what's so important about this letter."

Kurt said, "In the labour camp, an engineer told me about the first test and the location of Base Alpha. In exchange, I promised to deliver a letter to his father."

"That sounds to me like a debt of honour," said Pilgrim.

"Don't be ridiculous, Pilgrim. When will men grow up? You're all like little children, making crazy promises to one another."

"Who the heck is Pilgrim?" said Staerling.

On the road north of Lowenberg, a motorcycle roared past, ridden by a soldier wearing a greatcoat. He slowed and signalled for Staerling to pull over.

Erika's muscles tensed ready for combat. "Get ready, Kurt," she said.

Staerling drew up on the side of the road and wound down his window. The rider removed his gloves, helmet and goggles before approaching the car.

"*Guten tag,* Otto," said the rider. He was a small man with almost no hair, prematurely grey.

"This is Gutkind," said Staerling to his passengers. "He's one of the good guys."

"We've met," said Kurt. He nodded at the accountant from the factory.

"Stick close by," said Staerling to Gutkind. "We're taking a short detour to Carpin."

They drove on in silence, Gutkind keeping pace with them on his motorcycle. They were now a team of five but that thought was no comfort to Erika, and her unease increased with each passing kilometre.

#

SS-Sturmbannführer Manfred Necker headed north out of Berlin. They were ahead of the early morning traffic and could expect to reach the outskirts of the city with relative ease. Still, his driver took liberties with the suburban roads, throwing caution to the stars, taking corners on two wheels. It seemed Necker's excitement had communicated itself to his driver.

"Slow down," said Necker. "We will catch them. The only thing that will save them now is if we get involved in some stupid accident."

The driver eased his foot from the accelerator. They lost no more than 10 kph, but it was just enough to save the lives of a mother and baby who blundered out in front of them as they rounded a corner.

Necker looked back at the woman sprawled beside her overturned perambulator and sighed. He was sure the young woman would have been content to sacrifice her child if she had known the urgency of the quest he was on. But damage to the car would have been difficult to explain away so soon after his first car was stolen from the castle and burned out near the Swiss border.

Involving Lange in the pursuit was regrettable, but the Gestapo had virtually unlimited resources, while the SD had none. Necker ran a finger over the scar on his cheek. He liked to think of the SD as an épée. They had meagre resources, but they were an elite, relying on intellect to get the job done, every man hand-picked. The Gestapo, on the other hand, was a bludgeon. It had no finesse. To them everything was either black or white; they had no appreciation of the many shades of grey that confronted Necker daily.

And Lange was an idiot. Give him a sniff of an enemy agent and his first reaction was to load his gun and pull the trigger, ejaculating into his pants like an excitable teenager. Necker, on the other hand, was always open to the possibility of turning an enemy agent with carefully conceived methods of persuasion. 'Softy, softly catchee monkey' was his motto.

He took a few moments to dwell on his recent encounters with the delicious Miss Cleasby. She had a fine Teutonic figure – she was half

Swedish, after all. With his eyes closed he could picture her nipples and conjure up the smell of her.

Necker was confident that he would come upon the fugitives before they reached Lange's roadblock, but he suspected that Lange would attempt to intercept the spies personally. The fact that Necker had a head start on Lange was of critical importance, for it was essential that he should come across the fugitives first in order to claim the credit for the whole operation.

Lange's insolence in demanding the credit for his men made him smile. As if that was likely to happen! How could a captain claim the credit for a security operation initiated by a major? The man was a hopeless dreamer.

He took his Luger from its holster and checked it.

#

SS-Hauptsturmführer Lange's blood was racing through his veins. At last that insufferable, self-important dummkopf, SS-Sturmbannführer Necker had asked for his assistance. Lange knew that Necker would try to out-play him as usual, but this time he would lose, for Lange had an ace up his sleeve: Necker had no idea that von Schönholtz was the Abwehr deserter Kurt Müller.

The Gestapo was equipped for manhunts, the SD was not. Necker might outrank him, but, when it came to tracking down enemies of the Fatherland, Necker was hopelessly outclassed. Lange commanded an experienced and well-trained squad of men who knew how to get the job done. And now that Necker had called on him for help, Lange would make sure that Müller and his accomplices were captured – alive, preferably – to face the courts.

Lange bitterly recalled the last time he had worked with Necker. That operation had been a triumph for him and his men, and yet somehow the SS man had come away with all the credit. This time, Lange and his unit would get all the glory.

He lifted his telephone and gave the signal to start the operation. A single truckload of six crack Gestapo men, supplemented by four Waffen-SS troops, should be more than enough to handle any eventuality. To eliminate any possibility of the fugitives escaping across open countryside, two motorcycles would be included. Nothing must be left to chance.

Levering his ample frame from the chair, he hurried to the main door where his driver was waiting in the car. They headed north. He knew that he would probably meet the subversives on the road somewhere close to the town of Neusterlitz, but they would have to get their skates on if they were going to get there before Necker. Necker had a 10 minute head start.

The Berlin traffic was entering its usual morning snarl-up. Lange's driver switched on his blue light and siren and Lange watched with satisfaction as the people of Berlin stood aside to give him passage. It raised his spirits to see these spontaneous displays of national patriotism. The Third Reich had truly found its natural home in the hearts and minds of the German people.

As soon as they had cleared the city suburbs Lange signalled to his driver to give the car its head. The six-cylinder Mercedes Benz engine didn't disappoint.

#

Necker's driver passed two Gestapo motorcycles at the southern outskirts of Neusterlitz.

"Stop the car!" yelled Necker. "Those were Lange's men. Turn around and follow them."

The driver executed a three-point turn and chased back the way they had come. He overtook the motorcycles and waved them down. Necker jumped out of the car. The motorcycle riders dismounted.

One of the riders saluted. "Heil Hitler!"

"You are SS-Hauptsturmführer Lange's men?" said Necker, ignoring the salute.

The men confirmed that they were, and that they had come from the roadblock at Neubrandenburg. They had seen nothing of the fugitives' car.

"You must have missed them on the road," said Necker.

"They couldn't have passed us, sir. We would have seen them."

Necker leaned against his car, absent-mindedly fingering the itchy scar on his face.

"They may have taken a different route," said the rider. He signalled to his co-driver, who produced a map from his motorcycle's leather document bag.

Necker and the two Gestapo men spread the map out on the bonnet of Necker's car. Necker's driver joined them and all four men discussed their next move.

The route they had followed was the most direct from Berlin to Stralsund, but there were alternatives. Necker swore under his breath. Perhaps Erika and her nest of vipers had been aware of possible pursuit, in which case they could have taken a less obvious road.

Necker took charge of the situation, and gave orders to his driver and the motorcycle riders to cover a good number of the routes that the fugitives might have taken. They could still be found and the situation retrieved. In the last resort, they would be caught in Lange's roadblock at Neubrandenburg or the one at the bridge.

"I will remain here to meet Lange," said Necker. "A prize for the man who brings these runaways to me."

The motorcycles and Necker's car dispersed to carry out their orders. Necker strode to the opposite side of the road where he had seen a coffee shop.

Chapter 47

Tuesday, May 4 around noon

"I don't like this," said Erika.

Kurt drank in the tranquil scene. The farmhouse nestled among rolling hills and cultivated fields, a flock of sheep grazing contentedly in a lush pasture. A trace of smoke rose from the chimney and skipped away on a light breeze. "What are you worried about?" he said.

Erika shrugged. "I don't know. I just don't like it."

Staerling parked by the gate and signalled for Gutkind to take the motorcycle out of sight beyond a bend in the road.

"We'll wait in the car," said Staerling. "Don't take too long."

Erika said to Pilgrim, "You go with Gutkind."

Kurt and Pilgrim stepped from the car. Pilgrim followed the motorcycle. Letter in hand, Kurt approached the farmhouse and banged on the door.

The door was opened by an unshaven man in his forties wearing military breeches and boots and armed with a handgun.

"Dieter Khall?" said Kurt.

"Who're you?"

"My name's Frederick. I have a letter for you from your son."

The man opened the door fully. "You'd better come in."

Inside the farmhouse there was a massive wooden table standing on a floor made from flagstones and littered with the remains of a meal for four people. There was a fire in the hearth. A strange feeling in Kurt's gut told him to stay on his guard: something was missing here.

The man insisted on searching Kurt before inviting him to sit at the table.

Kurt handed over the letter and sat. His host remained standing.

"Tell me about this," said Khall, waving the unopened letter.

Kurt told him how he had met his son in the labour camp near the coal mines in the Ore Mountains.

"That's not possible. Those mountains must be 500 kilometres from here."

That was when Kurt realised what it was that had alerted him to danger: there was a flock of sheep outside, but no sign of a sheepdog. This man was no sheep farmer. He was not Dieter Khall. He was probably a deserter in hiding. Dieter Khall and his sheepdog were both dead.

"I can't stay any longer," said Kurt, getting to his feet.

"Tell me about your friends, the ones in the Gestapo car outside," said Khall, producing his handgun again and pointing it at Kurt.

"I promised your son I would deliver the letter. I've kept my word. Now I must leave."

"You're going nowhere. Take a seat."

Kurt sat down again.

The door opened. Staerling and Erika were bundled inside by a second man armed with a Schmeisser. This man, too, was wearing military breeches and boots. And there must be two more, thought Kurt. The table was set for four.

"They're not armed," said the second man.

Khall waved the gun, and Erika and Staerling joined Kurt at the table. Kurt glanced at Erika and got a frown and a slight shake of the head in return.

The second man ran hungry eyes over Erika. Erika averted her eyes.

"You need to let us continue our journey," said Staerling. "We are engaged in important work for the Reich."

"Shut your mouth!" said Khall.

The door opened and two more armed men entered. All four were dressed alike. These were deserters, no question about it. There was no chance that they would release Kurt and his companions to inform on them. Their only hope lay with Pilgrim and Gutkind, hiding outside.

"You." Khall pointed the gun at Staerling. "Tell me where you were headed."

Kurt noted the use of the past tense.

Staerling replied, "Rügen Island. If we don't arrive there within a few hours the Wehrmacht will come looking for us."

Khall turned to his men, "Search the car. Then put it out of sight behind the barn."

Two of the men left to carry out his orders.

"Now tell me what's so urgent that you have to get to Rügen Island."

Before Staerling could answer Kurt said, "My friend is lying. We're on the run from the Wehrmacht. We're deserters."

Khall tapped his teeth with the barrel of his gun while he considered this. The second man continued to leer at Erika.

"You don't look like deserters. Where did you get those clothes?"

"We stole them from a shop in Berlin," Kurt said.

"Lock them in the barn," said Khall, and when they all rose, he waved his gun at Erika. "Not you, Fräulein. You stay here with me."

#

"We need to do something," said Pilgrim.

Watching from the trees, Pilgrim and Gutkind had seen Staerling and Erika ordered from the car, searched and marched into the farmhouse by a man with a rifle. Then two more men had appeared and driven the car behind a barn.

"What would you suggest?" said Gutkind. "There are at least four of them and they have guns. I have a pistol. What do you have?"

"I'm not armed, but I have a few grenades." Pilgrim indicated the bag on his shoulder.

Gutkind said, "There's very little cover between here and the farmhouse. We'll have to wait until dark."

Pilgrim shook his head. "We're running out of time, and anyway, they'll all be dead by nightfall." Thinking of Erika, he added, "Or worse."

A few moments passed. Then Staerling and Kurt were marched from the house by two of the men and locked in the barn. The two men returned to the farmhouse.

"That's it," said Pilgrim. "I'm going in."

"We can't," said Gutkind. "What chance would we have against four armed men?"

Pilgrim spoke between clenched teeth. "You can stay here if you like. I'm not leaving Erika in there on her own."

#

Erika stood up as the two men returned from moving the car. She was under no illusions about what to expect from four deserting soldiers, but she would put up a fight.

The three men propped their Schmeissers against the wall by the door.

"I'm first," said one of them, stepping forward.

A second, bigger man pulled him back by the collar. "Get in line," he growled.

Khall, now the only one holding a weapon, pointed it at Erika. "Drop the slacks and get up on the table."

The big man swept the remains of the meal onto the floor and began to unbutton his trousers.

Erika stood her ground, and the big man reached a hand toward her. She grabbed his hand and spun him around twisting his arm behind his back.

The two unarmed men rushed forward. Erika pushed the big man from her and he crashed into the others. All three fell to the floor. Leaping over them, she grabbed one of the Schmeissers, cocked it and levelled it at Khall.

Khall laughed mirthlessly. "What are you going to do with that, Fräulein?"

The big man was on his feet again, moving toward her, a snarl on his ugly face.

She pulled the trigger. There was a loud 'click'. She threw the gun at the soldier, picked up another one, cocked it and pulled the trigger. Another 'click'. She dropped the second gun and grabbed the third.

"They're all empty," said Khall. "Take off your clothes and get on the table or I'll put a bullet in your leg."

Erika was out of options, but she cocked and fired the gun anyway. There was a loud 'crack!' and the big man fell, clutching his chest.

The other two men hurled themselves at Erika. Her head hit the concrete floor and she blacked out.

Chapter 48

"*Scheisse!*" said Staerling. "I knew this detour was a bad idea."

The barn door was solid oak, locked by a padlock on the outside. There were mouldy hay-bales and a rusty Volkswagen with no wheels occupied by a dozen chickens. The door was the only way out, although the chickens had a small hole in a wall plank that allowed them to come and go.

"Shut up and give me a hand," said Kurt. He wrapped his hands around the end of the plank at the chicken's exit and pulled with all his strength. The plank refused to budge.

Staerling found a two-pronged pitchfork and handed it to Kurt. Kurt stabbed at the wall, puncturing it. He tried twisting the pitchfork from side to side, until the prongs began to bend.

"Let me try," said Staerling. Jamming the handle into the hole, he placed a half-brick under it to create a lever and applied his considerable weight to it. The pitchfork bent and then snapped.

"*Scheisse!*" said Staerling again.

Kurt applied his shoulder to the door. It rocked, but remained closed. They both charged the door together without success. Kurt racked his brains for another way out, but could think of none.

"Stand back." That was Pilgrim's voice from outside the door. "I've set the fuse for 30 seconds."

Kurt and Staerling stood well back from the door. There was a loud explosion, deafening Kurt for a moment. The door flew from its hinges. Still clutching the broken pitchfork, Kurt ran out through the smoke. Staerling followed.

As two of Khall's fellow-deserters emerged from the house, Pilgrim and Gutkind pounced on them, and within seconds the two deserters were neutralised. There was no sign of Khall or the big man.

Pilgrim leapt through the farmhouse door and re-emerged supporting a half-conscious Erika.

"Did you see the other two in there?" said Kurt.

Pilgrim answered, "Just one, a big man, but he's been shot."

Erika sank to her knees, rubbing the back of her head. Pilgrim hunkered down beside her. At that moment, Khall emerged from the farmhouse, brandishing his pistol. He pointed the gun at Pilgrim. Kurt hefted the broken pitchfork in his hand and threw it at Khall like a spear. Half a second before Khall could pull the trigger, the pitchfork buried itself in his chest. The deserter fell back with a strangled cry.

Pilgrim nodded his thanks to Kurt.

Kurt ran inside the farmhouse where he found the big man dead on the flagstone floor and the letter unopened on the table. He tossed the letter onto the fire.

Erika took a few moments to clear her head. Then Pilgrim said, "If you're sure you're all right, we should get back on the road."

Kurt said they should split up, and they discussed who should travel in Staerling's car and who should ride on the pillion with Gutkind. Erika settled the argument. "Kurt, you have a KWIP pass, so you should stay in the car with Staerling. What about you, Gutkind? Do you have a pass?"

"I have a factory pass," said Gutkind. "And my boss, Blaue, is expecting me at the base."

"Right. You go in the car with Kurt and Staerling. If Zingler has raised the alarm, Necker will be searching for me. Pilgrim and I will take the motorbike. We'll bypass the bridge and meet again on the island."

#

While Staerling drove, Kurt questioned Gutkind. "How did you get posted to Germany?"

Gutkind laughed. "I had hoped for a South Pacific posting. One of those desert islands would have done nicely. But the brass had other ideas. My grandfather was German and I speak the lingo. I guess that's why they put me here."

"Are you really an accountant?"

"Afraid so. I was the nearest thing we had to a physicist in Germany, so I got lumbered with the project. Otto's my radioman."

Kurt took a moment to absorb this revelation. "How did you know that I was working for the British?"

"The OSS in London passed us your alias. We had a man on your tail as soon as you stepped off the boat in Wales. Then, once we knew your alias, all we had to do was sit tight and wait for Frederick von Schönholtz to show."

Kurt relaxed. That agreed with what Staerling had told him in the car on the way to Berlin from the camp. Gutkind could not know this unless he was part of the American operation, linked to the man in the library back in London who had discovered Kurt's secret alias and passed it to the OSS in London.

#

Lange found Necker sipping ersatz coffee at a coffee shop on the road north of Neusterlitz.

Necker greeted him with a scowl. "This is another of your disasters, Lange. I met your two motorcycle riders here. They came from the north, but found nothing. They must have missed them on the road somewhere."

Lange ground his teeth. The arrogance of the SS man was beyond belief! "What's more likely is that they were never on this road to begin with. Your information must have been faulty."

Necker touched the scar on his cheek. "There was nothing wrong with my information. This has all the hallmarks of one of your bungled operations. You will take the flak for this failure, and your office will bear the cost."

"Tell me, Necker, how long have you been on the trail of these desperadoes? You had this Monika woman in your custody in Haigerloch for several days and you let her go."

"Her name's Erika Cleasby. And she escaped."

Lange sneered. "You were interrogating a spy – a woman – and you let her escape! Now listen to me, you prick. You've been chasing her since she stole your car and burned it out. That was over two weeks ago."

Necker leaped to his feet, towering over Lange. "That is insubordination, Lange." His face was white with anger. "You cannot address a superior officer in those terms."

Try bringing me before a disciplinary board, thought Lange. Let's see who comes up smelling of apples when the strudel hits the fan. What he said was, "You've consistently refused to let me get involved, even though you don't have the resources to conduct any sort of efficient manhunt."

"The ORPO have been helping."

Lange snorted. "The ORPO! Right! And one officer from the city force was attacked and had his uniform removed at Leipzig railway station. Don't you think the Reich can do better than that? All you had to do was call me and these spies would have been safely and securely under lock and key in Prinz Albrecht Strasse by now."

"All right," said Necker. "I might have involved you sooner, I accept that, but you're just going to have to live with the fact that I chose not to. I'm sorry if you find that distasteful, but the only question now is how we should proceed."

Lange took a deep breath. "It's quite possible that the fugitives have been captured by my men at the Neubrandenburg roadblock. I need to go there."

Necker stood. "You can take me in your car. My driver and your motorcycles are combing the countryside."

"You sent my motorcycle riders on a wild goose chase? In that case you can wait here for them and tell them to report back to the roadblock."

Necker clicked his heels. "You have forgotten who you are talking to, I think."

"I have forgotten nothing," said Lange.

Chapter 49

With Erika on the pillion behind him, her arms around his waist, Pilgrim travelled east. After 10 kilometres he turned north again, keeping off the main roads. By the time they hit the coast the sun was sinking over the horizon to the west and the temperature had dropped three degrees.

They came to a sleepy fishing village. Erika was shivering, her teeth chattering. Pilgrim led her to a concrete shelter, built for lifeguards before the war. They huddled together under his greatcoat, staring across the sound, and Erika's trembling eased gradually. The island looked close enough to reach out and touch it. A finger of land jutting out from the island all but obscured the bridge shrouded in a sea mist 10 kilometres to the west.

When it was dark he left her to forage for a boat.

There was a selection of rowboats to choose from. He chose one that looked the most seaworthy, recently painted, chained to a rusty iron ring set into a wall. Smashing the padlock with a stone, he removed the chain and dragged the boat across the shingle to the water's edge. Then he returned to the shelter. Erika had fallen asleep, wrapped in the greatcoat.

"Ready to go?" he said, shaking her awake gently.

There was nobody about to stop them or raise the alarm, and the darkness was total. If there was a moon it was obscured by a heavy blanket of cloud.

Pilgrim wheeled the motorbike down to the boat, and between them they hoisted it on board. He threw in the helmet, gloves and goggles, they slid the boat the last few metres onto the water, and he helped her to climb in.

Erika kept the greatcoat on; Pilgrim wore the motorcycle gloves. Sitting side by side with an oar each, they headed out across the narrow sound toward the island, the weight of the motorcycle holding the stern of the boat low in the water, the prow tilted toward the sky.

The temperature was several degrees lower out on the water, the Baltic boasting its ever-present Arctic soul. The sky was totally black. Looking back toward the mainland, he could see flecks of light from the village catching the tips of the waves; behind them the island was nothing but a brooding grey mass against the darker sky. To the east, the water gave him nothing, and he had lost the horizon. No point of reference – nothing but a black abyss, impenetrable, endless.

Halfway across the sound, Erika pointed to a light moving over the water far to the east. "What's that?"

Pilgrim watched it for a while. It looked like a powerful searchlight sweeping the water. It could only have been on a boat. "It looks like a Kriegsmarine patrol boat," he said. It was too far away to concern them, but it gave Pilgrim an idea.

They continued rowing. Fifteen minutes out from the mainland shore, the motorcycle was lying in a growing puddle of water.

"It's leaking," he said. "Row harder."

After another 10 minutes water was lapping around their feet, and the motorcycle was half-submerged. The stern of the boat was seriously low in the water now, every passing small wavelet splashing in making matters worse.

"We need to bale," said Erika. A tin cup was tied to a length of twine lying on the boards.

"You bale. I'll keep rowing," said Pilgrim.

Pilgrim took both oars and put his back into it while Erika baled. Shifting her weight toward the stern did nothing to help, and Pilgrim quickly realised that they weren't going to make it.

They heard a roar, and a powerful motorboat rushed past from the west, its searchlight pointing straight ahead. Peripheral light from the searchlight gave Pilgrim a glimpse of the island shore. They were close – no more than 10 metres from a beach. But whatever chance the leaky boat had of floating, the wake from the motorboat sealed its fate. The stern of the boat slid under the surface.

\#

"Leave the talking to me," Staerling said. He wound down the window and handed their three identity cards and their passes to the soldier.

The bridge was bathed in a mist that softened the harsh lights of the roadblock giving the bridge an eerie, ghostly glow.

On the passenger side a second soldier shone a flashlight into their eyes. Gutkind sat up front. In the back seat, every muscle in Kurt's body went rigid.

"You are Staerling?" said the soldier, examining their papers.

Staerling replied, "Otto Staerling, recruitment manager for the Kaiser Wilhelm Institute for Physics. Take a look at the signature on my pass."

"Your reason for visiting Rügen Island?"

"We have urgent business at the military base."

"This pass is a factory pass for Auergesellschaft Oranienburg."

"Gutkind works with Herr Blaue at Oranienburg. Blaue is chief engineer on the project. He asked me to transport Herr Gutkind to the base, urgently."

"Which of your passengers is Frederick von Schönholtz?"

Before Staerling could reply the car was surrounded by armed soldiers cocking and pointing their rifles.

"Step out of the car," said the soldier.

\#

As the boat slid away from under them, Pilgrim grabbed his precious bag of grenades, holding it out of the water. His feet found the bottom. He reached out to steady Erika as she tumbled from the boat. They were in shallow water no more than waist-high. The prow and half the boat remained out of the water, frozen, pointing skyward. And then the boat shook itself free of the motorcycle, popped to the surface and floated upside down.

Together they waded to the island shore onto a sandy beach where they lay panting from their exertions.

Pilgrim poured water from his boots. "That patrol boat must be from the base. If we follow it we should find an entry point somewhere along the coast. But first we need to find some new transport."

They followed a path leading away from the shore and hiked inland for two kilometres until they came to an inn, with bicycles stacked outside. They wheeled two quietly away, and set off on the road north.

They followed the coastline, keeping their eyes on the patrol boat as it moved about at sea, sweeping the water with its searchlight.

After an hour they came to the village of Sassnitz, its wide harbour full of fishing vessels. The place was buzzing with military activity, and they could see roadblocks on all the approach roads.

Erika and Pilgrim took to the fields. They rode over a small hill and through several farms, lifting their bicycles over walls, wading through muddy patches. Once Pilgrim was satisfied that they had passed beyond the village roadblocks they rejoined the road and pressed onward. They came to the thick forest that grew along the top of the chalk cliffs.

"Is it much further?" said Erika. Her teeth were chattering again. They were both now feeling the effects of the cold seeping through their wet clothing.

"Not far now," he said. He hadn't the heart to tell her that he had no idea how much farther they would have to go.

Chapter 50

SS-Sturmbannführer Manfred Necker checked his watch. It was a little after 9 pm – just under five hours to detonation. He wasn't claustrophobic, but this underground base made him uneasy. He took comfort from the fact that Blaue, the project chief engineer, looked unconcerned, but he understood enough about physics to know that the test of an atomic bomb was no trivial matter.

A soldier entered and announced that the spy Fredrick von Schönholtz had been captured in a car with two other men at the roadblock on the bridge.

"The one calling himself Otto Staerling asked for you by name," said the soldier.

"Place them under guard and take them to me," said Necker.

The soldier hurried away, and Necker turned to Blaue, "I expect Herr Staerling will attempt to spin me a yarn. No doubt he will have some plausible explanation for why he helped these subversives evade lawful capture."

Blaue laughed. "If I had your knowledge of human nature, Necker, my friend, I wouldn't be wasting my time with engineering."

"Your work is of supreme importance to the Reich, Blaue," said Necker. "If this test is a success it will turn the outcome of the war."

"*When* the test is a success, you should say," said Blaue. "And it will change everything. The eagle will fly again."

Otto Staerling stumbled in, looking dishevelled, behind him came Frederick von Schönholtz and the accountant, Gutkind, sandwiched between two Waffen-SS men.

One of the soldiers handed Necker a set of car keys and a Luger, holding it by the barrel. "The prisoners were armed with this pistol, sir."

Blaue said, "This man works for me. His name is Gutkind and he is accountant for the project. I asked him to come to the base. I have urgent work for him here."

"Accounting work?" Necker raised a disbelieving eyebrow.

"Certainly," said Blaue. "Without Gutkind's oversight the costs of the project could run out of control."

"And why is he travelling with Herr Staerling?"

"Gutkind asked me to drive him," said Staerling.

"Very well," said Necker to Blaue. "Take him with you. But be warned if it turns out that he is an enemy of the Reich he will hang and you will hang with him."

Blaue and Gutkind hurried away together.

Necker took the gun from the soldier. "Secure this one in a cell. I'll deal with him later."

The guards marched Kurt from the room.

"Well Staerling," said Necker, examining the handgun. "I see you've brought me the spy. But it seems you have been complicit in aiding his escape, in transporting him to this base, and in several other crimes against the Fatherland."

"I assure you, Manfred, I have committed no crime. Far from it, I have been busy collecting intelligence which will prove that von Schönholtz is a British spy."

"Indeed?" said Necker.

Staerling took a deep breath. "You know that von Schönholtz is accompanied by two others, also enemy spies, a man and a woman?"

"I am aware of this, yes."

"Before Gutkind and I could start our journey, the three enemy spies produced that pistol. They seized my car and forced me to drive them here."

"Ah, I suspected as much," said Necker. "You were acting against your will."

"Yes, Herr Sturmbannführer. But, as I said, I used the opportunity to gather information about them and their plans, before finally managing to disarm von Schönholtz and make him my prisoner."

"Go on."

"First, you should know that Frederick von Schönholtz is an alias. He has revealed his real name as Kurt."

"Just Kurt. You don't have his family name?" The name stirred a faint memory in the back of Necker's mind.

"Just Kurt," said Staerling. "The woman has been operating under the name Marta Maynard. This is also a false name. Her real name is Erika."

"What can you tell me of the third member of the gang?"

"Apart from his name I know nothing about him, Herr Sturmbannführer, they called him Pilgrim."

"What sort of name is that?" said Necker. "And where are these two spies now?"

"They travelled separately on a motorcycle."

"What do they know of Base Alpha?"

Staerling replied, "They are aware that a new weapon is being tested. I'm not sure they know much more than that."

"You must cling to the hope that they do nothing to interfere with the test," said Necker. "If they succeed, you will shoulder the blame." Staerling began to protest, but Necker waved a hand to silence him. "You are the one who brought these spies among us. It was you who gave them the level of security clearance needed to work among us. And yours is the name that will forever be associated with allowing three spies into the very heart of the Reich's most secret project."

Staerling drew himself up to his full height. "Surely, delivering the prisoner has proved my good faith and loyalty to the Reich."

Necker ran a finger knuckle over his scar. "Producing one of the three spies has been helpful, but nothing you have told me has been of much value. I knew that we were dealing with three British agents, and I knew they were coming here to try to interfere with the test firing. Is there anything else you can tell me?"

"You knew that the woman, Marta Maynard was a spy?" said Staerling.

"Indeed. I interrogated her at Haigerloch where she was using the name Porsche Hoffbauer. I was aware even then, that her real name is Erika Cleasby. She broke out of Haigerloch Castle with the help of a man called Randau, whom we may presume is now calling himself von Schönholtz."

"Real name Kurt," said Staerling.

Again, that faint memory teased Necker. "I was aware that there was a third man in the group. It seems you have supplied his nickname. But why in the name of the Führer did you reveal the location of Base Alpha to these enemy spies?"

Staerling shook his head. "They knew where the base was. Perhaps von Schönholtz obtained this knowledge while working for Blaue at Oranienburg."

Necker decided to accept Staerling's word at face value. The man was too stupid to be anything other than an unwitting pawn in the larger game. He tossed Staerling his car keys and snapped his fingers. A soldier stepped forward. "Escort Herr Staerling from the base," said Necker.

#

Pilgrim and Erika stopped in the forest. The cliff here was not sheer. Covered in trees, it sloped down to the water's edge. A notice nailed to a post carried a skull and crossbones and the warning: "DANGER! NO ACCESS. CLIFF UNSAFE"

"What time is it?" he said.

Erika checked her watch. "Ten thirty. Why have you stopped here, Pilgrim? We need to find a way into the base. The test is in less than four hours."

"Just wait. You'll see," he replied. He peered out to sea and mouthed a silent prayer. It was 30 minutes since he'd last seen the motorboat and its searchlight. By dead reckoning this was as close as he could get to where he'd last seen it. He could be out by a kilometre – or two – but he was encouraged by the warning notice.

With a roar, the patrol boat shot from the tree-line below them and out to sea, its searchlight pointing straight ahead.

"This is the place," said Pilgrim.

The climb down the cliff took longer than it should have. It was no more than 20 metres from top to bottom, but they had no rope, footholds were difficult to come by in the dark, and their feet were wet and slippery. At the bottom they found a narrow stretch of stony shingle and a large cave obscured by the trees.

A concrete walkway led inside the deserted cave, where a line of powerful wall-mounted lights dispelled the darkness.

It was 11:05 pm, just under three hours before the planned test of the atomic bomb.

Chapter 51

Erika kept her back to the weeping walls of the cave. Pilgrim followed, carrying the bag with the grenades. The cold was paralysing.

They hurried to the rear of the cave and entered a tunnel leading deep into the island. After 10 minutes they came to a fork.

"Which way? Left or right?" said Erika.

Pilgrim shrugged. They went left and soon came upon a chasm 20 metres wide with a waterfall pouring from a hole in the rock above their heads and tumbling into a void 100 metres or more deep. There was no artificial light, and yet everything was clearly visible. She held out her hand, collected some spray and tasted it. The water was the sweetest she'd ever tasted and the clearest she had ever seen. There was no way around the chasm, and they had to turn back, returning to the fork in the tunnel.

They took the right fork, and soon the tunnel forked again, and again, and quickly became a maze of bewildering choices. There was nothing to show them where they should go. Every time they had to make a choice they selected whichever tunnel was lit or led uphill.

Facing another choice, left, right or straight ahead, they heard the sounds of a patrol coming rapidly from behind them. Erika pulled Pilgrim into the left tunnel where they hid and listened to the patrol passing by at the double.

Once the patrol was beyond earshot they followed the soldiers. Ten minutes after that, they picked up some faint sounds. Following these they came across what was clearly a billeting area, with about 20 soldiers cooking over an open stove, talking and laughing. Slipping past, they explored further into the labyrinth.

A new sound reached their ears, a regular, hollow, drumming sound that got louder and louder as they got closer. They turned a corner and found themselves beside a long ladder leading upward and downward. They peered down into a limestone cavern the size of 20 Berlin Dom cathedrals. The drumming, louder than ever now, was the combined cacophony of men and machines, like an industry in full operation. The cavern was roughly circular, 300 metres wide. It contained a convoy of five trucks as well as a gigantic stack of fuel in barrels and what looked like an ammunition dump.

"I don't see it. I don't see the bomb," whispered Pilgrim.

"There must be another, smaller chamber for the detonation," said Erika.

The floor of the cavern was alive with workers dressed in silver hazard suits, preparing for the test. Erika ran her eyes over the scene. She watched the men carefully and soon identified the entrance to the detonation chamber. She pointed it out to Pilgrim.

He directed her gaze upward, where he had identified a row of vertical ventilation shafts set in the roof of the cavern. "I will try to place a beacon at the top of one of those."

They embraced. Pilgrim handed her the bag containing the four remaining grenades and said, "You're clear about what you have to do? Place the radio activated grenade in the biggest electrical junction box you can find. I've set the time delay on the other three at 25 minutes. Pull the tabs and place them where they'll do the most damage."

"I know, Pilgrim. We've been over it a hundred times," she said.

Pilgrim climbed onto the long ladder "Take care of yourself, Erika," he said, and he started upward.

"You, too, Pilgrim," she whispered. "Good luck."

It was 50 minutes past midnight, an hour and 10 minutes before the test.

Erika watched her lover for a few moments before going back through the tunnel the way they'd come, searching for another way down. She found a tunnel branching left that sloped gently downward and followed that. It took her to a set of steps hewn into the rock. At the bottom of the steps, the tunnel went left and right, in a slow curve that Erika was sure followed the curve of the cavern. Many smaller tunnels branched off, left and right. Those on the left branched away from the cavern; those on the right branched inward toward the cavern, but they all had locked doors. She followed the curved tunnel until she came to another set of stone steps leading downward. There were 50 steps and they brought her to a deserted anteroom. Inside, she found a silver hazard suit and she put this on before stepping into the room next door.

This was the observation and telemetry room, containing a bewildering collection of remote measuring instruments set up in rows. There were six men in the room, all dressed as she was, in hazard suits. Some carried clipboards, others sat by their monitoring equipment, making last minute adjustments.

Projected onto one wall was a full-colour picture of the inside of the detonation chamber. As she watched she saw men moving about in the chamber – the projection was fed by a movie camera. Erika caught her breath at the sight. The chamber was the size of six ballrooms, with a height of 30 metres, and lit by rows of powerful lights. It contained several buildings the size of modest family homes, and between the buildings, arranged in regimented rows, stood dozens of mannequin dummies strapped to wooden stakes.

Suspended from a derrick in the centre of the chamber, and looking like a grotesque sculpture, was the bomb. Shaped like a gigantic pear with electrical cables protruding from the top, the device was tended by workers in hazard suits scurrying around like ants attending to their queen. On the wall directly opposite, a countdown clock showed 00:50:27, with seconds counting down, 50 minutes to detonation.

There were live pigs, too, moving about in a pen. Obviously the test was designed to show the effect of the blast on buildings and people. The effect on the pigs would approximate human flesh. Erika shuddered at the thought of what the bomb would do to those pigs – and to human flesh.

#

Wednesday, May 5 1:15 pm

SS-Sturmbannführer Necker put on his leather gloves and flexed his fingers. "You have two options, Kurt: You can answer my questions, or you can take a beating and then answer my questions."

Kurt struggled against the rope tying him to the office chair. The SS man had called him Kurt. But did he know his full name? He glanced at the burly soldier that Necker had brought with him. The man had removed his tunic. He was big enough to be a heavyweight boxer, and his nose was broken.

"First question," said Necker. "Who are you working for?"

"Go to hell."

The blow, when it came, was heavier than expected, a pile-driver from an iron fist across his jaw. Kurt tasted blood.

"Second question: Where did you and Miss Cleasby spend last night?"

He knows Erika's real name, thought Kurt. Does he also know mine? The sexual innuendo was obvious, as well.

"Don't know anyone called Creasy."

The second blow was a punch to Kurt's stomach. The soldier looked as though he was swatting a fly, but it made Kurt retch.

"Third question: What is Pilgrim's real name? What nationality is he?"

That's two questions, thought Kurt. "The only Pilgrim I know is from Chaucer."

Necker nodded to the soldier who delivered a second blow to Kurt's head. This one sent Kurt and the chair crashing to the floor. The soldier picked up the chair – with Kurt on board – in one hand and placed it back on its legs.

"Fourth question," said Necker. "Where are your two friends right now?"

Kurt spat blood. "You can be sure the whole base is awash with agents by now, working to destroy the bomb."

"You expect me to believe that? This base is tighter than a nun's drawers." Then realisation dawned in Necker's eyes. He picked up a telephone. "Patch me through to the Kapitan."

When the connection was made he said, "Check the cave for possible intrusion. Then conduct a thorough search of the tunnels. Report back to me if you find anything."

Necker disconnected without waiting for a response. Turning his attention back to his prisoner, he said, "Back to question one. I know you're working for the British. I just want to hear you admit it."

Kurt made no response and received another blow to his solar plexus.

"Go to hell," said Kurt, gasping.

"You sound German. Are you German? Why would a German side with the British against his own people?"

"The Nazis are not my own people," said Kurt. "I hate everything you've done and everything you are planning to do."

Necker massaged his gloved knuckles. "You admit your treason. What is your real name? I know von Schönholtz is a false name."

So, the SS man didn't have Kurt's full name. That was a relief.

"Klaus Randau."

"I asked for your real name. I know the name Randau is false."

"What was the second question?" said Kurt.

"You somehow evaded a Gestapo roadblock at Neubrandenburg. I want to know how."

Kurt shrugged a shoulder. "I saw no roadblock."

"Who told you about this base? Don't tell me that was Zingler. I know it wasn't him."

"Who's Zingler?" said Kurt.

The soldier slapped him across the head again.

Necker said, "Let's start again, shall we? What is your real name?"

#

Erika identified the main electrical conduit for the detonation chamber. As thick as the bole of a mature oak, it disappeared into the ceiling of the chamber. Turning on her heels she left the observation room, and set off to trace the conduit and place Pilgrim's vital radio-activated grenade.

It took her 10 minutes to locate the branch of the electrical conduit that ran through a narrow maintenance passageway into the detonation chamber. She followed it for 200 metres back to a junction box big enough to serve the whole base. Inside this junction box she placed Pilgrim's radio-activated grenade. Returning the way she had come, she went in search of the entrance to the main cavern.

The clatter of men approached ahead. Erika dodged into the nearest outward-branching tunnel and watched as four armed soldiers trotted past. She resumed her journey when the coast was clear, searching for an unlocked inward-branching tunnel that would lead her inside the main cavern.

It was obvious that the base was now on heightened alert, with teams of soldiers scouring the corridors and tunnels. Were they looking for intruders, or just being generally diligent? She wondered how Pilgrim was faring, and whether Kurt and the two American spies had made it onto the base. Perhaps they had all been captured and were being interrogated by Necker. The thought brought unpleasant recent memories bubbling up in her mind. She put them firmly aside and turned her attention back to her job.

She found one inward-facing tunnel that was not locked and followed it. It led her to an area of offices cut from the limestone. Peeping into the first one, she discovered Professor Heisenberg sitting at a desk with his eyes closed, wearing a massive pair of headphones. Erika guessed that the headphones were providing the great man with observational feedback of some kind.

She slipped past and crossed the main cavern. On the wall facing her, a gigantic countdown clock showed 00:35:06

Making sure no one noticed what she was doing, Erika planted Pilgrim's three delayed-action grenades. She pulled the tab and placed the first one under the rear axle of a truck. She waited until the countdown clock reached 00:30:00 before pulling the tab and placing the second one near a pile of ammunition boxes. The public address crackled and a voice announced: FIFTEEN MINUTES TO LOCKDOWN. A siren started up, soft, pulsing – and menacing.

Bending down, she placed the third grenade two minutes later between two barrels in a fuel cache. She straightened her back and had moved no more than two steps away from the barrels when a voice said, "Hands up, Marta!"

The voice came from behind her, but Erika knew who it was.

Chapter 52

SS-Hauptsturmführer Lange got out of his warm car. He needed to stretch his legs, as they were starting to cramp, but outside it was foggy and cold. The roadblock had been operating for hours, and in that time they had intercepted several local farmers moving small amounts of foodstuffs across the bridge in contravention of the rationing laws, and two teenagers acting suspiciously on bicycles. No enemy spies had come their way.

It struck Lange that SS-Sturmbannführer Necker may have sent him and his men on a wild goose chase for some nefarious reason of his own. Necker was the worst sort of slyboots. As a group, the SD were not to be trusted. They frequently operated under clandestine agendas designed purely for their own aggrandisement or to enhance their own personal wealth. Lange had direct experience of this sort of Machiavellian chicanery, but so far he had been unable to pin anything on Necker.

"Patch me through to Base Alpha," he said to his driver. "I want to speak with SS-Sturmbannführer Necker."

Five minutes later, the driver had made the connection. He handed the radio microphone to Lange through the car window.

"This is Necker."

"Lange at Neubrandenburg. This roadblock's been up for 18 hours and we've caught no one. Are you sure these enemy agents aren't figments of someone's overactive imagination?"

"We captured Schönholtz at the bridge three hours ago, Lange. I have him in custody here."

Lange had to take a moment to compose himself.

"Lange are you still there? The other two spies are still at large, the woman calling herself Marta Maynard and a man called Pilgrim. Call me back when you catch them."

"You didn't think to let me know that you had Schönholtz?" Lange was seething, but he spoke quietly.

"Was there some reason why you needed to know? The important thing is that we have him. With any luck you will catch the others there. Let me know when you do."

"Don't hang up, Necker!" said Lange. "Schönholtz is on our most wanted list. I insist that you hand him over to the Gestapo immediately."

"The name is an alias," said Necker. "How can you know who he is?"

"He is one of the most wanted men in Germany, a leading member of a notorious subversive organisation."

"Indeed? And what is his name?"

It pained Lange to play his trump card, but without it he might never get his hands on Müller alive. "Fredrick von Schönholtz is Kurt Müller of the Black Orchestra. You must hand him over. I will be there in 30 minutes."

"You will not gain entry. The base is in lockdown," said Necker. "No one is permitted to enter or leave."

"Must I remind you who I am?"

"I know who you are, Lange. As I said, you will not gain access."

#

Erika turned to face Franz Zingler. He held a gun, pointed at her belly. How long had he been watching her? Had he seen her plant the grenades?

Dressed in military fatigues, his sharp, frowning features gave him the look of a Kriegsmarine battleship under attack.

"Hello, Franz," she said. "I'm glad I ran into you."

Zingler jerked the gun at her. "Put your hands up and move to your right."

"It's good to see you, too, Franz."

"Walk!"

Erika moved forward. They were heading across the cavern, back the way she'd come.

"Where are we going?"

"We have unfinished business," he said.

"How did you know it was me in the hazard suit?" she asked over her shoulder.

"No talking."

They passed Professor Heisenberg in his office, still wearing his headphones.

"In here," said Zingler. They entered the office next to Heisenberg's. A wooden work-surface ran along one side littered with papers and equipped with a microphone. There was a loudspeaker high on the wall, and a table covered in technical drawings in the centre of the room. Some of these drawings were maps of the island and layouts of the base, but Erika could see that most were technical schematics of the bomb itself. At last! She fixed her eyes on one of the schematics, trying to read what she could.

"Take off the suit."

Erika removed the helmet and gloves and let the hazard suit fall to the ground around her.

"You're going to have to stop taking my clothes off every time we meet," she said with a coquettish smile. She stepped away from the suit.

"Now give me that bag."

She threw it to him. He caught it without the gun wavering a centimetre. Maintaining eye contact, he shook it upside down and grunted with disappointment when nothing fell out. He threw it to the floor.

There were a couple of chairs. Zingler indicated that Erika should sit.

"What are you doing here?" he said.

"You brought me here."

"What are you doing on the base? I know you are an enemy agent. What did you hope to achieve by coming here? Sabotage? Or were you planning to steal the schematics of the bomb?"

Erika said, "Look, Franz, I must apologize for what happened when we last met. I hope you weren't embarrassed by it."

"You have no idea," mumbled Zingler. "Now tell me who you're working for."

"You do realise that your bomb will open a portal in the space-time continuum," she said. "If it detonates successfully, this base and everyone in it will be sucked through a wormhole into another dimension. You need to stop the test."

"You're completely mad, woman, you do know that, don't you?" said Zingler. "There's nothing anyone can do to stop the test, Marta. The whole process is automatic now. No power on Earth can stop it."

"Then you will have all those needless deaths on your conscience," said Erika.

Zingler's eyes narrowed. He opened the door and waved the gun at her. "You're coming with me."

He led her along a narrow passageway, through two massive blast doors and down another length of tunnel into the detonation chamber.

The last three hardy souls in hazard suits attending to the bomb were packing up and leaving; all the others had gone. Fascinated and terrified by the proximity of the bomb on its derrick, Erika peered at it. It seemed to shimmer in the lights, and to call out to her, its voice a soft, pulsing siren.

The derrick was set directly over a gaping hole in the floor. Erika looked down and saw water below. "Why the hole?" she said.

"That's the Baltic," said Zingler. "A significant percentage of the blast energy will be absorbed by the water. Think of it as a safety valve. Without it the detonation could take the roof off the chamber."

The countdown hit 00:25:00, and the public address crackled into life again: ATTENTION ALL PERSONNEL. TEN MINUTES TO LOCKDOWN.

Erika was directly under the derrick, the bomb mere centimetres above her head. She had an irresistible urge to reach up and touch it.

#

Kurt had lost track of time. Still, he was convinced that the RAF should have put in an appearance by now.

The public address system announced: FIFTEEN MINUTES TO LOCKDOWN and a low, pulsing siren began.

He prayed that Erika and Pilgrim had evaded capture, that Pilgrim had managed to set up a beacon to guide the RAF bombs to their target, and that the RAF would start their bombing run soon.

The door crashed open and SS-Sturmbannführer Necker strode into the cell, wearing a broad smile. An armed guard stepped in behind him and stood by the door.

"I have it," he said. "I knew I'd seen your face somewhere before. You are Kurt Müller, the Abwehr deserter and subversive."

Kurt said nothing, setting his mind to the hopeless task of stilling his pounding heart.

"You don't deny it?" said Necker. "You are at the top of the list of the Reich's most wanted men, responsible for several killings. To those we must add two motorcycle riders killed on the road north of Haigerloch as well as two security guards in Oranienburg. I have a colleague in the State Police who will give a month's pay to get his hands on you, Müller."

Kurt said nothing.

"Tell me who this 'Pilgrim' is," said Necker. "Is that a nickname? What is his real name?"

When Kurt made no response, Necker continued, "Blaue's assistant, the accountant, Gutkind, perhaps?"

Again, Kurt made no reply.

"Nothing to say, Müller?" Necker turned on his heels at the cell door. "I'm turning you over to the Gestapo. You will be transferred under guard to Prinz-Albrecht Strasse in Berlin first thing tomorrow morning."

Chapter 53

Kurt heard the distant crunch of an explosion on the surface above his cell followed by a second and a third. The soldier guarding Kurt jumped to his feet, opened the cell door, and ran outside. Kurt got up to follow him only to have the door slammed in his face.

More explosions followed, getting closer. A fine white dust drifted down from the roof of the cell. The RAF had arrived at last! Kurt had no watch, but he reckoned it was close to 2 am. They were nearly an hour late, but he hoped not too late to destroy the base and put a stop to atomic bomb testing by the Third Reich.

A couple of moments passed in silence. Then the public address system announced ATTENTION ALL PERSONNEL. TEN MINUTES TO LOCKDOWN.

Without warning, a massive explosion blew a hole in the roof of the cell. Kurt was buried under a pile of chalk. Gasping for breath, he pulled himself from under the rubble, bruised and dazed but with no broken bones.

The cell door had been blown off by the bomb. Kurt leapt into the corridor and ran toward the centre of the base.

The bombing continued for close to five minutes. Kurt made good progress through the underground labyrinth to the main cavern. On his way he crossed a main arterial tunnel that curved around the outside of the cavern.

He crouched behind a packing case and looked around the vast cavern. The first thing that registered was that the RAF bombs had had no visible effect. The bombing raid had been a complete failure. There were men in silver hazard suits everywhere, moving about calmly. The test countdown was continuing as if nothing had happened.

Erika and Pilgrim were nowhere to be seen.

On the opposite wall a giant countdown clock read: 00:20:45 with seconds counting down. Kurt was trying to decide what action to take when the countdown clock reached 00:20:00, and the public address loudspeakers boomed: ATTENTION ATTENTION FIVE MINUTES TO LOCKDOWN. ALL PERSONNEL EVACUATE THE DETONATION CHAMBER.

The pulsing siren never wavered.

Kurt spotted the unmistakeable profile of Franz Zingler emerging from one of the tunnels on the opposite side of the compound. Kurt needed to make his way over there, but there was precious little cover in the centre of the compound. He hurried back, entered the curving arterial tunnel and ran.

#

Erika awoke to find the atomic bomb staring down at her from its derrick 50 feet from her head. She was tied between two wooden stakes, surrounded by mannequin dummies and close to where the pigs lay in their pen. The countdown clock read 00:19:58 and the public address system was booming: ATTENTION ATTENTION FIVE MINUTES TO LOCKDOWN. ALL PERSONNEL EVACUATE THE DETONATION CHAMBER.

She tried to work out what had happened. She remembered staring up at the bomb, Zingler standing behind her with a gun, but now she was secured to the stakes by her wrists and ankles, spread-eagled. Her head ached. And she was naked! She had been mesmerised by the bomb – she remembered that. Zingler must have knocked her out, stripped her and tied her up. The thought of Zingler's hands on her naked body sent shivers down her spine.

She struggled against her bonds, but they were too tight. She opened her mouth as wide as she could and shouted, "Let me out of here. Untie me."

No one responded.

Casting her eyes around she found the movie camera mounted high on the wall. He had positioned her directly in its gaze. A hot flush of embarrassment swept over her at the thought of all those men's eyes on her naked body.

"You can't leave me here. Let me out!" she shouted again.

A voice echoed through a loudspeaker, "I wanted you to know how it feels to be tied hand and foot and spread out like a starfish. I hope you enjoy it."

"Zingler? Is that you? Zingler, you bastard, untie me. Let me out of here."

There was a long silence. Then the voice returned, "Lockdown is approaching. Then the blast doors will be closed."

"You can't do this, Zingler! Stop the test and let me out."

Zingler's voice echoed around the chamber once more. "I thought you'd be pleased, Marta. You will be the very first member of the human race to be evaporated by an atomic bomb. Your sacrifice will make a memorable contribution to science."

"Cancel the test, you bastard! Get me out of here!" she yelled. "Can anybody else hear me? Stop the test!"

"That is impossible. I told you: no power on Earth can stop it. Everything that happens from now onward is fully automated. And, once lockdown has been initiated, no one can enter or leave the chamber."

"You can't do this. You can't leave me here."

There was no answer.

"ZINGLER!"

Erika struggled against her bonds, only making them tighter. She forced her mind to calm down. The RAF should have dropped their bombs by now. Where were they? She strained her ears for the sounds of bombs. All she could hear was the grunting and snuffling of the pigs and the waves lapping against the hole in the floor. It was about 15 minutes to detonation, which meant that the RAF was already 45 minutes late. She prayed that they might still come and blow the base to kingdom come. All she wanted was a chance – a chance to escape with her life.

Perhaps Pilgrim had failed to place the beacon above the ventilation shaft to guide the planes, and the bombers had come and gone home again without dropping their bombs. She prayed that the RAF had merely been delayed.

The public address system crackled.

ATTENTION! ATTENTION ALL PERSONNEL – THE CHAMBER IS NOW IN LOCKDOWN FIFTEEN MINUTES TO DETONATION.

Erika looked up at the bomb. It winked at her.

Part 7 - Countdown

Chapter 54

As the first RAF bomb exploded Pilgrim was close to the floor of the cavern. He had heard the five-minute lockdown warning during his descent. He barely registered the bombing raid, and knew immediately that it would be ineffective. He had rigged a spotlight at the top of the ventilation shaft as a beacon to guide the bombers to their target, but he realised now that the base was too deep underground to be damaged by bombs from above. The only way the test was going to be stopped was if he, Erika and Kurt sabotaged it from within.

He reached the floor of the cavern unseen, stepping from the ladder behind a row of troop transport and supply trucks. His next task was to locate the radio room. Everywhere he looked he saw men in silver hazard suits busily preparing for the test. Pilgrim would have to find a hazard suit too. Without one he would stand out like an overripe banana in a barrel of apples.

Keeping his head low, Pilgrim moved forward and hid behind a mountain of fuel barrels. He waited until a lone worker in a hazard suit passed by, carrying a clipboard. Pilgrim pounced on the worker, wrapping an arm around his neck and dragging him behind the fuel barrels. A quick twist of his head snapped his neck.

Pilgrim removed the worker's hazard suit and put it on. Picking up the clipboard, he set out across the cavern in search of the radio room. He passed by the entrance to the detonation chamber, and explored the next three tunnels. They all ended in locked doors. The fourth tunnel led to a flight of steps leading upward. He climbed these steps and came across a group of offices hewn out of the limestone. This looked more promising.

Inside the first of the offices he saw a middle-aged man with his eyes closed, wearing a pair of headphones, lost in the sounds coming through them. The man in the second office Pilgrim recognized from Erika's description. The slim build, curly hair and pointed nose were unmistakeable. Without question this was Franz Zingler, the perverted sexual sadist.

Pilgrim took a couple of deep breaths and passed on. Focus. He would deal with the pervert later.

The next office in line was the radio room. Pilgrim slipped inside. The radio operator was at his radio, dressed in a Wehrmacht uniform. Sitting with his back to the door and wearing his headphones, he never heard Pilgrim approach. A double-fisted blow with the heavy gloves of the hazard suit knocked the man unconscious. Pilgrim tied him up with a length of electrical flex, stuffed his Wehrmacht cap into his mouth and dragged him behind the radio stack.

The public address crackled to life. ATTENTION! ATTENTION ALL PERSONNEL – THE CHAMBER IS NOW IN LOCKDOWN FIFTEEN MINUTES TO DETONATION.

Pilgrim glanced at the countdown clock on the wall above the radio: 00:14:52. He selected the frequency of the radio receiver in his radio-activated grenade. Now all he had to do was transmit the short Morse code signal, and the grenade would detonate. Assuming Erika had played her part and placed it well, the explosion would interrupt the electricity supply and prevent the atomic bomb from going off.

Acutely aware that any one of a number of things could go wrong, he itched to transmit the code, but he couldn't do it yet. He had to wait until much nearer to the time of the test when it would be too late for the Nazis to repair the damage, and until his three time-delayed grenades started to go off. Hopefully Erika had planted them and found a safe place to hide.

#

Kurt heard a shout. "Halt!"

Looking backward he saw a group of four armed guards in Wehrmacht uniform emerging from one of the branching tunnels. All four were preparing to fire their weapons. Kurt accelerated. Loud gunfire echoed all around him, and bullets tore chips from the white walls close to his head.

His pursuers were no more than 30 metres behind him, but the curve of the corridor kept him out of their line of sight. He raced through the corridor for 300 metres, frantically looking for a means of escape. Rounding the curve of the corridor, he was suddenly confronted by another group of soldiers directly ahead. He was sandwiched between two groups intent on killing him. He had seconds left to live. Then to his right, a short flight of steps appeared, leading upward from the corridor. He bounded up these steps. At the top there was another tunnel to his left. He turned into this as a volley of bullets from below tore at the chalk walls all around him.

He ran along the tunnel. Forty metres ahead he could see a chalk wall – a dead end. He turned to face the soldiers as the first of them emerged from the top of the steps.

With little hope that he would be allowed to surrender, he lifted his arms. The soldiers raised their Schmeissers.

Chapter 55

"Don't shoot! Put down your weapons!" shouted a voice from behind Kurt.

He spun around to see Necker stepping from an office cut from the limestone wall, holding a palm toward the soldiers.

"This man is my prisoner," he shouted. "I need him alive."

The soldiers lowered their weapons to their hips, keeping them trained on Kurt.

"You four take him to my office. And take this one as well," said Necker, pulling Gutkind out of the office. "The rest of you resume your patrol. Well done, men."

All but four of the soldiers left.

Blaue stuck his head from the office. "I need Gutkind here with me, Necker. We have work to do."

Necker snorted. "Accounting work?"

"Yes. Important accounting work."

"I'm not satisfied with Gutkind's papers. Your work will have to wait." Necker stepped into the corridor, indicating to the four remaining soldiers to proceed.

#

Necker and the four guards led Kurt and Gutkind down the stairs and out into the cavern. Halfway across the compound the public address system announced: ATTENTION ATTENTION! TEN MINUTES TO DETONATION. The pulsing siren's note rose half a tone.

Pilgrim's first grenade went off with a crash. A troop transport exploded with a loud *crump* and burst into flames.

Necker swore, "*Scheisse!* Hurry along." But when a second truck caught fire and its petrol tank exploded, the four guards dived for cover.

Kurt and Gutkind took off. One of the soldiers fired after them – another shouted, "Leave them! Grab a bucket!"

As they reached the far side of the compound, Kurt looked back. Attempts were being made to quench the flames with buckets of water and a pressure hose was being prepared for use, but the fire had already spread to a third truck. A driver climbed aboard the next truck in line and tried to move it, but when it too burst into flames, he leapt for his life and the guards scattered, dropping the hose.

Kurt and Gutkind passed by an office where Professor Heisenberg sat listening to his headphones. They found Franz Zingler in the office next door, dressed in a hazard suit without a helmet, sitting at a table covered in blueprints and technical drawings.

When he saw Kurt his eyes widened and he frowned, his face resembling a ship's keel even more than usual, the deep furrows on his brow like the ship's wake. "Frederick, what are you doing here? You don't have sufficient clearance for this base."

"Herr Blaue sent for me to help Gutkind with the accounts," said Kurt.

"With the professor's approval?"

"Oh yes," said Gutkind, backing Kurt's story. "In fact it was the professor's suggestion."

"That's highly irregular," said Zingler. "He usually consults me before moving staff around. No matter. You will both need to put on hazard suits. The detonation is in less than ten minutes."

Kurt spotted Pilgrim's bag on the floor. It looked empty. He wondered how Zingler had got his hands on it, and if Erika and Pilgrim had planted all the grenades.

Zingler seemed unaware of the chaos in the compound where the fifth and last truck was now blazing. "You do know there is a fire raging out there?" said Kurt.

"The men will handle it," said Zingler. "I have more important matters to attend to."

Kurt heard a whimper, barely audible.

"What was that?" It had sounded like a child calling through a tube. "Help me."

Zingler crossed the room and flicked a switch off. "It was nothing."

Kurt pushed him aside and flipped the switch on again. On the wall above the switch was a speaker, and below it a microphone.

"Who is that? Who needs help?" said Kurt into the microphone.

"Kurt! Is that you? Help me, Kurt." It was Erika's voice.

"Where are you?" said Kurt.

"I'm locked in the detonation chamber with the bomb."

Gutkind turned on Zingler. "What have you done?"

Zingler sneered. "Marta is a spy. She's obviously interested in the atomic bomb. I gave her a ringside seat."

Kurt drove a fist into Zingler's stomach. Zingler folded and collapsed on the floor.

Pilgrim ran in from the radio room next door dressed in his hazard suit with the helmet under his arm. "Erika! I heard Erika's voice. She's in trouble. Where is she?"

He saw the grenade bag on the floor and picked it up.

"She's in the detonation chamber," said Kurt.

Pilgrim dropped the empty bag, and turned on Zingler, dragging him to his feet by the collar of his hazard suit. "This is your doing, you depraved monster!"

"What's happening? Get me out of here!" Erika shouted.

Pilgrim picked up Zingler's gun and stuck the barrel against his forehead. "Stop the test or I'll blow your brains out!"

Gasping for breath, Zingler said, "It's too late. The chamber is in lockdown. You cannot save her."

"Say a prayer, so." Pilgrim cocked the pistol.

Kurt said, "Leave him, Pilgrim. We need to talk to Professor Heisenberg."

Pilgrim dropped Zingler and tossed the pistol away. Then Kurt and Pilgrim ran next door to Heisenberg's office where the professor sat with his headphones on, his eyes closed.

Kurt ripped the headphones from his head and caught a snatch of Beethoven's pastoral symphony. "We need your help, Professor. We have to stop the test."

The professor took a moment to recover his composure. "That is impossible. We have passed lockdown."

Waving his arms about, Pilgrim shouted, "There's a girl trapped inside the detonation chamber. We have to stop the test and get her out."

The professor shook his head. "You must be mistaken. The chamber was cleared of all personnel five minutes before lockdown."

"Nevertheless, the fact remains that someone is trapped in there," said Kurt with infinite patience.

"How is that possible?" said the professor. "I don't see how–"

"We're wasting time!" yelled Pilgrim. "Stop the test, now!"

Kurt said, "Franz Zingler locked her in there."

"My god!" said the professor. "That is appalling."

"Yes," said Kurt. "What can we do to get her out?"

"I can't stop the test. All systems run on automatic from lockdown. But..."

"But what?" screamed Pilgrim.

Chapter 56

"I can unlock the blast doors. But be warned the doors will close again automatically two minutes before detonation." The professor glanced at the countdown clock. 00:08:03.

"Open the doors!" yelled Pilgrim.

The professor pressed a button on his desk. A warning red light began to flash, and the public address announced: WARNING WARNING BLAST DOORS OPENING WARNING WARNING.

From the corridor outside came Necker's voice. "Come out with your hands up, Müller."

Kurt grabbed the professor and marched him to the door. Fires had started all over the cavern. Necker was there, and he had ten armed soldiers with him now, their guns cocked and ready to fire.

"God in heaven! What's happening. The base is on fire!" said the professor.

"Tell Necker to back off," said Kurt.

"But you don't you understand, we are all in danger. If those fires reach the explosives dump..."

"Tell Necker to let us pass," hissed Kurt.

"Lower your weapons," shouted the professor. "Give these men safe passage. Someone is locked inside the detonation chamber."

"Give yourself up, Müller," said Necker.

Kurt shouted back, "Do as the professor says or I'll break his neck."

Necker hesitated, then he ordered the soldiers to lower their weapons.

Kurt dragged the professor with him back to Zingler's room, where he found Zingler sitting against a wall hugging his knees. Kurt spoke to Erika on the intercom. "Professor Heisenberg has opened the blast doors. Get out of there as soon as they open."

"I can't, Kurt," she shouted. "I'm tied up. I can't get free."

"I'm on my way," said Kurt.

Erika shouted back, "No! Send Pilgrim!"

"I'll go," said Pilgrim, struggling out of his hazard suit.

"You can't go," said Kurt. "You have to man the radio transmitter."

"You can do that, Kurt," Pilgrim replied. "I've already set the frequency on the radio. Wait as long as you can. The blackout may interfere with the blast doors."

"Blackout? What blackout?" said the professor.

Pilgrim ran from the room.

"Wait!" Kurt shouted. "You haven't given me the code."

But Pilgrim was gone.

The countdown clock showed 00:06:50. Pilgrim had less than five minutes before the blast doors would close again.

Kurt activated the intercom. "Pilgrim is on his way."

"Thank god!" she said. "Tell him to hurry."

Professor Heisenberg suggested he should make an announcement over the public address. Kurt loosened his grip and the professor flipped a switch on the microphone: "This is Professor Werner Heisenberg. A young woman has been trapped in the detonation chamber. I have opened the blast doors. We are sending a runner to get her out. Give him clear passage."

00:06:00.

"Where is he? I don't see him," Erika called out.

"He'll be there in a minute. Stay calm," Kurt replied.

"That's all very well for you to say, Kurt. You're not trussed up like a Christmas turkey under a ticking bomb."

"Let me know when you see him," said Kurt.

The countdown clock reached 00:05:00 and the public address announced: ATTENTION ATTENTION! LOCKDOWN IN PROGRESS. FIVE MINUTES TO DETONATION. BLAST DOORS WILL CLOSE IN THREE MINUTES. The siren's pulse rate grew faster and its tone rose another half tone.

In the cavern, the second grenade went off. This one caused a gigantic explosion in the ammunition store followed by the sound of bullets ricocheting at random throughout the cavern.

"What was that?" said Zingler. "Are we under attack?"

Kurt guessed what it was. "Come on, Pilgrim. What's keeping you?" he muttered.

"I'm in!" yelled Pilgrim through the intercom.

"Give me the code," Kurt shouted through the microphone.

There was no answer.

"Pilgrim, can you hear me? I need the code." Kurt glanced at the countdown clock 00:04:27. He shouted down the microphone again, "Pilgrim? You never gave me the code for the radio-activated grenade."

Pilgrim said, "These bindings are tight. I should have brought a sharper knife. Hold on, Kurt. There! That's two."

"For God sake hurry up, Pilgrim!" that was Erika's voice.

At 00:02:50 the third grenade blew up the fuel dump with a massive explosion that they all felt. The soldiers outside the door dropped their guns and ran for their lives. Necker ran with them.

"Get out of there now!" Kurt yelled. "You have less than 60 seconds left."

There was no response.

Kurt sat Professor Heisenberg beside Zingler. "Don't either of you move." Then he went into the radio room.

The clock reached 00:02:00

ATTENTION ATTENTION BLAST DOORS CLOSING. DETONATION IN TWO MINUTES.

Kurt racked his brain. The instructor in London had used the code PILGRIM. He waited until the clock showed 00:01:30 and keyed PILGRIM into the radio. Nothing happened. A lone bead of sweat trickled down his back. If the code had been set by the boffins in London it could be anything. On the other hand, if Pilgrim had chosen the code, it was just possible that he might be able to guess it. The countdown clock reached 00:01:05. With trembling fingers Kurt keyed in the code. ERIKA.

There was a flash like lightning and all over the base the lights went out. The pulsing siren stopped.

'Thank God!' thought Kurt.

Ten seconds later the lights came on again. The siren remained silent.

Standing behind Kurt, Gutkind said, "All you've done is wipe out the monitoring stations and the siren. The test is entirely automatic. Look at the countdown."

The countdown continued at 00:00:40.

Chapter 57

Erika watched as the blast doors swung closed. The countdown clock read 00:02:00.

"We could have made it," said Pilgrim.

Erika gave him a withering look. "You took too long to cut me loose."

"There was still time, even then."

"You expected me to run out there with not a stitch on?"

"Okay, but did you really have to put your lipstick on?"

She smiled weakly. "How can you make jokes at a time like this?"

"What better time?" said Pilgrim. He looked at the clock. "We have less than 90 seconds to live."

Erika took his hand and squeezed it. "Have faith in your radio-activated grenade, Pilgrim. I'm sure that will stop the detonation."

"If you placed it in the right place."

"Don't worry about that," she said. "Worry that Kurt keys in the code correctly and that your radio-activated grenade works."

At 00:00:50 the lights went out and the siren stopped. Pilgrim gave a small cheer, but 10 seconds later the lights came back on, and the clock continued the countdown.

"What happened?" said Pilgrim.

Erika shook her head. "The base must have a backup electrical system."

"Is there anything else we can do?" he said.

A voice began the final countdown "30, 29..."

"Nothing," said Erika.

She swallowed. She was 32 and had barely started her life. It seemed unfair that it should end so soon. She had so many plans. She had wanted to return to Sweden and maybe travel to Canada to trace all her distant relatives. She had hoped to have children one day, when the war was over.

An ominous rumble reached their ears, the ground shook and a fine powder of chalk dust fell from the ceiling.

"What was that?" said Pilgrim.

"Come on, Pilgrim," said Erika. "If this bomb is going to kill us, I want to see it. I want to watch it go off."

"22, 21, 20..."

"Are you mad?"

"No, I'm a scientist." she released his hand. "You stay here if you like. I'm going inside the chamber to stare the thing down." She grinned. "Maybe I can scare it into submission."

Erika re-entered the chamber as the countdown reached 13 and another, much louder rumble shook the chamber. The derrick shivered and the bomb swung lazily from side to side.

Erika stood facing the bomb, her chin held high. At 00:00:07 Pilgrim sidled up beside her.

"I love you, Erika."

"Me too, Pilgrim.

Pilgrim closed his eyes and put his fingers in his ears.

"3, 2, 1..."

The clock stopped at 00:00:00. Pilgrim opened his eyes and took his fingers from his ears.

Erika said, "Nothing happened."

There was a huge explosion and the roof of the chamber fell down around them. Pilgrim grabbed Erika's hand and jumped into the hole. As they hit the water Erika was aware of pieces of metal splintering from the derrick, the bomb toppling toward them.

#

Kurt watched in horror as the roof of the detonation chamber collapsed with a roar. The atomic bomb was destroyed, but it had taken Erika and Pilgrim with it.

Base Alpha was in chaos. Bullets were firing at random from the ammunition dump, five trucks were ablaze and the fuel dump was a conflagration that had spread to the packing cases of supplies. Thick black smoke filled the roof and rolled down the walls, threatening to engulf the cavern. Bodies lay strewn on the floor of the cavern. Everywhere, soldiers had dropped their weapons and, together with men in hazard suits, were running for their lives toward the exit.

Kurt ran back to Zingler's office where Gutkind was stuffing Zingler's schematics into Pilgrim's bag.

"We've got to get out!" Kurt shouted.

"I need a minute," Gutkind continued stuffing the bag with drawings. Then, "Okay, I have what I need. Let's go."

Professor Heisenberg was still sitting on the floor where Kurt had left him.

Kurt hauled him to his feet and said, "The route to the main exit looks impassable. Is there any other way out?"

The professor said, "There's an emergency exit. Follow me."

He led the way to a small tunnel that ended with a steep flight of steps, and all three scrambled to safety.

They emerged into the fresh air and starlight, their eyes streaming from the effects of the acrid smoke. Kurt's eyes cleared to reveal Franz Zingler standing under an oak tree, his face blackened by smoke.

Heisenberg was muttering to himself, "I thought we had all of the systems covered by the emergency power supply, but we must have missed something, some failsafe..."

At that point the roof of the base collapsed inward with a deafening roar, sending a shower of sparks and a cloud of black smoke high into the moonlit sky.

Chapter 58

As soon as they hit the icy water Erika's hand slipped from Pilgrim's. Forcing her eyes open, she looked for him, but visibility was zero. He found her, pulled her to him. She reached for his belt and held on. Crashing down behind them, the massive bomb creating a pressure wave that propelled them forward.

After about a minute they came to the surface in a small air pocket. It was dark and cold enough to freeze her eyeballs. Erika could barely see him beside her.

"Are you all right?" he said.

Erika's teeth were chattering too much to speak. She squeezed his shoulder in affirmation. They both took deep breaths and submerged again. They swam. After a couple of minutes Erika signalled that she could go no farther. They surfaced and found a larger air pocket.

"The water's warmer, here," he said, shivering.

Erika couldn't feel any difference.

They dived again. Keeping her eyes closed, she held onto Pilgrim's belt. By the time he pulled her to the surface again her lungs were bursting.

She heard a rushing noise that she couldn't identify and opened her eyes. They had surfaced in a brightly lit cave of sparkling crystal, a waterfall cascading down into a pool of clear blue water. The water was warmer, as Pilgrim had said. She tasted it. It was fresh and sweet.

Erika took a last look at the crystals and they dived again. The river wrapped its warm waters around them guided them down a sink hole, and the current swept them out into the Baltic.

They scrambled ashore and sat filling their lungs and shivering on the sand 100 metres from the cave where they had first entered the base.

"We can't stay here. The patrol boat will find us," she said.

Using the same gentle tree-covered incline that took them down, they climbed the cliff. The going was tough with wet footwear, but they made it. At the top they found the two bicycles among the trees where they had left them.

"I'm going to light a fire," said Pilgrim. "We need to get warm."

"We can't afford to draw attention to ourselves, Pilgrim," she replied.

Pilgrim pointed to the sky where a plume of black smoke rose from the remains of Base Alpha. "I don't think one more small fire will be noticed, do you?"

Erika gathered dry wood, and within minutes their wet clothes were steaming in front of a crackling fire.

"As soon as daylight comes we'll cycle back to Sassnitz," said Pilgrim, turning their socks on a branch over the fire. "If we can pay a trawler skipper we could get to Sweden..." His voice was hopeless.

"Where did you learn to start fires without matches?" said Erika.

"Didn't you know I was a boy scout?" Pilgrim replied.

They dozed for a couple of hours. It was a fine night with no moon, the sky peppered with a million blazing stars. Erika let her mind drift. Watching Pilgrim as he slept, she tried to imagine what life would be like after the war. He was a good man. She would marry him, and they would set up house together in England somewhere. She could find work as a teacher, he as an electrician. They might raise a family.

Chapter 59

Staerling's car drew up near the entrance to the base, and he prised his portly frame from it like a cork from a bottle.

"I hope someone grabbed the schematics," he said.

Gutkind held up the bag. "I have them."

Kurt said, "London has first call on those."

Staerling produced a handgun and pointed it at Kurt. Kurt wasn't sure what to expect next. The expression on Staerling's face was unreadable.

"I don't think so," said Gutkind. "Washington will be mighty pleased to get their hands on them. But don't worry, I'm sure they will share the knowledge with our allies."

Stepping toward the car, Gutkind said, "It's been fun knowing you all, but Rocky and I have a boat to catch."

A shot rang out, and Gutkind hit the ground like an axed tree.

Kurt was stunned. His first thought was that Necker or some Nazi sniper must have shot Gutkind, but then he saw a telltale trace of smoke drifting from the muzzle of Staerling's gun.

Kurt checked Gutkind for a pulse. There was none. "What's going on, Staerling?" he said. "Why did you shoot your own man?"

"It's a long story," said the portly American. "I have to go, I have a boat waiting."

Kurt followed Staerling around the car.

"Stay back," said Staerling. Keeping his gun trained on Kurt, he opened the car door and climbed in. Before he could pull his arm inside, Kurt slammed the car door, catching Staerling's hand. The gun fell to the ground. The American gave a shout of pain. Kurt picked up the gun. Then he reached into the car and retrieved the bag of schematics.

"You're going nowhere," said Kurt.

Staerling said, "I have a boat waiting at Sassnitz. Come with me. We can get out together."

"I'm not leaving without Erika and Pilgrim," said Kurt.

"They're dead," said Staerling. "I know they were close friends of yours and I'm sorry, but they're gone. You need to forget about them, Kurt, and get out of Germany while you still can."

Kurt thought about it. Staerling was probably right. A glance at the huge hole in the ground confirmed it. Base Alpha was still burning with occasional minor explosions. He got into the back seat, keeping the gun trained on Staerling.

While Staerling drove Kurt thought about what had happened. The cold-blooded killing of Gutkind made no sense. He needed to hear an explanation.

Without prompting, Staerling said, "If I hadn't taken him out he would have killed me and given the schematics to the Soviets."

"Gutkind was working for Moscow?"

"He was a double agent. I've known about him for a couple of months. I couldn't do anything until today, not until I had the schematics."

Kurt didn't believe it. What Gutkind had said about picking up his secret alias in London from the left luggage office at Euston station rang true. If anyone was a double agent, then Staerling was.

"You were only ever interested in the schematics," said Kurt.

Staerling shrugged. "Sure. Those plans will be of great interest to the scientists back home. They could shorten the war by several years."

"But why did you need my help? Couldn't Gutkind have taken those at any time?"

Staerling replied, "Gutkind's involvement was limited to the uranium enrichment plant at the factory, and he had some responsibility for the project accounts. But Blaue only ever told him what he needed to know to do his job."

"So the mighty United States of America was depending on the three of us?" said Kurt, open-mouthed.

"We had our own plans, but when you Brits showed we just stood back and watched. And you did a pretty good job, if you don't mind my saying."

#

They abandoned the car at Sassnitz harbour, and Staerling led Kurt to an old wooden trawler tied up at the quay.

"Anybody home?" Staerling called out.

The skipper of the boat emerged from the wheelhouse. "I thought you'd never get here. Climb aboard."

He started the engine. Kurt and Staerling climbed onto the trawler. The skipper opened the throttle, pointing the old trawler at the mouth of the harbour.

Inside the harbour the sea was flat calm, starlight reflecting off the water. The boat reeked of fish, but the fresh breeze was strong enough to dispel the worst of it. Still, Kurt was sick to his stomach, not from the smell, but at the prospect of leaving Germany without Erika and Pilgrim.

Outside the harbour the water was choppier. Staerling took on a strange colour and was soon leaning over the side. They steamed a kilometre to the east before the skipper turned the brow of the ship to the north and into a headwind. After that Staerling began to deposit the contents of his stomach into the Baltic.

Running parallel to the chalk cliffs, Kurt could discern little progress.

"How far is it to Sweden?" he asked the skipper.

"Sassnitz to Trelleborg is 120 kilometres. I can do 12 knots at a pinch, so that's 6 hours 40 minutes at sea. Your friend asked me to take you to Malmö. That's 30 kilometres further."

Kurt did a quick calculation. Another hour and a half to get to Malmö.

Kurt kept his eyes on the chalk cliffs. There was no moon, but the stars lit the scene. It was difficult to discern any movement over the water, but he could tell that they were making progress as the cliff scenes changed.

Twenty minutes out a column of black smoke tinged red showed Kurt where Base Alpha had been. Then he spotted a small fire at the top of the cliff at a point where the trees swept down to the edge of the water. Grabbing a pair of binoculars from the wheelhouse, he trained them on the trees and saw two figures huddled over the fire. Kurt's heart skipped a couple of beats.

"It's them! Captain, take us over there to the cliff." He pointed. "Two of my friends are there. We need to pick them up."

"That'll cost extra," said the skipper.

"We can pay," Kurt replied.

Staerling grabbed the binoculars from Kurt. "It's them all right, but we don't have time. Keep going, Captain."

Kurt squared off in front of the American. "We have plenty of time, Staerling. What's your hurry? I'm not leaving them behind."

The skipper turned the wheel hard to port. The boat rocked in the water. Staerling lost his balance and landed on his backside on the deck. "All right," he said. "Pick up your friends if you must, but I'm warning you, you will regret the delay."

#

Pilgrim spotted the trawler and pointed it out to Erika. Erika showed no interest. But when the boat turned and began to steam toward them, Erika shouted "It's Kurt! It must be. Come on."

They pulled on their clothes – reeking with damp and wood-smoke. Pilgrim kicked sand on the fire, and they climbed down the sloping cliff face, reaching the water's edge just as the trawler was drawing in.

Kurt helped them to climb on board.

Chapter 60

They resumed their journey.

"Drop us at Trelleborg," said Kurt to the skipper.

"Your friend paid for Malmö."

"That's all right," said Kurt. "You diverted to pick up my friends. That should make us even."

The skipper pulled a bottle of vodka from behind the wheel and passed it around. "Warm yourselves a little."

Three hours out from Sassnitz, when Rügen Island had disappeared from view, Pilgrim spotted a light moving over the water in the mist behind them. As it got closer he could see that it was a boat moving toward them at speed. Ahead the Swedish coast was nothing more than a flat strip on a mist-shrouded horizon.

Erika liberated the binoculars from the wheelhouse. "It's the patrol boat," she said. "And it's coming up fast."

The skipper opened the throttle as wide as it would go. With a cough and a plume of black smoke from the exhaust, the trawler responded, shuddering like an old horse under the whip.

The skipper checked his instruments. "We're close to Swedish waters," he said. "It'll be touch and go, but we should make it."

Erika watched as the patrol boat grew larger and larger in the binoculars. "They're gaining on us."

Two minutes later, Kurt could see the patrol boat clearly. Mounted high on the superstructure was a large machine gun, a sailor perched behind it.

Erika shouted, "I can see Necker."

Closer and closer came the patrol boat until Kurt could the SS man, wearing his peaked cap, standing like a figurehead in the prow, his duelling scar clearly visible.

The patrol boat barked at them through a loudspeaker: "Cut your engine!"

The skipper ignored the order.

"In the name of the Reich, heave to and prepare to be boarded."

A tense minute went by, the trawler coughing more black smoke across the waves. Then Kurt thought the patrol boat seemed to slide backwards.

"It's slowing down," said Staerling.

Erika said, "They're stopping. They're turning back."

Pilgrim gave a whoop of delight.

The skipper hammered a fist on the helm in triumph. "We've made it. We are now in Swedish waters. They can't follow us here, not without creating an international incident."

For the first time since leaving Ireland, Kurt began to relax. They were on the homeward journey, safe at last! "Won't you be in trouble when you go back?" he said to the skipper.

The skipper shrugged. "I can fish Swedish waters. They can't touch me here."

The machine gun flashed. A line of tracer bullets hit the water and ran across the stern of the trawler.

As the rattle of the gun reached them, Kurt shouted, "Get down!" and threw himself onto the deck. Staerling, Erika and Pilgrim did the same.

Peering over a pile of nets in the bow, Kurt saw the patrol boat complete its turn and head back toward the island. He got to his feet.

"Skipper?" he called out.

"I'm all right," said the skipper.

Kurt turned back to check the others.

Pilgrim was on his knees by the wheelhouse, clutching his side. "Erika? I've been shot."

A dark stain was spreading from the side of Pilgrim's shirt. He looked at his hands. They were covered in blood.

With infinite care, Erika helped Pilgrim to lie down on the deck.

The coast of Sweden was clearly visible now, looming out of the mist ahead.

Weeping quietly, Erika sat on her heels with Pilgrim's head in her lap as Pilgrim slipped from consciousness, his face turning a deathly grey.

"How is he?" said Kurt.

She shook her head, big teardrops coursing down her face.

Kurt sat beside her. He gripped Erika's arm and felt her body tremor.

Pilgrim opened his eyes briefly. The pupils looked glazed, as if he had the cataracts of an old man.

"Hold on, Pilgrim," said Erika. "We're nearly there."

Thirty minutes after that, with the port of Trelleborg within their sights, Pilgrim gave a last sigh and succumbed to his wounds. His head fell to one side. His eyes remained open in a fixed stare.

The skipper put the trawler engine into neutral.

"We'll have to let him go," he said. "We can't make landfall in Sweden with a body. I'd be tied up in paperwork and red tape for months."

Erika gave Pilgrim a last kiss and they lowered him gently into the water. Erika said a prayer as the body slid beneath the waves.

Kurt wiped a tear from his eyes. "He was a good friend. I'll miss him."

He had known Pilgrim for no more than five weeks, and yet it felt like half a lifetime. Pilgrim had been a good and loyal friend from the day they met until the day he died. He put his arms around Erika and held her tight.

"We had plans to marry. He would have made a great father," she said.

Erika discarded her blood-stained tunic and washed Pilgrim's blood from her hands. The skipper provided a bucket on a rope and Kurt used it to scoop up seawater and wash the blood from the deck. Before they entered the harbour Kurt threw the handgun and tunic into the sea.

By the time they landed at Trelleborg all traces of Pilgrim were gone.

Chapter 61

As they disembarked from the boat Staerling said, "This is where I must leave you. Hand me the schematics and I'll be on my way."

Kurt refused.

"We had a deal," Staerling said. "I rescued you from the labour camp and found you a position at the Institute. You agreed to let me have the schematics."

"Not as long as we have just a single copy. After I've given them to London, I will ask them to send copies to Washington. That's the best I can do."

Staerling's colour deepened. "You would never have completed your mission without my help. Give me that bag. I'll see that London gets a copy of everything. You have my word."

"I think it's time you told us the truth," said Kurt. "Gutkind was never a Soviet spy, was he? Why did you kill him?"

"Gutkind was stupid. I couldn't work with him. He couldn't see beyond the end of his nose."

Erika glanced at Kurt. "I think we're dealing with a little old-fashioned enterprise, here," she said. "I'd be willing to bet that Otto intends to hold an international auction and sell the schematics to the highest bidder. They must be worth a small fortune on the open market."

"A large fortune," said Staerling, a glint in his eyes. "Now hand them over."

"I don't think so," said Kurt.

"Give them to me," said Staerling, his face distorted in desperation. "I'm willing to give you both a share. We can all be rich!"

"Is that what you offered Gutkind?" said Kurt.

"He knew the value of those drawings, but he lacked the imagination to cash in on them. God knows I gave him enough opportunities to join me."

"I expect he was a man of principle," said Kurt.

Staerling snorted. "You could say that. He wore his principles like a straightjacket. And that's what killed him."

Staerling's eyes narrowed. He grabbed Erika's arm and pulled her to him. Kurt saw the flash of a knife. "Hand me the bag or I'll cut her throat."

Part 8 - Homecoming

Chapter 62

Erika reached out, took the bag from Kurt and handed it to Staerling. Staerling released Erika, tucked the bag under his arm, and began to walk away toward where the crowd was densest. Kurt moved to follow him.

Erika put a hand on his arm. "Leave it, Kurt. Let him go."

Staerling disappeared into the crowd.

"We can't let him get away with it," said Kurt. "You know what could happen if those schematics get into the wrong hands."

"Don't worry about it," she said. "Remember the discussion we had about giving the schematics to the British? You said that we would be risking the spread of atomic weapons around the globe."

"You didn't agree with me."

"I did agree with you, Kurt. While Pilgrim and I were on the trawler I removed all the schematics of the bomb and dumped them into the sea. That bag contains nothing but maps of the island and the base."

Kurt grinned. "Staerling's going to get a nasty surprise when he tries to sell those."

"I expect he'll check them before that," she said. "But if he ever shows his face again, the OSS will be waiting for him. They'll make him pay for the murder of Gutkind."

#

They were met at the quay by two Swedish policemen. Erika spoke to them in their own language. They were escorted to a police station. As neither of them had identity papers, it took 30 minutes of hard talking for Erika to convince them to let her use the telephone.

Within another hour they were in a car with an attaché from the British Consulate heading for Malmö airport where British Intelligence had a plane standing by.

#

SS-Hauptsturmführer Bismarck Lange sat behind the desk in his drab third floor office in Prinz-Albrecht Strasse 8. He was dressed in full uniform, and was sweating into his collar. Apart from his telephone and one thick file, his desk was clear. The noticeboard on the wall was also clear.

Lange was expecting a visitor. His career in the Gestapo was teetering on a knife edge. The notorious traitor and Abwehr deserter, Kurt Müller, had returned to Germany as a British agent. This man, whom Lange had been chasing for almost a year, had completed an audacious espionage mission for the British, resulting in the catastrophic destruction of a secret military facility. And he had slipped clean through Lange's fingers.

For the hundredth time he searched his mind for some mitigating factor that he could offer to counter-balance the disaster. He could find none. The whole sorry affair was the fault of the SD man Manfred Necker, of course, but he could hardly put that forward as an excuse. Necker should have asked for help from the Gestapo much earlier, but Necker had acted in his own interests, as he always did. And now that the reckoning was at hand, Necker was nowhere to be seen.

Lange considered resignation. Better to find a plausible reason to leave than have his superior officer remove him from his post with all the ignominy that would entail.

With a sigh he opened the file to gaze once more on the face of his nemesis, Kurt Müller, Superspy.

The door burst open and Lange's visitor stormed in. The SS-Standartenführer looked greyer than usual about the temples. He was wearing a suit, and an indescribable expression on his face.

"You're still here, I see," he said.

Lange leapt to his feet and stood to attention.

"Have you any conception of the effect your incompetence has had in high places? Everyone above you in the chain of command – and I mean everyone – is suffering the consequences. The Führer is beside himself with fury."

Lange saluted. "Heil Hitler!"

"Nothing as catastrophic as this has happened since the foundation of the Third Reich. The path of this one man through the Fatherland from south to north can be seen by the death and destruction he has caused. In Haigerloch there was a prison break and the death of two Wehrmacht motorcycle riders. A staff car was burnt out near the Swiss border. Two killings followed at Oranienburg, and, at Rügen Island he brought about the complete destruction of the most secret of military bases."

Lange opened his mouth to respond, but thought better of it when he saw the look on the SS-Standartenführer's face.

"SS-Sturmbannführer Necker has provided a full report of the whole sorry mess. It seems you knew the identity of the ringleader and kept the information to yourself." He shook his head solemnly. "I have to tell you, Lange, there are those who believe you must have been acting in concert with this subversive. How else could this man have wreaked such a trail of destruction without being apprehended and brought to book? I have done everything I can to protect you, but..."

"Thank you, sir."

"Don't thank me, Lange. Your career in the security service is over. You will be stripped of your rank and your membership of the SS revoked, effective immediately."

#

Ten minutes later, the SS- Standartenführer was in Necker's office on the fourth floor, towering over Necker.

"Have you any idea how disappointed I am in you, Necker? When you were promoted to your present rank, every senior officer in the organisation from the Reichsführer down was confident that you would fulfil your role with distinction."

Necker tried to stem the flow. "But Herr Standartenführer, Lange knew that the ringleader was a member of the Black Orchestra. He kept that vital piece of information from me."

"I have read your report. Don't think that your attempts to blame this catastrophe on others have gone unnoticed. As the senior officer, you must shoulder the blame. Lange has told us how you kept him in the dark until the situation was beyond recovery."

Necker plucked an envelope from his desk and offered it up. "My letter of resignation."

The SS-Standartenführer ignored the letter. "You have your service weapon?"

Necker blanched. "I have."

"Your failure has inflicted a grievous wound on the entire *Schutzstaffel.* And a serious wound must be cauterized. Do I make myself clear?"

Necker nodded. The SS-Standartenführer spun on his heel and left.

#

A Swedish Air Force Junkers W34 was waiting for Kurt and Erika on the runway. They climbed in and sat on either side of the aisle in the centre of the plane. They were the only passengers. The engine started. Erika and Kurt strapped themselves in and the plane took off.

It was twilight, and they rose quickly above the clouds, catching sight of the sun retreating in the western sky.

"We made it," said Erika. "I just wish he was still with us."

"I miss him too," said Kurt.

"It was fate," she said. "We were never destined to be together, Pilgrim and me. I should have known."

Kurt could see the grief etched in her face. "He will be remembered. We could never have completed the mission without him. Pilgrim was a good friend and a brave man."

Erika closed her eyes. Kurt turned his face to the window. Through a break in the cloud he could see the lights of occupied Norway far below. He watched as they cleared the land mass and set off across the North Sea. He let out a deep breath. Now they were safe; nothing could stop them reaching the safety of London.

Fifteen minutes out across the sea, the plane went into a sudden steep dive. Erika's eyes snapped open and she sat up. "What's happening, Kurt?"

Gripping the seat in front of him, Kurt peered out the window again and caught sight of a Messerschmitt fighter racing toward them from behind and to the side.

"We're under attack by the Luftwaffe!" he shouted.

Their plane levelled off close to the ground. Now the attack aircraft was above them. They had little chance to evade it, and, if the fighter opened fire on them, they would be unlikely to survive. The Swedish markings on their own plane should have kept them safe from attack. This was personal. Someone knew they were on board and wanted to stop them from getting back to London.

"We're going to die!" whispered Erika.

Chapter 63

Kurt and Erika heard a short burst of machine gun fire. The pilot immediately put the plane into a steep climb, pinning them into their seats. Banking left at the top of the climb, they entered a thick blanket of cloud and levelled off. The machine gun was silent.

Kurt watched through the window as they emerged from the cloud and the enemy aircraft came at them again. They heard another rattle of a machine gun. And then there were three fighters in the air. Two of them were RAF Spitfires.

The Messerschmitt turned and ran, chased by one of the Spitfires. The second Spitfire drew alongside and waggled his wings at them.

Kurt gave a cheer. "Hurray for the RAF. They've come to save us."

"A little late, as usual," said Erika.

#

The landing was rough, and when they climbed out of the plane it was clear why: the tail was riddled with bullet holes, only half of the rudder still attached. Kurt shook hands with the pilot and thanked him for getting them onto firm ground.

A waiting car took them directly from the landing strip to Kensington Palace Gardens in London. Once inside 'The Cage' they were separated. Kurt was placed in an interrogation room on his own.

Colonel Scott came in and took the seat across the table from Kurt. He opened a notebook and unscrewed the cover from his pen. "Welcome back, Kurt. And congratulations on a mission successfully completed." The smile on his face would have lit up the room if they'd had a blackout.

"Thank you, Colonel."

"Tell me you have the schematics for the atomic bomb hidden somewhere."

"I'm sorry, Colonel. I don't have them. They were destroyed when the base collapsed."

The colonel's smile vanished at this news, his face a picture of disappointment, but he gathered himself and continued with the debriefing.

Kurt described the first few days of his journey. He said nothing about his failed parachute.

Colonel Scott interrupted him at the first mention of the Auergesellschaft factory at Oranienburg and the uranium enrichment operation there. "You had an opportunity to destroy that enrichment operation at Oranienburg. Please explain why you eschewed that opportunity. Pilgrim was carrying sufficient explosives and all the materials necessary to complete that task."

"I didn't know the significance of that factory at the time," said Kurt. "In fact, I was very poorly briefed from the outset. Why was I told nothing of Erika's mission, nothing about the development of a fusion reactor by the Reich, and nothing at all about the atomic bomb?"

Scott made a note in his notebook before fixing Kurt with his beady eyes through the circular lenses of his glasses. "All of that was mere theory and speculation before you left here, and before Erika was sent from Leipzig."

"Even so, you might have given me some warning."

"We were unsure of you, Kurt. You will remember that I was in two minds about trusting you. We only sent you back to Germany because there was no one else available at the time."

Kurt recalled that the alternative to the mission might well have been the noose-end of a rope.

The Colonel broke eye contact. "You disappeared from our radar for a week in April. Where were you during that time?"

"In a labour camp in the Ore Mountains, working in a pitchblende mine."

Again, the pen visited the notebook. The colonel said, "I see, and the purpose of that detour?"

"It was not planned, Colonel, but it proved useful."

"How did you escape from the camp?"

"I was rescued by an American OSS man called Otto Staerling."

"We know that the OSS had an agent codenamed 'Musicman' there, but our information is that his cover name was Gutkind, not Staerling."

"Staerling was Gutkind's radioman. He was the recruitment manager for the KWIP and the factory. He also seemed to have some influence at the camp, so maybe he recruited workers for the mine as well."

The colonel wrote 'Otto Staerling' in his notebook. "I take it that's how you found work in the Kaiser Wilhelm Institute in Berlin – Otto Staerling helped you? And it was Staerling who took you to the island in his car?"

Kurt nodded.

Colonel Scott asked Kurt to draw a sketch of the bomb.

"I never saw it," said Kurt. "Better ask Erika. She got a good look at it."

The colonel removed his glasses and cleaned them. "What can you tell me of the trigger mechanism?"

"I'm sorry, Colonel," said Kurt. "I'm not a physicist, or an engineer. Erika may know more."

"Where is the bomb now?" said the colonel. "What happened to it when the RAF bombing raid destroyed the base?"

Kurt didn't have the heart to tell him that the RAF bombing raid had left the base unscathed. He said, "It's at the bottom of the sea."

The colonel tucked his notebook and pen away in his breast pocket. "The Americans are accusing you of shooting Gutkind in the head. They're calling it cold blooded murder."

Kurt shook his head. "That wasn't me. Otto Staerling did that."

"Why would Staerling kill his partner?"

"For personal gain. He planned to sell the bomb schematics to the highest bidder, and when Gutkind refused to go along with him, he shot him."

"I thought you said the schematics were buried in the rubble of the base," said the colonel.

"Yes, that's right, Colonel, but Staerling didn't know that. He took away what he thought was the schematics, but in reality what he had was of no value."

"I see," said the colonel. "Now tell me how Pilgrim was killed."

Kurt felt a stabbing chest pain at the memory. He retold the events as they occurred on the trawler. "We were in Swedish waters when they fired, and any of us could have been killed. Pilgrim was the unlucky one. We were too far from land to save his life."

Colonel Scott got up to leave. "There's just one other piece of the jigsaw that I need you to clarify for me. Around about the time that you turned up in the factory, my counterpart in the OSS got word that a British agent using the alias Frederick von Schönholtz had arrived. We knew it had to be you, but the alias was not one we were familiar with. I assume this was one that Erika arranged for you in Leipzig?"

Kurt considered replying 'yes' to this, but he doubted that Erika's story would back him up. He opted to tell the truth, and told Colonel Scott that the alias was one he'd brought with him from Ireland.

"And your purpose in keeping it from us?"

Kurt returned the colonel's probing gaze with one of his own. "Call it my instinct for self-preservation, Colonel. Just as much as you were unwilling to put your whole trust in me, I was unwilling to trust you – British Intelligence – completely. That alias was a small element of insurance."

Chapter 64

By the time his debriefing was over at 3 am, Thursday morning, Kurt was exhausted. He collapsed onto his cot in the quarters that he had shared with Pilgrim, and slept through until bright sunlight and birdsong streaming through his window woke him at 10 am.

He went to the canteen in search of breakfast and found Erika eating a bowl of grey porridge. She had been grilled as thoroughly by Major Weir as he had been by Colonel Scott. Kurt took the fact that they were both still at liberty as an indication that Scott and Weir were satisfied with their stories.

"Bertie Weir asked me if I arranged your von Schönholtz alias," said Erika. "I wasn't sure what to say, so I stuck with the truth."

"Good choice," said Kurt.

"He was disappointed that we had no schematics." She shrugged. "You can bet they'll pencil that in as a mission success on the basis that German know-how would have been of no help anyway. They'll say whatever they might have learnt from those schematics would have set their own research back a couple of years."

"You think the British are building their own atomic bomb?"

"It's a fair bet," said Erika. "The Yanks too, and the Ivans."

"So it's a race to see who can build the first one!" Kurt shuddered. "I'm still hoping that none of them ever succeeds. The last thing the world needs is a new bomb with a yield of 1,000 tons."

"They'll build bigger ones than that," said Erika quietly. "You can bet your bottom dollar on that."

After breakfast Kurt went in search of Major Weir and asked permission to return home to Dublin to spend some time with his family. The major gave Kurt £15 and a seven-day pass in the name Kevin O'Reilly starting from Tuesday. It seemed Kevin O'Reilly was now a fully enlisted member of the Intelligence Directorate of his Majesty's Armed Services.

Erika and Kurt met again in the two rooms set aside for the medical officer. There a doctor checked them for the possible long term effects of exposure to radioactive emissions. The doctor was unable to give either of them an absolute guarantee that they would live long and healthy lives, but he assured them that they were showing no signs of radiation poisoning.

They had lunch together, and afterwards they went for a stroll along streets that had been beautiful, now scarred and gapped from the nights of bombing.

Erika stopped to stare at the ruin of a house, its front facade stripped away and lying in rubble, curtains flapping at the side of what had been a window, a fireplace gaping halfway up a wall, with a teacup and saucer balanced on the mantelpiece. She turned to Kurt. "I keep thinking about how strange it was that Necker picked me up immediately in Haigerloch. And how did he know my real name? And how easily the ORPO found my apartment in Leipzig. I think you're right. There must be a mole within The Cage."

Kurt said, "I knew it from the moment half my parachute failed to open properly."

"Have you any idea who it could be, or how to expose him?" she said.

"I have a few ideas, but I'm going to need help to flush him out."

"I'll do whatever I can."

"Thank you, Erika, but I'm going to need help from inside British Intelligence. And there's only one person I can trust."

"Colonel Scott?"

"I was thinking of Sir Hugh Anderton."

\#

At noon that Monday a Luftwaffe troop transport landed at a remote landing strip in the desert near Tunis. One hundred German infantry men jumped down from the aircraft, formed up into ranks and set off at a brisk march across the sand. Each man was dressed in full battle fatigues, carrying a rifle, a full military backpack, and enough water for two days. These men were reinforcements for Germany's Afrika Korps, now in retreat. Throwing them into the conflict at this late stage was a foolish and pointless gesture by the generals of the OKW. One hundred fresh troops could make no difference; 10,000 new troops would have made no appreciable difference. The battle was already lost.

Of the 100 infantry men, all but one was aged under 20. Some were as young as 16. The exception was 36-year-old Franz Zingler. He had taken the lion's share of the blame for the destruction of Base Alpha, and a posting to the battle front was his punishment. He was grateful for the chance – however slim – to redeem himself.

Chapter 65

𝑓irst thing on Tuesday morning Kurt said goodbye to Erika and left The London Cage. A car took him to Euston station where he could catch a train to Holyhead and the mailboat from there back to Ireland. He waved goodbye to the driver, waited until he was out of sight, and then ran the half mile to King's Cross station.

On the way he racked his brain for the telephone number that Professor Hirsch had used to contact the head of British Intelligence, General Sir Hugh Anderton. By the time he reached King's Cross he had the number. Lifting a public telephone, he asked the operator for Huntington two-six.

"Anderton House."

"I'd like to speak to the general. My name is Kevin O'Reilly. He will remember me as a friend of Professor Stephan Hirsch."

"The general does not accept unsolicited telephone calls. If you care to leave your number he will call you back in a day or two."

Kurt could feel his toes curling. Obviously the general would take calls from a select number of callers but Kevin O'Reilly was not on that list.

"Tell the general I'm on my way from London to speak to him on a matter of great urgency."

"The general does not receive unsolicited visitors."

"Nevertheless, I shall be there in about an hour and a half." Kurt replaced the telephone in its cradle.

He bought a return ticket for Huntington and boarded the train.

He arrived at Huntington at 9 am, asked a passer-by for directions, and walked the two miles to Anderton House. He buzzed the intercom on the gate post and gave his name. The gates swung open.

The general received him in his study, a couple of stocky types in suits hovering about.

"Thank you for seeing me," said Kurt.

"I hope you don't mind," said the general. He nodded to one of his bodyguards who stepped forward. "We can't be too careful."

"I understand," said Kurt, lifting his arms for the body search.

Once Kurt was declared free of concealed weapons the general dismissed his bodyguards. He offered tea.

Kurt declined. He took a seat. "I come to you to report that your intelligence service may have an enemy mole operating within the London Cage."

The general poured himself a cup of tea. "You have evidence to back this up?"

"I'm assuming you know of my recent mission in Germany?"

The general nodded. "I have received a detailed report."

"First, Erika Cleasby was picked up as soon as she arrived in Haigerloch. Second, my parachute was interfered with. I was lucky to survive the drop."

The general raised an aristocratic eyebrow. "There was no mention of that in the report."

"I thought it best to keep that to myself. Also, the picture that was printed in the German newspapers was one taken in London."

"You're sure about that?"

"Yes. And our return flight from Sweden to London was attacked by the Luftwaffe over the North Sea. If it hadn't been for the timely intervention of the RAF I wouldn't be talking to you now."

The general sipped his tea with a raised pinkie. Kurt was struck by the man's demeanour. He was in his early fifties. Obviously a wealthy member of the British aristocracy, no doubt he could trace his ancestry back a thousand years. Men like this could never countenance defeat in the war with Germany; they had too much to lose. And yet they could have been discussing a cricket score.

A full minute went by before the general said, "I have been aware for some time that security in the London Cage may have been compromised. This is why I arranged an escort of fighters for your flight home from Sweden."

"You arranged that? Thank you, General. You saved our lives."

"I was hoping that you might have something to help identify this mole, as you called him, this enemy within."

"I have given the matter a great deal of thought," said Kurt. "You should be looking for someone with access to my parachute, and someone with knowledge of my and Erika's missions."

"That list would include Colonel Scott, Bertram Weir on the Germany desk, and Pilgrim. Even Melissa, my personal private assistant would qualify."

Kurt said, "Whoever this was had no knowledge of my real name. The mere mention of my real name to the German authorities and the full force of Nazi internal security would have been mobilized. On that basis we can exclude the colonel and Major Weir."

"That eliminates me as a suspect," said the general with a thin smile. "Bertie Weir has been with me in one capacity or another for twelve years. I have absolute faith in him. And Colonel Scott served in the last war. Did Pilgrim know your real name?"

"No, but I can tell you, sir, that Pilgrim was a loyal member of our mission to the end. He died a hero. I am sure he was no double agent."

"And yet Pilgrim was never betrayed. Was his parachute interfered with?" said the general.

"No, General."

"There you have it. Pilgrim was the mole."

Kurt shook his head. "I believe the mole's plan was to deflect attention from himself by throwing suspicion on Pilgrim."

"His plan seems to be working," said the general. "If Pilgrim isn't our double agent then we've run out of possibilities."

"Tell me, General," said Kurt, "does Melissa know my real name?"

"No."

"How long has she been your personal private assistant?"

The general blanched. His hand shook as he replaced his cup in its saucer. He reached for the telephone.

Chapter 66

Travelling back to London, Kurt looked out at the devastated countryside. Great houses that had once been surrounded by parks now had fields with teams of 'Land Girls' working in them; the stations had no name plates and some had been bombed and never rebuilt; and everywhere thin plumes of smoke rose into the sky. War-ravaged Germany had looked exactly the same.

He was surprised to find Major Weir waiting for him at King's Cross. "Colonel Scott wants you back at The Cage," he told Kurt.

"I'm on leave, remember," said Kurt. "My family's waiting for me back in Ireland."

"This will only take one day," said Weir.

In his office in The Cage, Colonel Scott waved Kurt to a seat. "The Americans have been on the blower," he said. "They have detained one of their own in Rio de Janeiro and they need your help. The man's name is Arthur 'Rocky' Stone. You knew him as Otto Staerling. The OSS has taken him back to Washington –"

"You mean they've kidnapped him and smuggled him onto US soil?"

"Not to put too fine a point on it – yes. They intend to charge him with treason and the first degree murder of their agent Gutkind, but they need your evidence. I've set up a meeting with Captain Johnson, their man in London. You will be required to give them a sworn statement that they can present in court in Washington."

"How long will all that take?" said Kurt. "I'm on leave."

"It shouldn't take long," replied the colonel. "The meeting's at four o'clock this afternoon."

Kurt sighed. He would miss the train to Holyhead and have to spend one more night in The Cage. He said, "Have you heard from General Anderton?"

"Yes. The police have been alerted to watch for our mole."

"She's not here?"

"We haven't seen her for a week."

Kurt said, "You didn't think that was odd?"

"She splits her time between here and Anderton House. We assumed she was with the general, and he assumed she was here with us."

"She's probably drinking schnapps in Berlin by now," said Kurt.

#

On his way back to The Cage from his meeting with the OSS, Kurt passed down a bombed-out street – two parallel rows of houses flattened, with Civil Defence teams clearing the smouldering rubble. Half-way along the street he discovered a couple of buildings still standing, and on the ground floor of one of these, a shop, its window heavily criss-crossed with protective tape. The sign over the window read: 'Toys and Fancy Goods'. The outside of the shop was covered in grey dust, but a sign in the door read 'open'. He pushed the door, and a small bell tinkled.

It was dark inside. Kurt ran his finger through a layer of dust on the counter. "Hello," he called out. "Is there anyone here?"

An old woman wearing a headscarf and fingerless gloves emerged through a bead curtain from the back of the shop. "Can I help you?"

"I was looking for furniture for my daughter's dolls house," said Kurt.

"How old is your daughter?"

"She's ten. Her name's Anna."

"Wait a moment," said the woman. She went back behind the bead curtain and re-appeared clutching two small items. She placed these on the counter. "I'm afraid I don't have a good selection. Before the war…"

Kurt picked them up and examined them. There was a bed and a chest of drawers, both obviously homemade from empty matchboxes and scraps of material.

"These are perfect," he said, placing a pound note on the counter. "I'll take them, thank you."

"Keep your money," said the woman, putting the items in a paper bag. Kurt tucked the bag inside his jacket and left the money on the counter.

Major Weir was waiting for Kurt back at The Cage. He handed Kurt a slip of paper. "There was a telephone call for you while you were out. It was Erika. She wants you to call her back at this number."

Kurt dialled the number and Erika answered.

"Kurt, I'm at the Turkish baths in Jermyn Street. I need you to meet me here."

"What's going on?" said Kurt.

"Don't ask questions, please. Just get here as fast as you can. I'll be meeting Pilgrim later."

Erika terminated the call. Kurt redialled the number, but there was no answer.

"What did she want? Where is she?" asked Major Weir.

"She's in the Turkish baths in Jermyn Street. I think she's in trouble. She said something about meeting Pilgrim."

The major pointed out the location of the baths on the London map pinned to his wall. "Those baths were demolished by a German bomb at the start of the blitz. I know she's been depressed since Pilgrim died. You don't think she could be thinking about killing herself?"

Kurt shook his head. "It's not that. It's something else. She needs our help."

"Right, I'll put a squad together," said the major.

Kurt said, "Let me go in first. Give me ten minutes to see what's going on."

He ran the two miles to Jermyn Street. Most of the buildings in the street had been destroyed and those few that were left teetered precariously. Part of the facade of the Turkish baths was still standing, behind the facade a mountain of rubble.

"Down here," called a voice. Kurt followed the voice and discovered a makeshift entrance behind the rubble leading down some steps to a dark underground chamber. Placing his feet carefully, he picked his way through the debris and followed a couple of rats down the steps.

The tiled baths were still in evidence under a high vaulted ceiling, although all the water had long since drained away. Kurt took a couple of moments to allow his eyes to adjust to the gloom. Then he saw Erika in the bowl of a dry bathing pool, gagged and tied to a chair, surrounded by lumps of masonry and broken shards of wood.

Melissa appeared behind him and poked the muzzle of a handgun in his ribs. "Welcome to the party, pussy cat. Get in there and join your girlfriend."

Kurt spun around and grabbed for Melissa's gun hand, but lost his footing in the loose rubble and fell into the pool. Winded by the fall, he took a moment to get his breath. Then he said, "You know the whole of British Intelligence is out searching for you, Melissa?"

Looking down at him from the edge of the pool, Melissa laughed mirthlessly. "British Intelligence! There's a contradiction in terms if ever I heard one. They couldn't find a teat on a sow."

"I thought you would have been in Berlin by now," said Kurt.

"I knew I would have to get out if you made it back to London, and I thought I had an escape plan ready. But when I tried to use it, it collapsed. It seems the Third Reich has no further use for me. Why couldn't you have died in Germany like you were supposed to? You're like a cat with nine lives."

"Sorry to disappoint you. Releasing my picture to the Nazis very nearly did the trick, but I shaved off my beard and slipped through their fingers."

"You should have been captured in Erika's bolt hole in Leipzig. Didn't they come looking for you there?"

"That was a close call. I barely escaped that time."

"The parachute should have killed you. How did you survive that?"

"I was lucky. I landed in a tree and the local people helped me."

She grunted. "That I don't believe."

"It's true, Melissa. There are lots of Germans willing to stand up to the Nazis."

"That may be so, but some day they will be called to account. They will regret their betrayal of the Fatherland."

"You still believe that the Third Reich will prevail?"

"Of course. I know I won't be here to see it, but one day the Wehrmacht will march down the Mall and the Führer will take possession of Buckingham Palace."

Melissa seemed lost for a moment in her vision of a perfect future. Kurt edged closer to Erika and removed her gag.

Melissa shook herself and jerked the gun at Kurt. "There is one last service I can perform before they hang me. I can rid the world of two German traitors."

"We may be traitors to the Third Reich," said Kurt, "but not to Germany." He picked up a piece of masonry and flung it at Melissa.

Freed of her gag, Erika shouted, "If there is a traitor here, it's you, Melissa. You are English and yet you work for the enemy. How could you?"

The first two bullets ricocheted off the tiles, uncomfortably close to Erika, strapped in the chair. A flurry of rats scattered in all directions.

Kurt kicked Erika's chair onto its side and leapt away to the other end of the pool. Melissa turned her gun toward him and fired again. Kurt picked up a loose plank and threw it at Melissa. She ducked that, but he followed it with two more chunks of brickwork and another length of wood embedded with rusty nails. That found its mark. Melissa swore at him and moved along the edge to get closer to her target.

She stopped within eight feet of Kurt and raised her gun. Kurt stood his ground. As long as he had Melissa's full attention Erika was safe. Using a dusty plank as a makeshift shield across his head and body, he shouted at Melissa. "You're dead, Melissa. Drop the weapon and give yourself up. This is pointless."

She fired again, and the bullet struck the plank, knocking him onto his back. She stepped to the edge and prepared to finish him.

"Drop the gun!" shouted Major Weir from the doorway as his squad of soldiers swarmed in.

Melissa turned her gun toward the soldiers and they opened fire. She went down in a rain of bullets, toppling off the edge into the dry pool.

Kurt righted Erika's chair and untied her. "Sorry for kicking your chair on its side. I thought you'd be a smaller target that way."

"I suppose I should be grateful," said Erika. "But I didn't enjoy being that close to a pack of hungry rats."

#

It wasn't until he got back to The Cage that Kurt remembered he was still carrying Anna's dolls furniture inside his jacket. Sitting at a table in the canteen, he opened the bag to discover the contents squashed, battered and torn beyond recovery.

"What do you have there?" said Colonel Scott.

"It was dolls furniture for my daughter, but it's ruined."

"Never mind," said Erika. "She'll be delighted to see her Papa again, with or without presents."

"Ah! About that, Kurt," said the colonel. "I'm afraid I'm going to have to cancel your six-day pass. I have a new assignment for you, and it can't wait."

THE END